THE THIRD WAY

AIMEE HOBEN

a novel

SHE WRITES PRESS

Published 2022
Printed in the United States of America
Print ISBN: 978-1-64742-095-6
E-ISBN: 978-1-64742-096-3
Library of Congress Control Number: 2022902746

For information, address:
She Writes Press
1569 Solano Ave #546
Berkeley, CA 94707

Interior design by Tabitha Lahr

She Writes Press is a division of SparkPoint Studio, LLC.

For my sister Beth, the revolutionary

CHAPTER 1
MORAL HAZARD

ARDEN FIRTH DUCKED INTO THE STUDENT union before class to check her mailbox, hoping her grandmother had sent some cash. She was broke again. Although room and board were part of her scholarship at the University of South Dakota, Arden desperately needed a new pair of jeans—her only pair was wearing dangerously thin in the seat and the knees.

Instead, she found the letter with a blue seal from the US Department of Education, marked "Important Information About Your Federal Student Aid Package."

"We regret to inform you," the letter began, "that your federal education grant through the Pell Grant and Federal Supplemental Educational Opportunity Grant programs will not be renewable for the next tuition year due to changes in funding. To explore options for covering your college tuition needs, we encourage you to explore the new privatized loan programs available from YouthBank Corporation, with flexible repayment plans."

Arden's gut clenched as she realized what this meant: in order to finish college, she'd now need to borrow the whole of her tuition and expenses for the remaining two years, at more than twenty thousand dollars a year.

She stumbled over to the sitting area in the corner of the student union, tossing her backpack on the floor and slumping into the ratty couch. Numbly, she watched the other students unlocking their mailboxes. Some gathered their mail and went on their way; others ripped open the same letter with the same blue seal, their faces registering the same shock Arden's had. Eventually, Arden's best friend Ophelia sauntered in.

"What's your deal?" Ophelia asked. Arden let her head fall forward so that her unruly dirty-blond hair covered her face, suddenly afraid she might cry, and handed the letter up to her friend.

"Oh, shit," Ophelia breathed, scanning the letter and then glancing around the room to see several other students staring dumbfounded at the same letters. O dropped the letter in Arden's lap and turned away to check her own mailbox. Arden watched as Ophelia fumbled with the combination and with the overstuffed mail jammed into her box. *Typical*, Arden thought, Ophelia didn't think much of housekeeping—her dorm room was always a mess. Catalogs fell to the floor as she ripped open her own blue seal.

"Shit," she repeated, joining Arden on the couch, leaving her unwanted junk mail on the floor. "This is bad."

Arden nodded. *This is bad for you*, is what Ophelia meant. Arden knew her friend's grant was only for a few grand, not for the whole thing like Arden's. Ophelia had only gotten financial aid because her mom had been between jobs when O applied for aid, and she didn't expect to qualify next year anyway. Her mom had been on unemployment for almost a year before they made the move to Sioux Falls so she could start work at the hospital. And though Ophelia's parents had split when she was in high school, her dad had money and would help her, as long as not a penny went to her mom.

Arden was on her own for college. Her dad had never been in the picture—she had no idea who or where he was. Her mom had died when Arden was fourteen, and her gram, Emma, had her own financial problems. She had almost had to sell off the farm to pay her hospital bills when Arden was in high school, but instead she'd taken out a mortgage on the farm for cash to pay her debts, and now the mortgage payments were more than she could afford. She barely got by on her social security checks, and there was nothing to spare.

"It sucks," Ophelia sighed. "You'll just have to borrow . . ." She broke off abruptly when she saw the look on Arden's face. "What? Lots of people borrow, and USD is cheap. Most of my friends from New York are paying twice what we are. You just pay it back once you get a job."

Arden wasn't so sure about that. What would college get her, other than being saddled with debt? She knew that she didn't want a desk job. She'd had a taste of that working as an office temp last summer. Standing in as a receptionist or administrative assistant at the big bank headquarters in Sioux Falls, she'd had a window into the working world, and it scared her. Even the supposedly good jobs, the sales or analyst roles, with the better office real estate and VIP parking, seemed meaningless and utterly dreary. It all came down to corporate profit and impressing the executives, chasing access and recognition, making money. A silly golden ring. She'd spent her days there uncomfortable in itchy pantyhose, wondering, *Isn't there something more worthwhile all these people should be doing with their days?* Arden didn't want to indenture herself to that kind of life, just to go to college.

Maybe USD was cheap compared to some schools, but what was she really getting for it? She didn't have the first idea of what she wanted to do with her life. Hadn't she read online some famous entrepreneur saying he regretted going to college? He claimed it squelches critical thinking, teaches rule following, and is a waste of time and money.

Once, she thought she'd be a farmer, like her grandmother. As a child, she had loved putting seeds in the ground and waiting for them to emerge, unfurling tiny hopeful shoots. Later, in 4-H, she had pressed her grandmother to start selling at farmers markets, instead of the local auction house that she stubbornly stuck to even as she made less and less. Farming in the old ways Emma practiced, without bioengineered seeds and designer chemicals, was getting harder every year. More and more of their old neighbors were selling out to the mega-farms, which were slowly squeezing out small farmers who couldn't compete.

Arden thought of the last conversation she'd had with Emma, where her grandmother mentioned that she had received a foreclosure notice on her mortgage. Emma had tried to avoid selling out by borrowing money, and look at where that had gotten her.

And what would she actually get for the forty grand in tuition that she couldn't learn on her own, if she put her mind to it? The vo-ag classes were all about factory farming and chemicals, which turned Arden off. The history classes were the same old self-satisfied patriotic stories she'd learned in high school. In English lit, she'd already read most of the books. Other than poli-sci, her classes were crap.

"Poli-sci!" Arden exclaimed, and both girls grabbed their stuff and set off at a run across the quad to Old Main, still crusted with snow in late March. They pushed open the door of the lecture hall and were relieved to see Justin Kirish, the graduate student teaching assistant, standing in the front of the hall at the lectern rather than the professor who would have recorded them being late.

"Arden, Ophelia, nice of you to join us," he said in a serious tone, but when his back was to the class, he flashed them a smile. Ophelia headed for the one remaining seat in back and Arden eased into an empty seat in the front row.

"Although Professor Atwood's lesson plan today calls for a lecture on the Second Amendment"—Kirish wrinkled his nose slightly at the enthusiastic murmur that rumbled from the men slouching in the back of the class— "I'm going to take us a bit off-syllabus and focus instead on freedom of speech." The right to bear arms, they all knew, was the Second Amendment. Arden thought Kirish was from the Northeast, so he was probably for gun control, not a popular view at USD.

Arden took out her laptop and began tapping away, numbly taking notes but not really absorbing the lecture. Instead, she found herself watching Kirish. Only when he was lecturing did he seem fully involved in the class— maybe because he despised the professor.

"Did you see him roll his eyes when Atwood said millennials don't save money? Does he know how much college costs?" O had shrieked after class once. Kirish was the subject of some speculation around campus. How had an East Coast liberal (people assumed) who drove an expensive foreign SUV with Pennsylvania plates ended up at a place like USD? The school was mainly South Dakotans, and although some out-of-staters attended the law school, he still stuck out. Was he not smart enough to get in anywhere close to home? That didn't seem likely once you heard him talk. There was a rumor that he had dyslexia, but he wrote on the chalk board quickly while he spoke, so Arden didn't think that was right either. He also had this weird thing about people not using his first name, Justin, insisting that people call him by his somewhat odd last name.

All of a sudden, he was calling on her with a question. "Arden, does the Constitution only protect humans?"

"Uh, I think so," she responded, annoyed that he was singling her out yet again. *What is he talking about? Why does he always call on me?* "I mean, what else would it protect? Animals?" Classmates snickered.

"Well, many of the rights protected by the US Constitution relate to property ownership. . . ." he prodded, giving her a hint. It was not helpful. He waited. "Who else can own property?"

"I don't know . . . businesses?" she guessed.

"Exactly! Certain types of businesses, such as corporations, have independent legal status under the law, so they can own property and enter into contracts. And in certain circumstances, a corporation is considered a legal 'person' under the US Constitution and is entitled to protection. The City of Vermillion couldn't bulldoze your house to build a highway without going to a court hearing first and then paying you its fair market value, because the Constitution assures you due process and just compensation. And because corporations are considered legal persons, the same would be true of the Subway sandwich shop on Main Street."

Despite her annoyance at being called on, Arden was drawn into the lecture. The young student teacher paced back and forth across the front of the classroom as he spoke, bright brown eyes periodically fixing on her. He was lean, with an aquiline nose and brown hair that stood up in strange angles when he raked his hands through it. His well-worn and slightly rumpled white button-down shirts, half tucked into khakis, and gum boots made him look like he just stepped off the campus of a prep school, but twenty years ago.

Justin Kirish came alive when he taught class, whereas around campus he often seemed harried, walking briskly with a furrowed brow. When simply attending Professor Atwood's lectures, he often looked pained, as if he were repressing a better way of explaining things. Like Ophelia, he talked faster than most people Arden had grown up with, like he had somewhere to be. He was one of those smart people who could, when he wanted to, make you feel like you were in on the joke. As opposed to the professor, who treated them like children. But if he was tested, like when obnoxious Clyde Henderson got political during Kirish's first lesson, he could be withering. Clyde cut class for two weeks after that, everyone had laughed so hard at his stupidity, because not laughing meant you were as dumb as him.

If Arden were honest with herself, she'd had a minor crush on him earlier in the semester. That was before the graduate student's house party off campus in Vermillion. It had been a warm October Friday night, and Ophelia had gotten invited to the party by a history grad student she'd met at the library. He was brainy and liberal, so it made sense that Kirish would be there too. Arden noticed him right away when they got there, standing in the hallway laughing with a short older guy, but it wasn't until her second beer that she got up the nerve to approach him. She'd tapped Kirish on the shoulder, smiling up at him. "This commons is pretty tragic, eh, professor?" Arden had nodded to the swill of plastic cups and bottles on the kitchen table.

He had taught a section in poli-sci that week on the idea of tragedy of the commons: where people use up a common resource because no single person owned it. In the old days, he'd explained, the "commons" had been the town green, and the "tragedy" was that everyone let their sheep overgraze. There had been a long pause, after which he turned to his friend and introduced them, formally, as if to show he felt forced to do so by her continued presence.

"Jim, this young lady is a freshman in my undergrad poli-sci with Atwood. Her name is . . ." Kirish flicked a disapproving eye at the cup of beer she gripped in her suddenly sweaty hand, and then down her green halter dress.

"Uh, Arden," she'd stammered, feeling embarrassed in the sexy dress she'd borrowed from Ophelia. "I'm a sophomore." Which he must have known; poli-sci was a second-year class.

"Oh really?" He feigned surprise. "How old does that make you?" Like Clyde Henderson, she'd crossed some invisible line.

She mumbled an answer as he turned away, leaning in to hear what his friend was saying over the din of the loud music. She'd stood there for an awkward moment, thinking he might turn back to her, but instead, he said goodbye to his friend and left the room. Arden had been stuck talking to his friend, who had terrible breath and went on about how she had no idea how hard law school was for twenty minutes before she could get away.

SINCE THEN, HE'D CALLED ON HER OFTEN in class, which she hated. Trying to drive home that he was her superior, it felt like.

Arden had that buzzing feeling she got when called on in class that made it hard to think as she strained to follow the lecture. Kirish polled the class on the characteristics of a corporation, thankfully leaving her alone. Corporations were owned by stockholders, someone volunteered; they could be traded on the NY stock exchange or privately held. "Limited liability?" someone else called out. Arden tapped her keyboard to wake up her laptop, suspecting this part was important.

"That's right," Kirish responded. "Although the shareholders own the business, they are only liable up to the amount of their investment. So they can only lose the value of their shares, and can't be sued in a way that extends to them personally for the company's wrongdoing. Historically, prior to the late 1800s, a corporation could only be created with a charter from the government, and would often be granted a monopoly. Anybody know why?"

"They needed a 'Get Out of Jail Free' card?" a hockey player in the back quipped, to scattered laughter. Arden hated that guy; he always made stupid jokes and expected everyone to laugh.

"Yeah, in a way," Kirish forced a laugh. Arden watched as he steered the lecture back to his point, explaining the reason for a monopoly. "Monopolies were granted to corporations to encourage investment in a project that had a public benefit, like a railroad, or a new town, or a fire insurance company. The East India Trading Company, one of the earliest charter corporations, is a classic example. The British government wanted Far East spice routes to be built out and wanted private investment to make it happen. The limitation of liability is important because it allows investors to put their money to work without risking everything." Arden had never heard that before; she'd only thought all monopolies were bad.

Kirish shoved his hands in his pockets and surveyed the crowd. He continued, "One criticism, however, is that people are less careful with other people's money than with their own and that private entrepreneurship is better."

The hockey player in the back interrupted, "O—P—M," he chanted, "Otha People's Mon-ayy!" Was this a rap song? Arden saw Ophelia rolling her eyes.

"Exactly," Kirish said dryly. "Yes, it's easier to be reckless with someone else's money. But being less careful could actually be one of the strengths of a corporation, if you need a level of risk-taking, like with the railroads, which the government or individuals acting alone won't take."

Ophelia called out a question from the back of class. "But there's a big downside to limited liability, right? If no one is really responsible for the acts of the corporation, it ends up making decisions that hurt people, or the environment. Like those oil pipelines on Native American lands, keeping us addicted to cheap fossil fuels."

Arden felt a swell of pride for her friend, speaking loudly, without trepidation. Arden turned to see her backlit against the window at the back of the classroom, the thin white winter sun reflecting off the snow in the courtyard outside. Her straight brown hair was pulled back in a sloppy bun that stuck out in spikes, and her olive skin was slightly shiny—O rarely bothered with makeup. As always, she had no qualms speaking up. It seemed to Arden that Ophelia was never afraid, in class or anywhere else—or if she was, it just made her more resolute.

Ophelia and Arden had been assigned to the same dorm hall in their freshman year and quickly become friends. Ophelia was the first true New Yorker Arden had ever met, and she'd been to the opera, been to Broadway, eaten Korean barbeque, been to Paris, and been scuba diving. At first, Arden had been intimidated at her relative sophistication and self-conscious about being broke all the time. Ophelia always managed to casually throw things Arden's way without making it seem like charity. *Oh, I don't like how this lotion smells—do you want it?* Or, *They gave me two burritos by accident—please take one.* Like Arden, poli-sci was Ophelia's favorite subject. She loved a good political argument. She never became snarky or dismissive, but rather was witty and charming even when Arden knew she vehemently disagreed with her opponents.

"That's a good point, Ophelia," Kirish responded. "It's a kind of a moral hazard, right? A moral hazard is when financial or other pressures push people to ignore the moral implications of their decisions. Anyone ever come across one of these?"

"Like if you find a twenty in the dryer at the laundromat, and you know who used the machine last. . . ." someone volunteered. Everyone laughed.

"Yes." Kirish nodded. "Exactly. But how about if you don't know who used the machine last? It's much easier just to pocket the money then, right?"

Kirish went on to explain how stock ownership, removed from the day-to-day decisions of a corporation, allowed investors to divorce themselves from the actions of the enterprise while still reaping the financial rewards of these actions. Back when corporations had public charters, they were created because they served the public good. In the late 1800s, however, the laws changed so that *any* business venture could incorporate.

"All of a sudden, with a simple paperwork filing with the state, a separate legal entity was created that shielded investors from personal liability—and even, as Ophelia suggests, from moral responsibility for the actions of the corporation. The stage was set for the second industrial revolution and a massive expansion of the influence of corporations in America, and the concentrations of wealth that went along with them."

Arden thought of the companies her mother had worked for before her death, five years ago. Jill's last good job had been at a call center—she'd actually enjoyed helping people with their complaints about the appliances they'd ordered from Sears. When the company announced it was sending its customer service jobs overseas, the employees had been shocked that such an iconic American company would abandon American workers. Its flagging stock price briefly rallied at the news of the outsourcing, billed as part of a cost-cutting measure, and Arden could still remember how this had angered her mother and grandmother, Emma. *Investors liked this?* they had railed. Moral hazard indeed.

After the Sears layoff and thirteen months on unemployment, Jill had gotten a job in an internet retailer's distribution facility. Her job was to race around an enormous warehouse plucking orders to be drop-shipped in the night. *Off to the fulfillment center,* she would say sarcastically, as she left for work, which was anything but fulfilling. The pickers were timed on filling orders, punching in and out when they got onto the floor and even when they went to the bathrooms. They wore tracker bracelets to gather their performance data, which was then ranked and posted on a public performance board. They were compared against each other for their efficiency and speed in team meetings, and periodically told how their facility as a whole compared to the company's flagship, fully-automated, robotic fulfillment facility. Not well.

Jill had already been suffering from lower-back pain when the cherry picker fell under her. She had operated the picker only once before, after watching a training video. The union rep told Arden's grandmother that the picker had fallen because Jill had used the remote control to extend the bucket arm too far forward, and then had herself leaned too far to reach the toaster on the top of the warehouse shelving. There was also the suggestion that she hadn't been sober, but Arden believed it had been the pain meds the workers-comp doctor had prescribed her, and the fact that it was three in the morning. After three ruptured disks and a broken shoulder, and a sixty-day supply of OxyContin, Jill hadn't had much interest in getting better.

Arden forced herself to pay attention as Kirish shifted the lecture back to the Constitution. "Should a corporation have the right to the pursuit of life, liberty, and happiness?" he asked. The class was in agreement that this did not make sense. "What about privacy? Or the right to marry? What about the right to bear arms? How about voting? Freedom of religion?" Again, general consensus in the negative.

"Okay, those are easy. What about free speech? Or equal protection?" Kirish asked. He laid his palms flat on the empty desk next to Arden's, looking expectantly around the class. When no one volunteered, he raised an eyebrow at her, inviting her to answer the question. To her immense frustration, she felt a flush of heat at his attention. She shook her head slightly and raised her chin to answer.

"On equal protection, well . . . corporations should be treated fairly. I mean, one shouldn't have an unfair advantage over another."

"So they should be treated equally to people, then?" he quizzed her.

"No," she said, stubbornly but unable to articulate more.

"Should they have the same right to free speech?"

"No. . . ."

"Why not?"

"Well, corporations don't have, like, a . . . human . . . right to speak," Arden forced herself to say, silently cursing her fumbling.

"Why not?" He was leaning toward her now.

Arden wasn't sure. "Well . . . I think we learned that the most important, or most protected speech, is political speech, right?"

He nodded, smiling.

Arden continued, "Well, since corporations don't vote, and therefore don't have a political say, it seems like they shouldn't have the right to political speech."

"Interesting," Kirish responded. "The US Supreme Court did not agree with you. In the 2010 case of *Citizens United v. Federal Election Commission*, the highest court held that a law prohibiting corporations from 'electioneering,' or trying to influence the outcome of an election before Election Day, was unconstitutional. The court held that the not-for-profit corporation Citizens United had a right to political speech that could not be restricted, and it was allowed to air a negative biographical movie it had made about a candidate. It didn't matter if the movie allegedly included misrepresentations—because it was the most protected form of speech, political, the court would not restrict it."

Ophelia spoke up, "How can a *thing* that can't vote have a right to political speech?" Arden wasn't surprised to hear O's distaste; she'd heard her trash corporate America before, going on about how it caused environmental destruction and exploited workers. Arden had always taken Ophelia's politics with a grain of salt—she wasn't sure that labor unions and higher taxes and big government were the way to go. She thought of herself as more of an independent voter, like her grandmother.

But now, this anger, Ophelia's condemnation, felt right to Arden. Hadn't it been her mom's downfall, being used up by corporations? Hadn't it been this phenomenon of limited liability that made it so no one had to answer for the outsourcing of her job, and the injuries that had ultimately destroyed her?

The TA explained the basis for the court's decision— that the individual members of a corporation had free speech rights, and they were permitted to amplify their voices by banding together around a common goal. She considered the student aid changes that had eliminated her grant, so that now students like her had to resort to loans from corporate banks. She didn't see how those changes could possibly reflect the will of voters, banding together to amplify their voices. Rather, it was the will of corporations, seeking to increase their profits, at the expense of people. And the voices of these corporations—already so loud, with their lobbyists—drowned out the voices of the people, to the point that the politicians no longer worked for the people. They worked for the corporations.

This isn't how a democracy is supposed to work, Arden thought. Somebody had to do something. But what?

CHAPTER 2 · THE FARM

OPHELIA HAD JUMPED AT THE CHANCE to spend Easter with Arden and Emma, happy to get out of a weekend with her mom and her new boyfriend in Sioux Falls. Arden was glad to have O coming home with her. She planned to tell her grandmother about the financial aid letter and needed moral support.

The two-hour drive went quickly, and soon Arden was speeding past her old regional high school, two towns west of Badger. Seeing the low-slung brick building with its parking lot full of rusted pickups brought back her first couple weeks there, as a freshman, just months after her mother had died. She'd hardly been able to speak to anyone, which was fine because most people avoided her anyway. Especially after the incident in chorus.

On the second day of chorus, Arden had a splitting headache and had rooted around in her backpack, finding a foil packet with two half-disintegrated aspirin, which she had tossed back with a swig from her water bottle.

Bonnie West, with her perfect blond hair and her jean skirt and her white eyelet blouse, had eyed her and said, "Oh, you're like your mother, aren't you?"

Arden had snapped, knocking the girl's chair over backward with a shove on each shoulder. Luckily the girl just lay moaning on the floor, cradling the back of her head where it hit the linoleum. If she'd fought back, Arden didn't know what she would have done.

Later, the girl explained to the principal that she'd only meant Arden was like her mother in that she liked to sing.

"Her maw used to come sit in with our church choir sometimes, at the First Lutheran in Boalsburg. I believe she was attending the AA meetings in the basement there. You know, for alcoholics." Bonnie West and the principal had exchanged a knowing look.

Sure, that was what she meant.

Principal Hanlon was willing to let her off with a warning, given Arden's "difficult circumstances," if she apologized to Bonnie. But Arden had never been much for apologizing.

For that, she'd spent two weeks in after-school detention, which meant she missed the bus. For the first two days, her grandmother, Emma, had to come and pick her up each afternoon when it was over.

"It's hard to break away," she'd sighed in the car, clearly resentful of the forty minutes she had spent away from the farm. She was falling behind. Arden had noticed the broken tractor, awaiting repair. The weeds. The bills. Emma had been more tired than usual. It would be months before she found the lump in her breast.

After that, Arden had resolved to find another way home from school. She surveyed the other students rotating through the detention hall, proctored by the frightening tenth-grade math teacher. Mostly boys, they leered at her, having heard the story of the freshman girl with the mother who had overdosed, now fighting in school. She needed someone who had their license, obviously, and a car, and who lived in her direction, east of Regional 10. Also, someone who could be trusted not to grab her, or tell stories about her putting out. She settled on Scott Bouchard, whose family farm was on her bus line outside of Badger, ten minutes from Emma's. She knew him slightly from Grange picnics. He was a senior, she thought, so possibly had a car. His younger brother rode the bus, but not him. Probably not a good sign that he wasn't giving his brother rides, but worth a try.

She'd turned around in her chair when the proctor stepped out into the hall, asking whether he'd give her a ride home the following day so that Emma wouldn't have to pick her up.

"What makes you think I'll be here tomorrow?" he'd sneered.

"Oh, you only got one day?"

"I skipped school. It's not like *I* was fighting," he answered.

"Right, I get it, girls aren't supposed to fight. Whatever. Can you give me a ride or not?" Arden insisted, her voice rising. Asshole.

"Sure." He smirked. He held her eye, and then made a show of returning to his history textbook with a sigh, as if she'd interrupted him in the midst of something important.

That night, Emma had been visibly relieved that Arden had figured out a ride home.

"Well, isn't that nice of Scotty Bouchard!" she'd remarked, looking a bit surprised.

But the next day, in detention, he was not there. Arden walked out to the parking lot afterward, looking around.

She stood where the school buses drop off, scanning the parking lot, not knowing what his car might look like, not seeing anyone she knew. Damn. Arden felt like a fool for trusting him; he probably planned the whole time to leave her stranded. She was just about to walk back into the school to call Emma from the office, knowing that the phone would just ring and ring. Emma wouldn't be back in the house until suppertime, six o'clock at the earliest, at which point it would be dark and she'd be exhausted.

"You all right?"

She had noticed the boy in the back of detention the first day. He was scruffy, quiet, with bloodshot brown eyes and dirty jeans. He had been there each of the three days Arden had, and she wondered what he had gotten in trouble for.

"Yeah, just waiting for someone." Arden wondered if the boy had overheard the exchange yesterday in detention. "Someone who's probably not going to show."

"Where do you need to go?" he offered.

Although she didn't know him at all, she didn't have a lot of options.

His truck was a rusted out old Chevrolet, which Arden was relieved to see could easily be Scott Bouchard's pickup. She didn't want Emma to know she'd gotten stood up and taken a ride from a stranger. The boy told her that his name was Matt Johnson. He was a junior. He'd gotten detention for smoking weed, he explained, eying her. She nodded, not surprised. They hadn't said much to each other that first day and he drove too fast, but he'd offered her a ride the next day too, and she'd gratefully accepted. He was more talkative Thursday, smoking a joint as he drove and talking about school, how he thought it was bullshit, how the principal was a prick. Arden didn't like the smoking, but it made him drive more carefully, and she had to agree with him about school—it *was* bullshit, and she resented all the other students watching her walk through the halls, judging her because of her mom. Matt's ideas were interesting. He didn't like consumerism, which he thought was an unavoidable result of capitalism. He didn't like the internet, social media, or smartphones.

"It's like *The Matrix*—everyone is plugged in, and they think it's real life, but it's not. This isn't what life is supposed to be about." He became philosophical when he smoked.

"What is it supposed to be about?" she asked him, genuinely curious. Going through high school so she could get a job so she could pay the bills felt pointless, but what else was there? She liked farm life, but the work was so hard and uncertain—with one storm a whole year's profits could be washed away. Emma never seemed to get above water, always writing checks from the dark-green checkbook against the farm equity line, which Arden knew she hated, feeling like she was losing a bit of the farm each time.

"I don't know the meaning of life, but I know it ain't that," Matt said, passing the joint, which she accepted without realizing what she was doing. She looked at it for a long time, feeling no pressure from him like grownups had always warned that she would. Was Matt's different way of looking at things from the weed? She took a careful drag and waited. Although the change wasn't very strong, she could feel a relaxation in her body, a warmth, and a spinning in her thoughts. She took another drag.

The next day, Matt brought her a book, which she read in detention, *A People's History of the United States*. This offered a different angle than her textbooks: unsettling, unpatriotic, critical. She read about the genocide of Native Americans, about slavery and racism, unions, the robber barons, and much more. The government screwing people, the powerful accumulating power, the rich getting richer at the workers' expense. There was a moldy underbelly to the American dream.

After those two weeks of detention, Matt offered to keep driving her home. Arden wasn't sure whether he liked her or just liked having someone to talk to. She'd begun to look forward to their conversations, and to the way she felt in the time they shared on the drive home, which became a bit longer each day as he took more and more meandering routes. With Matt, she felt relieved of social expectations—for example, how she was supposed to look as a girl. Never one for makeup, Arden had dutifully applied eye shadow and cover-up those first days of high school, because that was what high school girls did. Looking at her face in Matt's passenger-side visor mirror, she saw the artifice in the plum-colored shadow on her lids, the sparkle of jewelry on her earlobes when she felt flat, without sparkle. Just like the consumerism Matt railed against, the primping and grooming, the shaving and plucking, the blow-drying and the dieting, all of it was phony. After smoking with Matt, Arden felt any obligation to do these things fall away. Why bother?

Arden thought for a long moment about Matt's offer to keep driving her home, as they sat in Emma's yard. What would come next, if she said yes? Would he become her boyfriend? Had it been like this for Jill, when she'd been a girl? She could see now how easy it would be to slip into a relationship with him, smoking joints and driving around, stepping outside of the pressures and artificial demands of life. It was deeply appealing, and that scared her. This was the first step down the road to following in her mother's footsteps.

"No thanks," she'd said.

She could tell that his feelings were hurt when she stopped saying hi to him in the halls, but it was better that way. Arden spent her time studying, reading more about the history and counterculture that Matt had introduced her to, and philosophy too, but stayed clear of him and his friends. They were trouble, smoking in the bathrooms and getting suspended. The first two years of high school she just tried to keep her head down, and after her sophomore year, she realized she could graduate after only three years if she took a class that summer. Matt was there in summer school too, although not for the same reason she was. He'd flunked biology, and couldn't graduate until he passed it. Arden tried to help him with some of the assignments—science came easily to her, like most subjects—but Matt didn't seem as smart as he had two years before. His thinking, which had seemed to her to be flexible and unbound by convention, just seemed flabby and unorganized now. She suspected he'd moved on to the harder stuff. Arden was never sure if he passed the summer biology class, but he was not back at school the following year.

Thinking of Matt always made her feel unsettled, and reminded her how easy it was to step off the path, how easy it is to let your life take a dark turn, like her mother's had. The University of South Dakota had been a relief for Arden, to be anonymous, to not be *that girl*. She didn't tell many people that she'd done high school in three years, and even fewer about what happened to Jill. Ophelia was one of only a handful who knew.

Now, Ophelia sat in the passenger seat looking expectantly at her. Arden shook her head to clear her thoughts, turning to Ophelia, "Uh, what?"

"I said, what's up with you? You've been in outer space for the last five minutes. Was that your school we drove past?"

"Uh, yeah, sorry, just old memories."

Soon they were pulling into Badger and flying down the straight dirt road that led to her grandmother's farm. Despite the cold April day, Emma was out scratching around in the large vegetable patch behind the house, getting things ready for planting. Behind her stood the small white farmhouse Arden loved, which had been her refuge as a child. To this day, she could close her eyes and see every room, with their low ceilings and simple, sparse furnishings. On the rich farmland surrounding the house, Emma typically grew corn or sunflowers, but in the vegetable patch, she experimented, growing potatoes, parsnips, ground cherries, and cabbages. Each season had been a treasure hunt for Arden as a girl. Emma rotated crops, always growing several different things to protect against a single blight knocking out all of a season's efforts. She was a firm believer in letting fields lie fallow. Those resting fields, as Emma had called them, were often the most interesting, full of insects and wildflowers.

After Emma's cancer and the mortgage she'd taken out to pay her bills, she'd leased half her acreage on the other side of the road to "the AGM," a Big Ag conglomerate. Emma's half still included her house, vegetable patch, orchard, and barns, and the richer farmland containing the cold stream that bisected the southern parcel behind the house. AGM had wanted that parcel too, for the water source, but Emma had refused. As it was, she worried about her well now with the chemicals AGM sprayed on their crops. For four years, they had planted nothing but soybeans. There were machines for watering, spraying, seeding, tilling and harvesting, looming on the leased land across the dirt road like massive insects. Sometimes it felt like they were waiting to descend on them, to dismantle the house and whisk it away. Why did they have to park them right across from Emma's house, when they could be anywhere along the road? Arden didn't like the uniform fields, scraped bare now for spring planting, so different than she remembered. They felt like occupied territory.

Seeing the girls arrive, Emma bustled over to the car, dropping her gloves and gardening tools in her wake, and scooped Arden into a huge hug. Arden wondered how often her grandmother thought of Jill, her own daughter, when Arden returned for holidays. Did Emma compare the two of them? Was she reminded of other homecomings, some happy, some probably involving the kind of fucked-up drama that used to follow her mother wherever she went? Did she think Arden was like her mother? She must miss Jill. Arden didn't.

After a moment of Arden and Emma hugging, Ophelia elbowed in. "Gimme some of that!"

Ophelia and Emma embraced, laughing.

"How's my other girl?" Emma asked, beaming at O. "Are you staying out of trouble?"

"Mostly," Ophelia said with a grin.

Emma led them into the house, helping with their bags. Arden took a lap around the house, touching the picture of her grandfather on the mantle, avoiding the smaller frame with Jill's picture. The pile of boots by the back door, the crocheted afghans folded on the back of the couch, the firewood neatly piled by the woodstove, all was familiar and in its place. She sighed and plopped down at the kitchen table, knowing that next Emma would make coffee and try to feed them stale potato chips and hard candies gone soft with age that would stick in her teeth.

Arden watched with satisfaction and maybe a tiny bit of jealousy the friendly banter that continued between her grandmother and her best friend. Ever since they first met during their freshman year, Emma and Ophelia had been close. Arden was struck by how much Ophelia preferred

Emma to her own mother, whom O had diagnosed as a narcissist. Ophelia had grown up in Brooklyn. She and her mom had moved to Sioux Falls midway through her last year in high school. After a long job search yielded nothing closer to home, and a bitter divorce, her mom took the job at the big hospital in the city. It seemed like a good job to Arden, but Ophelia was prone to making snarky jokes about the hospital, as if she blamed it for uprooting her life. She still hadn't forgiven her mother for insisting she attend a Midwestern college, as opposed to somewhere back East. Ophelia liked USD fine now, but she resented her mother's selfishness.

In Brooklyn, during her last two years of high school, Ophelia had worked on a political campaign that had completely consumed her. The candidate was a woman named Sophia Mendez, a thirty-two-year-old lawyer and community organizer, who was brilliant, articulate, passionate, and dedicated. At first Ophelia hadn't realized that she had fallen in love with Sophia—everyone was bewitched by her. Ophelia had proven herself as a volunteer; she was hardworking, bold enough to talk to anyone, and able to argue all the policy points. Sophia had come to rely on her as a focus group of one: Ophelia represented the next generation and could provide their view on the big issues. One day, however, Sophia cut her loose, telling Ophelia to focus on her studies and herself. Ophelia had argued, she wanted to see the campaign through, she could handle "the crush." Sophia demurred, however, explaining that such entanglements happened in every campaign. They were part of politics, she had explained, but she couldn't risk it, not with a young person, not with Ophelia.

The rest of her senior year was rocky. Until then, she had only ever considered herself straight, and she was confused about whether one infatuation made her otherwise.

She did some things trying to figure that out that Arden knew she wasn't proud of. Starting a new school halfway through the year, halfway across the country where the kids were very different, hadn't helped. With her GPA, she was lucky to have gotten into USD.

However O had ended up there, Arden was glad that they were together. They tossed their bags into Arden's room and sat down with Emma for lunch. Emma fussed in the kitchen, serving egg salad sandwiches on toasted home-made bread. There were half-sour pickles from Emma's garden and apples from the orchard. To drink, they had Emma's signature herbal iced tea, bright red from her hibiscus flowers. Almost everything served came from Emma's own homestead, Arden reflected, except the flour for the bread. The pantry shelves were stocked with tomatoes and other vegetables and condiments, jarred and set up for winter. Although Arden shuddered at the memory of being stuck in a hot kitchen, spending hours and hours preparing and preserving food, she was impressed that her grandmother was still so self-sufficient.

Arden considered broaching the topic of the financial aid letter, but couldn't bring herself to disturb the peace of the meal.

"Follow me, buttercup, I have a surprise for you." Emma bustled around them, clearing the plates, and then led them out to the barn. Arden felt dread slow her feet as they approached the barn—she hadn't spent any time in the barn since the summer after her mother died.

After Jill died, Emma had forced herself to be cheerful for Arden's benefit. Arden remembered thinking to herself, *Don't do that, it must hurt.* But Emma had to keep moving, keep the farm running, fix the tractor, prune the fruit trees, get the apples picked, get the crops in, get the vegetables put up in jars. It never stopped. She allowed Arden exactly one month of lying around in bed after Jill died, and then picked her up and shoved her outside. She informed Arden that she had a job for her for the summer, and it had been that forced work that had helped her put Jill's death behind her. She was put in charge of a herd of sheep Emma had agreed to take for a neighbor who'd had a barn fire. It was easy to empty her mind when Arden was feeding sheep, or wrestling them to the ground and shearing them with the electric clippers, or her favorite, picking the bits of straw from the wool to prepare it for the yarn house. She had been sad to see them go when, at the end of the summer, the neighbor came with his livestock trailer and loaded the sheep on, to take them back. The neighbor paid her fifty dollars for watching the sheep for the summer. But it hadn't been about the money, Arden knew. It had been to get her moving again. To get her from June to August.

Arden wondered now for the first time if the barn fire had even been real, or if it had all been something Emma cooked up as therapy. Arden stepped gingerly into the barn, expecting to be hit by the wave of anger that had followed her that summer. Instead, she saw the intricate cobwebs, outlined in dust, making dirty lace along the ceiling, with gleaming motes floating in the air where the sun streamed in the door behind them. It felt safe. Arden heard a low nicker as they stepped into the dim warmth.

"I took in a boarder," Emma smiled, stroking the horse's long head. "This is Nick. He's Jimmy Bouchard's horse. Arden, do you remember him from school? He's the foreman at the soybean operation next door, went upstate for vo-ag. He's paying me to keep this fella here, takes him out to ride the fields when it suits him."

Arden nodded, remembering vaguely a solid, dark-haired boy, cowboy boots and jeans, dirty fingernails. He was the younger brother of Scott Bouchard, the boy who'd agreed to drive her home from detention but never showed. On the long bus rides to school, Jimmy had sat alone, doing his homework in the mornings. They had been in FFA together, Future Farmers of America. She remembered bringing rabbits to the state fair. Had he raised goats? She wondered whether he liked the soybeans.

"He's so big!" Ophelia exclaimed.

Arden eyed the horse. "Probably almost sixteen hands?" she asked Emma, who nodded.

"What on earth does that mean?" O laughed. Arden explained that a "hand" was the width of a hand, four inches, measured up to the horse's withers, or the shoulders at the base of its neck. She could see that the horse was gentle, so Arden slipped into the stall to point out the withers, which were about level to her nose. The horse was a bay, dark chestnut in color with a tangled black mane. She felt a physical pull to ride, remembering wistfully the many hours spent at her cousin's place out by the Black Hills, riding through scrubby plains and trails.

Emma went to the next stall, serving as feed storage for the horse, and scooped a handful of grain. Watching her gram feed the horse, Arden was happy to see an animal back on the farm. Emma could make a little cash, and although she would have argued otherwise, the chickens weren't good company, not like a horse.

Later, at dinner, Arden broke the news to Emma about her Pell grant. Emma demanded to see the letter, not wanting to believe it.

"*To explore options for funding your college tuition needs, we encourage you to explore the new privatized loan programs available from YouthBank Corporation, with flexible repayment plans,*" Emma read aloud in an outraged tone. "So there you have it—that's who's going to benefit from this— YouthBank Corporation! Those bastards." Emma stood up and paced around the small kitchen. "It's probably those damn corporations behind this, with their lobbyists getting the laws made in their favor," she muttered. Emma hated lobbyists.

"For sure," Ophelia responded, "I read that the college funding cuts were made to pay for the recent tax overhaul, which lowered the corporate tax rate."

Arden nodded, thinking of Kirish's lecture on *Citizens United* about corporations with all their constitutional rights and influence. After Ophelia shot her a loaded look, Arden wondered if O was thinking the same thing.

"When I was your age," Emma said, "we passed a ballot initiative to keep corporations out of farming in the state. Now it looks like somebody needs to kick them out of the universities!"

Arden's mom had once told her something about the ballot campaign. *Your gramma marched on the state capitol to keep factory farms out of South Dakota*, she remembered her mother telling her once when they drove by the capitol in Pierre. She knew Emma sometimes got fired up about politics, especially corruption in politics, but mainly she was rabid about making sure everyone she knew voted. She would drive her elderly neighbors to the town hall each Election Day, pestering them on the phone until they agreed to go. Arden remembered how hard it had been for Emma to sign the lease with AGM for use of the land, because of her belief in keeping corporations out of farming in the state. But Arden really didn't know much about the ballot campaign itself.

Ophelia was intrigued as well. "A ballot initiative? I've always wanted to work on one of those. There was that one in Denver to legalize marijuana—it had just passed when I moved out here, and everyone was going bananas about it."

"Well, that's hardly something I'd know about," Emma snorted. The girls exchanged a smile. Emma could get going on her opinions about the *devil's weed* if they weren't careful.

"But I do know about ballot initiatives. South Dakota was the first state in the union to have them," she told them proudly. "Our state invented them! They put the power in the hands of the voters, when the politicians aren't minding us. Now, our cause, back in the seventies, was the anti-corporate farming act. It prohibited corporations from owning agricultural land in the state of South Dakota, and a whole bunch of other states did it too, following our lead again! And it protected the family farms pretty well, for a long time. I'd never have been able to buy the back forty with the money from your grandfather's life insurance if I'd had to compete with Big Ag."

Arden thought of the forty wooded acres on the northernmost tip of the farm, where she used to take long walks. It had been her escape in high school, wooded and remote. She hadn't been out there since the land had been leased to AGM and wondered what it looked like now.

"The anti-corporate farming law also leveled the playing field when selling corn for animal feed at the local co-op. I would have never been able to compete with the factory farms with their modern turbines and patented seeds."

"What was the campaign like?" Ophelia asked eagerly.

Emma smiled broadly, nodding, reliving the past. "Well, we went door to door, talking to folks about it. We went to Grange Hall meetings and county fairs, collecting signatures. And come Election Day, it became a law!" She jumped up from the table again and went into the living room, digging around in the bottom of her cedar chest and producing a photo album. There was a picture of

Emma marching at the state capitol, ironically carrying a pitchfork with her curly brown hair pulled back in a yellow bandana.

"You look amazing! I've never seen this before," Arden exclaimed, astounded at how young and fierce Emma looked. She could see herself in Emma's set jaw, as well as Jill in her eyes, crinkling with a smile.

"That's so cool!" Ophelia said. "But . . . I'm confused. Isn't your land across the road leased to a . . ." She trailed off, seeing Arden wince.

The excitement drained out of Emma. "Over the years, the damn corporate lobbyists and lawyers got one loophole after another put in the law, till it didn't mean much anymore. Those bastards can't wait to get their hands on this farm for good—every year they send me a letter trying to buy me out. They bought the Johnson place last year. They'll be the first in line at the foreclosure." She scowled darkly, getting up from the table and clearing dishes with a shaky hand.

Arden and Ophelia exchanged stricken looks. Arden hated how this triumph of Emma's youth, the anti-corporate farming act, had ultimately failed to protect her own farm at the end of her life. It seemed so wrong. And was she serious about the foreclosure or was she just being dramatic?

After dinner, Emma turned in, worn out from their conversation. As the girls made up the couch with sheets for Ophelia, they talked more about Emma's story.

"I love the idea of a ballot initiative," Ophelia said. "It's like a political campaign for an idea." She wanted to be a campaign organizer when she graduated. She'd looked into grad schools, but lately she'd been thinking the best way to learn was to just do it.

"When Emma was talking about the anti-corporate farming act, I was thinking about that poli-sci class that

Justin Kirish taught, remember, on corporations being people under the law?" Arden said.

"I know!" O exclaimed, "Me too."

"If corporations have all the rights people have, but so much more power, maybe it's these ballot initiatives that can keep them in check," Arden mused.

"But it seems like they don't hold. Didn't Emma say that the corporations got loopholes put in the bills by their lobbyists? And now a corporation is trying to push her out?" Ophelia shuddered.

"What about a ban on corporations entirely?" Arden asked, and they looked at each other for a long while, considering it. Arden remembered that feeling she had at the end of Kirish's class, that this wasn't the way the country was supposed to work, and that somebody had to do something.

They talked about the idea late into the night. If the anti-corporate farming statute had protected family farms (at least before it got ruined), wouldn't an anti-corporation statute protect the political process from corruption? The fact that Emma's initiative had only covered farmland, rather than everything, was its flaw. Corporations still had an outsized ability to influence the state legislature, chipping away at the law's protections when people weren't looking. If there were no corporations, there would have been no corporate lobbyists to undo the work of the people. A total ban on corporations in the state would be a message to the politicians that they worked for the voters, not corporate interests. Under the law, corporations and people had the same rights, but corporations had resources and lobbyists to drown out the voices of regular people. This could fix things.

"What about Walmart and Amazon? Wouldn't people freak out if they couldn't get all that cheap stuff they sell? Delivered?" Ophelia asked, skeptically.

Picturing Emma's pantry, Arden thought about self-suf-ficiency. What would she be willing to sacrifice in order to change the world? All the consumerism fed by stores like that was destroying the planet, but would she be willing to spend her time canning and gardening instead of an easy trip to the grocery store? There must be some kind of middle ground, where you could still get what you needed but everything wasn't controlled by corporations.

"What about all the stuff those corporations own? All the land and businesses?" Arden wondered aloud, thinking maybe people could start up shops or farms from the corporations' land and stuff, and could become self-sufficient. Instead of relying on corporations to spoon-feed them things, they would relearn how to make things for themselves, with their hands. She thought of Emma's land, in jeopardy from the bank and AGM.

"Ophelia, that's it!" she exclaimed. "The thing that would make it good for people, to make up for what they'd miss, without corporations selling them stuff and orga-nizing the economy. The thing that would make people vote for a corporation ban. All the land and belongings of corporations in the state—it would all go back to people."

Ophelia nodded, looking pensive. This felt like a radical idea to Arden, but why? Why should it be so shocking? Only if you accept the premise that corpora-tions are people.

"Let's sleep on it," O said, climbing under the covers they'd made up on the couch.

THE NEXT MORNING, EMMA KNOCKED on the door to Arden's room. She was sitting on her bed, thinking about her conversation with Ophelia the night before, about the corporation ban. Was it a crazy idea? What would Emma think of it? Before Arden could ask her, she stopped, seeing what Emma had in her hands.

"I was cleaning out the closet. . . ." Emma hesitated, almost nervously. "I found this jacket of your mom's, and thought you might want it," she continued, holding out the jean jacket. Arden did not reach out to accept the denim bundle, knowing exactly what it was. She remembered her mother embroidering the back of the jacket with richly colored flowers. Emma shook out the folds and held it up so they could inspect the handiwork. Arden's memory of them as garish and flamboyant must have been tinted with teen embarrassment; she saw that the flowers were quite beautiful.

"You're going to have to forgive her at some point, you know, honey. I know that's not exactly your strong suit, but you're only hurting yourself." Emma's words were light, but they stung. "You can't hold a grudge against a dead woman."

When Arden did not respond, Emma deposited the jacket at the foot of the bed, patted Arden's knee, and walked out of the bedroom. After a moment, Arden touched a violet flower—a peony, perhaps—with the tip of her finger before shoving the jacket in the back of a dresser drawer. She knew she wouldn't be able to think straight with that thing around.

"Wait, Gram," Arden called. When Emma popped her head back in the doorway, she asked, "Were you serious about the foreclosure? Is everything okay?"

Emma's smile fell away. "I'll figure something out, hon. I always do."

LATER, AFTER THE HAM WAS IN THE OVEN, and the pies made, Emma went to take a nap before the big feast. Ophelia had set up camp with her laptop in the living room, researching the ballot initiative process. She had the papers from an old shoebox of Emma's full of materials for the anti-corporate farming initiative laid out around her. Arden sat at her feet, fingering an old clipboard with a yellowed sheet of paper, lined for signatures. *I support passage of a law prohibiting corporations from owning agricultural land in South Dakota,* it proclaimed across the top.

"Could we do it?" Arden asked her friend.

"Running a campaign like this is a big deal. It would take a serious commitment of time and effort. I can't have a repeat of high school, where I barely passed my classes." She cast Arden a glance, and continued, "Unlike you, I actually have to study. But it would be an amazing learning experience. Not to mention something big to put on my resumé. I'd be that much closer to getting a paying job on a national presidential campaign. Maybe we wait until after we graduate. . . ." Ophelia chewed on a nail.

"What if I didn't need to worry about my classes?" Arden said softly.

"What?" Ophelia glanced surreptitiously at Emma's bedroom door. "If you drop out, your grandmother is going to freak."

"It's like a hamster wheel. You borrow money for college so you can get a good job. You need a good job to pay college debt," Arden protested, getting up from the floor to look out the window. "I don't want to borrow money from that fucking YouthBank, not unless I know damn well what I'm going to study and what I'm going to do with it."

She turned back to O, practicing for Emma, "I can always go back to school after the campaign."

"You'd have to be out in front," Ophelia warned her. "You're from South Dakota, so it would need to be you as the spokesperson. I'll be your campaign manager, and I can design the game plan, but I can't take charge. Unlike you, I've got to graduate. For what I want to do, I need a degree."

"But you're so much better in front of a crowd than I am." The thought of public speaking made Arden's stomach clench.

"That's not the deal, Arden. You better think long and hard about this. Dropping out of college is a big step. Do you care enough about this to change your life? If so, you've got to be willing to step up and be a leader."

Arden nodded. She had a lot to think about.

"And one more thing," Ophelia pushed her chair back from the table and gestured toward her research. "If you are serious about this, I think you should talk to Justin Kirish. He's in law school. I'm on top of the process stuff, but whether the corporate ban would be legal and how to word the ballot question is something we'd need to figure out before we do anything."

ARDEN WENT OUT TO VISIT THE HORSE and mull things over. Standing outside his stall, she said, "Hi, buddy," in a low voice, and he turned in the stall. She stood scratching his neck and stroking his whiskery nose for a while, which he seemed to like, murmuring to him.

"Seems like Nick has taken to you."

Arden spun to face the man standing behind her, leaning against the far wall near the door. She recognized Jimmy Bouchard, who'd been a year ahead of her in school. He was taller, more filled out, but still angular.

"He's beautiful," she said. "I'm Arden, Emma's granddaughter."

"I know." Of course. She had a reputation. "I'm Jim. I remember you from 4-H. You raised rabbits, right?"

Arden was pleased his image of her was not the fight in chorus.

"That's right. You were goats?"

"Yup. Best way to keep land clear there is," he nodded, smiling. He had a kind crinkling around his eyes. "What brings you back here—aren't you in college?"

"Just visiting Emma for Easter."

"Oh, right, Easter. Forgot about that." He looked grim for a moment. "Hey, since you are here, want to keep Nick company for a minute while I muck out that stall?" She noticed the wheelbarrow and pitchfork at his side.

"Of course! What can I do?"

"Well, if you felt like giving him a treat, you could put that halter on him and graze him a bit in the yard there. He'd be mighty happy to get some grass. I've been meaning to fix up the fence out there so he can pasture, but haven't gotten around to it." He handed her a lead line, which she clipped onto the halter after slipping it over the horse's nose and ears.

"You know your way around a horse," he commented.

"A bit," Arden answered. The bay perked up with the halter on, and she led him through the barn and out onto the grass outside. Arden stood beside him holding the lead rope, watching his square teeth rip the grass off neatly at the stem. The sun was low in the sky, casting a golden glow on the tops of the trees and warming the back of her neck.

"Arden!" Emma called out from the house. "I need you to make the salad! The ham is almost done!" There was a note of panic in her voice, the anxiety of timing a big meal with an expensive ham. Jimmy appeared in the doorway of the barn.

"Here, I'll take him, you'd better go." He held out his hand to take the horse. She saw him lift his nose in the air.

Suddenly she could smell the ham, wafting from the house, fragrant and homey. Did he have nowhere to go? He'd forgotten it was Easter, earlier. Should she invite him to stay?

He watched her look back and forth from him to the house and chuckled, somehow reading her mind. "That's very kind of you," he said, even though she had not in fact invited him, "but I've got somewhere to be. Here, give him to me. I'm done."

Arden handed him the horse's lead, and from the way he watched her walk away into the house, toward the feast, she thought maybe it wasn't true that he had an Easter supper of his own, somewhere, waiting for him.

THAT NIGHT, ARDEN LAY IN BED with a full stomach, turning things over in her mind. The ballot initiative idea had sparked something in her. It felt foretold that she would do it. That Emma's work on the anti-corporate farming act was a baton that had been passed. But the idea of standing up in front of a crowd or positioning herself as the leader of something made her heart pound. She hated public speaking with a passion. Still, Ophelia was right—if it mattered enough for her to do it, it must also matter enough for her to put herself out there.

And dropping out of school would not be easy to explain to Emma. But Arden could always go back, right? Once she knew what she wanted to do. She felt duty bound to weigh methodically the pros and the cons, but in her heart she knew she had already decided.

They left the next day for Vermillion without talking to Emma about the idea. Ophelia had wanted to, but Arden begged her not to. She feared that Emma would smell a rat that Arden was thinking of dropping out, and she wasn't ready to defend it.

As they drove, she thought of Kirish. *Next, you need to go talk to Justin Kirish*, Ophelia had said—and she was probably right. Arden wondered what his reaction to the idea would be. If she dropped out, it might be the last time she saw Kirish. She found that she wanted to see him one more time. But she worried, would he be the friendly TA, eager to teach, or the cold law student she'd affronted at the party? More importantly, would he judge the corporation ban to be a good idea, legally or otherwise?

CHAPTER 3 · **INTERESTED**

ARDEN WENT LOOKING FOR KIRISH WHEN the semester
ended. She'd seen him in class a few times, and at the
final he proctored, but he hadn't taught another class.
She surprised him in his tiny graduate student cubicle
in the library, piled with books. When he didn't look up,
she'd rapped on the wooden dividers, and he'd jumped.
A flowering tree outside the old paned window pressed
enormous pink flowers against the glass. He'd looked
back between her and the flowers, as if she'd found out a
secret. *I won't tell*, she thought.

"Hi . . . uh. . . ." she began awkwardly, "Do you have
a minute?"

"Arden," he said, surprised. "What brings you in?"
He leaned back in his chair, smiling lightly, and glanced
behind her.

"I've got something I want to talk to you about."
Arden wasn't quite sure how to begin.

"Okay, something about poli-sci?"

"Well, the idea kind of started with poli-sci, in a way, with the *Citizens United* lecture, but no, it doesn't really relate to class. It's about . . ."

He interrupted her, "I'm really sorry, Arden," seeming genuine, "I'm slammed finishing this paper for my Bankruptcy Law final." He turned back to his desk as if that concluded their discussion.

"Wait, please, it's really important, and you are the only one who can help me," Arden blurted out.

"Arden, I really can only help you with things relating to class. Anything else is . . . not my purview," he finished coldly.

"What do you mean?" Arden asked incredulously.

"It's not my job to help you with anything else," he repeated, gritting his teeth. "I'm not interested in getting involved with any undergrad drama."

"I'm only asking for twenty minutes of your time," Arden said, getting pissed. "And I've dropped out of school, so you don't need to worry about the fact that I'm an undergrad. Because I'm not anymore."

"What do you mean, you've dropped out? You're such a good student! Why?"

Arden was surprised at his concern, especially after a moment ago, when he so coldly said helping her wasn't his job. He waited for her to answer.

"I lost my scholarship. I don't want to borrow," she responded. "I have an idea for a ballot initiative banning corporations in the state."

This got his attention. He sat for a long moment looking at her, first a smile playing across his face at the idea, then furrowing his eyebrows.

"You have dropped out of school?" he confirmed.

"After my finals last week, I filed the paperwork."

He sighed. "I can't talk with you now." He gestured to the stack of books on his desk but also flicked a glance around the library, as if to make sure they were alone. "I can meet you later, after I'm done with this paper. Tomorrow, at the Spine."

ARDEN ARRIVED EARLY AT THE COFFEE shop the next afternoon, staking out a quiet table in the back among the books and plants. She browsed the books, feeling guilty she'd never bought a book here, only lattes. When Kirish arrived, he waved to her from the entrance, plastered with posters and band flyers, and got in line to order a coffee. When he sat down at the table with his cup and two cookies, he was much more relaxed than when she'd seen him last.

"Sorry about yesterday," pushing the cookies toward her as a peace offering. "On top of the bankruptcy final, I was dealing with something that got messed up on my transcript. Which I had to get out for a summer law clerk application. Nightmare," he said with a friendly shrug of his shoulders that seemed to say, *you know how it is.*

"So," he said, "what's going on? Why are you dropping out?"

She told him about the grant letter, and Emma's anti-corporate farming law, and their ballot initiative idea. Kirish sat back and looked at her for a while, really looked at her, until Arden couldn't take it anymore.

"What do you think?"

"Interesting," was all he said, still looking at her.

"So, we wanted to ask you," Arden fumbled, feeling vulnerable all of a sudden, and drawing on her instruction from Ophelia to speak to Kirish, "we wondered whether there were legal problems with the idea? And if it passes, do you think there's a way to stop the legislature from whittling away at it, like the lobbyists did with the anti-corporate farming law?"

"Who's we?" he asked. "All I see is you."

"Ophelia."

"Was it your idea or hers?"

"Both of ours."

"Really, the two of you had the same idea? At the same time?"

Arden thought back to that night at Emma's. "Well, I guess it was initially mine. But we came up with the plan together."

He nodded, and Arden felt the heartburn sensation she got when she was about to raise her hand in class.

He broke into a smile, almost suppressing a laugh. "I thought so."

"What is that supposed to mean?" Arden demanded, thinking he was making fun of her.

"Don't get like that. Only means that I thought there was something different about you."

Different being a positive attribute here? It was hard to tell if she was being made fun of, but there was no mocking in his expression.

"So what do you think?" she asked again. "Is it legal? Could it work?"

He nodded, contemplating. "I'm going to need to do some research. Seems like there would be problems with it being a taking of private property. Do the owners of the corporation get compensated for what they've lost?"

"We were thinking that the land they owned, the things, the businesses, they would revert to the people. It would get doled out somehow."

He let out a low whistle. "That's pretty radical, Arden Firth."

Something about his using her full name made her heat up, but she responded coolly. "Well, not really. I mean, wasn't it that way before corporations?"

"I suppose. Some folks will see that as government overreach, taking private property and redistributing it. For a lot of people, that smacks of communism. Is that what you're proposing?" he asked.

"How can it be government overreach if it's the people doing it? We're taking back what should have been ours, if the corporations hadn't been skimming off the top for so long!"

Kirish grinned, enjoying her flare of temper. "You know, it's not *more* regulation, it's less," he mused. "It's actually less government bureaucracy *not* to have corporations. The laws that create and regulate corporations would just be taken off the books."

He swigged the last of his coffee, apparently inspired by the idea. "Okay, what about folks who rely on Walmart or Amazon to get diapers, or printers, or coffee? Without a free market or an interstate distribution model, how will people get the things they need?"

This question had been troubling Arden. "We'll have to work that out," she told him. "We'll have to find a way to set people up with livelihoods that keep a working free market, like general stores and independently owned shops. But do we really need thirty different kinds of toothpaste? I don't think so." Arden insisted. She always felt paralyzed having to choose among so many brands; it felt like wretched excess to have so much choice when so many people in the world had nothing, or lived so much more simply. Arden hated to grocery shop, it felt like an existential crisis. Some products were endangered species, she'd read, like sea bass, or mated for life, like swordfish. Should she stop eating beef because of its environmental impact? Which was the brand of apple juice with high arsenic levels? Was it better to buy local or get something not packed in Styrofoam?

"Anyway," she continued, "the fact that we can have perishable food from all over the world, whenever we want, wastes natural resources. We take it for granted to get an avocado or pineapple or banana in South Dakota in January. Maybe people's expectations should change."

"Hmm," he said, looking doubtful, "that's going to be a hard sell. I mean, I try to buy local when I can, but there's not a lot of local food to choose from, as you say, in South Dakota in January. And what about all the other things people rely on Walmart for?"

Arden pressed on. "Before there was Walmart, what did people do? The Sears catalog, right, back in our grandparents' day? And the general store. If there was no Walmart to compete with, there would be general stores again. There's no Sears catalog anymore, but the whole worldwide internet marketplace has replaced it. Just 'cause there's no corporations in South Dakota anymore doesn't mean people can't buy things made or sold elsewhere. And as far as your *distribution model?*" Kirish smiled wryly as she parroted his academic language. "Something new will take its place. Isn't that how the free market works? Maybe like Uber drivers, but truly independent, delivering packages? Or maybe the US postal service will be revitalized and hire tons more people."

"So there'd still be internet sellers delivery then?" he pressed.

Arden paused. She'd been struggling with this. "Definitely no warehouses. No fulfillment centers." She thought darkly of her mother's accident. "That's exactly the kind of exploitive corporate model we don't want in the state. But we can't stop people from ordering something in the mail, right?" Arden didn't like this devil's compromise, but after long conversations with Ophelia she was willing to try it out. What would Kirish make of it?

"Hmm," he said again, noncommittal. "What happens to those big box stores?"

"Ophelia and I have been researching co-ops. Do you know Cabot Cheese? It's owned by the workers. Maybe each of those existing big box stores will be returned to the workers to build into a co-op. Now those employees make so little they have to work two or three jobs, or take public assistance despite working full time. What if they got to own the store?"

Kirish looked pensive. "Interesting. But we'll need things from other states to fill those shops. Will corporations still do business with South Dakotans if they are not recognized as having rights in our courts? I suppose there could just be a choice-of-law provision in every contract that the law of another state applied. But what about exercising personal jurisdiction over the South Dakota resident to enforce those contracts. . . ."

Arden got lost as Kirish talked himself through some incomprehensible legal jumbles. She liked how he kept talking to her as if she understood, forgetting she was just an undergrad. His sleeve was a bit short on his arm, which had sandy brown hair on it, and long bones with square joints at his wrist and knuckles that were strangely interesting to her. She was aware of his arm brushing hers as he reached for his empty coffee, and she forced herself not to jump at the warmth of his touch.

"It's a really interesting legal question, actually. Could a state ban corporations? Corporations are formed by state law, so arguably, they could be ended if the state laws change. I'm not sure how you deal with out-of-state corporations, though."

"You keep using that word, *interesting*," Arden ventured to tease him back. He smiled again, looking at her.

A group of students approached and pulled out chairs

at the table behind them, bumping Arden's chair and saying, "Excuse me." She slid her chair in, putting her arms on the table, and her knee touched Kirish's under the table. He jerked back abruptly, knocking the table and upsetting her untouched coffee, spilling some. Arden grabbed her knapsack to keep it dry, and he stood up, looking at the new patrons darkly.

"Yes, well, I'll think about the legal issues and let you know. It's probably unconstitutional in several different ways, but let me do some research and get back to you."

Arden looked up at him, confused by his change of tone. He was the cold law student again, unsmiling, collecting his things.

"I presume you still have your student email for at least a few more weeks?" He shot another glance at the students behind them, now laughing loudly. *What is he worried about?*

"Uh, yeah, I think so."

"Okay, then, I'll be in touch. By email." He stood up and walked out without a backward look.

Arden sat for a while, sipping her cold coffee. *What just happened?* She was flummoxed. He had been so friendly, so *interested*. Was he embarrassed to be seen with her? What had she done?

A FEW DAYS LATER, ARDEN MOVED onto Ophelia's couch. She'd stayed in the dorm until all the other kids were gone, until they basically kicked her out. Just as Arden had feared, Emma had gone ballistic when she heard Arden was dropping out. Her grandmother was adamant that finishing the last two years of college was an investment in herself that Arden had to make. It was so frustrating to Arden that Emma would push her to take on debt, when her own experience with borrowing had been so bad. Even before her mortgage troubles, Emma had borrowed on the farm equity line, and it had always terrified Arden. Arden's grandparents had once owned the land outright, but each time the tractor broke or the crops didn't do well, Emma wrote a check off the green checkbook, sometimes paying the monthly payments on the farm equity line with more borrowing. Arden would never forget how desperate it had felt, when the monthly minimum on the loan couldn't be paid and the medical bills kept piling up.

Emma had always been a stable influence in Arden's life, but this fight had been emotional and bruising. *You can't give up or you'll be just like your mother,* Emma had growled. *You're too bright not to go to college.* And then again, *You never could forgive anyone, you're going to just take your ball and go home, then? You always were a wet grudge, and let me tell you, that didn't make things any easier on your poor mother.* Something about Arden dropping out had unhinged Emma. It would be a long time before they spoke, and Arden sure as hell wasn't going home for the summer. She wasn't even sure it was home anymore.

Weeks later, she got the email. She had begun working as a waitress at a local burger joint, trying to save enough to get her own place, and beginning to second-guess herself. The email was addressed to both of them, although sent to Arden's account.

Arden and Ophelia,
I've considered the legal issues raised by your proposed corporate ban and I think I've found a way that it could pass constitutional muster. Success is by no means assured, but I believe that there are strong arguments for the proposition that South Dakota voters should be

permitted to abolish corporations, if a ballot initiative is properly crafted and passed by a majority of voters.

I would be willing to consider being the legal advisor to the campaign, if you wish. First, I'd like to meet to discuss the main legal hurdles the initiative will face, as well as some policy considerations that I see that the campaign will need to address. Please let me know of a time that would be convenient for you both.

Sincerely,
Justin Kirish

They met him the next day in The Spine. As they joined him at his table, he was courteous, like a lawyer to his clients. He began to brief them on the legal issues that the corporate ban would encounter, mainly ways in which it might be unconstitutional. The two central obstacles were whether the ban would be a governmental taking of private property without just compensation, and whether it would violate something called *interstate commerce*.

"Under the US Constitution, the federal government has the sole power to regulate interstate commerce, and there are limits on what states can do to block it," he explained. "But there are exceptions to these rules, for matters of public policy—basically, things of public social importance—which I believe arguably applies here."

"And what about the just compensation part?" Arden asked, sipping her coffee. "Does that mean we need to pay executives and stockholders for their stock? Because that wouldn't work. Our plan is that land and other assets are surrendered into a fund that gets distributed to South Dakotans. We think this is a key reason people will support the initiative, because they see value in it for themselves. Also, we think it's fair because it counteracts the way corporations have exploited people like my mom.

It gives things back to people that should have been theirs all along."

He nodded, beginning to relax his formal legal advisor mask as he thought about it. "Yeah, that's going to be a tough one. Our argument will be that since corporations aren't people under state law, which is where corps are created in the first place, they aren't entitled to just compensation. It's got some holes, because that doesn't address compensating stock owners, who actually are people. And some of those plaintiffs will be pretty sympathetic—the family-owned business loses everything? No one's going to go for that. The law will need an exception for family-owned corps, where their businesses just revert to being privately owned, and are not subject to redistribution."

"Yeah, we were thinking something along those lines," Ophelia agreed.

"The rest of the just compensation piece will have to be the argument that the plan of redistribution itself is a type of just compensation," Kirish reasoned. He turned to address Arden. "As you said before, Arden, the distribution is fair because it addresses the past harm of corporations. It's perhaps not just compensation in the legal sense of paying shareholders the value of their property, but we argue it's a different type of fair, nevertheless. We'll have to build in some protections, like hearings and an opportunity to be heard, into the implementation of the plan, so that we can avoid being challenged on due process."

Arden looked at Ophelia, who was leaning back from the table, scratching her chin. They'd been talking a lot about fairness, and she thought it fit here to support Kirish's argument. "We've been researching the social effects of corporations for the last month, and I think that could go a long way toward showing what's fair," responded Arden. "Did you know that less than half of US citizens have *any* investments in the stock market? When you look at South Dakotans, it's less than one quarter. And the vast majority of wealth is concentrated among a very few. Over the last fifty years, the differential between the CEO's salary and the entry-level worker has increased almost exponentially."

Arden heard her voice becoming hard as her anger built. The more they had researched corporate economics, the more right their idea felt. She pressed on. "Corporations have become more and more profitable, pushing for efficiency at the cost of their workers, until there's nothing left. And did you know that the success of corporations is measured by how much and how fast they grow? How creepy is that? Nowadays, they can only achieve that kind of growth by outsourcing and automating. Which results in environmental destruction and people working two or three jobs just to maintain a living wage."

Arden halted, seeing the look on both their faces. "What?"

"That's it, Arden, that's your stump speech!" Ophelia exclaimed.

"Yeah." Kirish nodded, looking at her across the table with new respect. "That was powerful."

"Stop distracting me!" Arden said, dodging the compliment. "What I am trying to say is that the way corporations work has historically been unfair to people, real people as opposed to the legal fiction of corporate people. Massive gains in corporate wealth and power have not benefitted South Dakotans. Our redistribution plan is just a way to put that right."

They both grinned at her. "There it is," said Kirish, "that's our argument." He moved the salt shaker sitting on their table as if it were a chess piece, as if to say, "checkmate."

Kirish and Ophelia talked for some time about the process of filing a ballot initiative. For a voter-initiated law, they'd need fourteen thousand signatures collected over the course of sixty days, which had to be filed with the Secretary of State by mid-December. They had five months before the filing deadline, or they'd have to wait another year. First, they'd need to draft the ballot question and the actual law itself, and get it certified by the State Attorney General. After getting on the ballot, the initiative would need a simple majority of votes cast to pass during the general election the following November. Based on voter turn-out for past elections, Ophelia figured that would be about 140,000 votes.

"What about a voter-initiated constitutional amendment?" Arden asked. "We've been wondering whether that would be a better route. Wouldn't that make it harder to poke holes in the corporation ban, like happened to the anti-corporate farming law, with all the loopholes the legislature has snuck in over the years?"

"I don't recommend that," Kirish warned them. "We'd need to collect twice as many signatures to get on the ballot, and I think voters are more wary about passing constitutional amendments. The default is 'no' on those for most voters, where on legislation, people are more willing to experiment. People will just have to stay vigilant, to keep the legislature from weakening it, the way they did with the farming bill."

Kirish paused, and looked out the window of the coffee shop pensively. "Also, a voter-initiated constitutional amendment is more likely to trigger the interest of the US Supreme Court, where a voter-initiated law could fly under the radar."

Arden wasn't entirely convinced. Hadn't they learned about state laws found unconstitutional by the Supreme

Court? It still felt to her like a constitutional amendment would be stronger. But Ophelia didn't seem concerned.

"Wow, you really think this could end up in the Supreme Court?" Ophelia asked.

"Yup," Kirish said with a grin, clearly excited by the prospect.

"This is awesome, Kirish, thanks for doing all this work," Ophelia said. Arden could tell by her friend's tone that a "but" was coming. "But what's your angle, here? Aren't you worried that working on a campaign like this would hurt your chances of getting a job when you graduate? Isn't it mainly corporations that hire lawyers, other than the personal-injury kind?"

He sat up straight. "I want to teach law, rather than be in private practice—although those professorships are definitely hard to come by," he responded.

Arden had to assume that attending USD didn't put him in line to teach at many law schools, but perhaps he could teach poli-sci or law to undergraduates. She knew he was an excellent teacher.

He continued, "My father is a partner in a big firm in Philadelphia, and I've seen what that life is like. Entering your time in six-minute increments, working fifteen-hour days. My dad is fifty-five but looks seventy. My mother's already pulling his strings to get me into one of those jobs." Kirish shook his head. "Honestly, making me less marketable to a law firm would be a good thing in my book."

"Why don't you just tell your mother you don't want to work in a place like that?" Ophelia challenged him.

He laughed. "You haven't met my mother. And also, getting the chance to be involved with something that has the potential to end up in the Supreme Court would be a really cool experience."

"Makes for a more interesting resume than just the University of South Dakota, too," Ophelia observed. She cast a glance to Arden, thinking of something. "By the way, how is it that you ended up here, Kirish? Seems a strange choice for a guy like you."

He sat back, crossing his arms. "It's the only school I got into. Obviously. Why else would I be here?"

"Boy, law school must be competitive, I'd have thought you'd be a strong candidate," Ophelia pressed.

He said nothing, starting to look angry. Arden could see that he was embarrassed by the topic, and she was relieved when Ophelia didn't push it further. Arden wondered what he wasn't saying.

That August, the three of them spent long hours in Kirish's apartment, planning the campaign. Ophelia drew up a meticulous battle plan for getting the required signatures, and they worked on letters to the editors of the college papers around the state. They researched state and local land-use laws and town ordinances to think about how the distribution might work, how to fit it into existing governing structures. Kirish patiently explained to them, more than once, the specific constitutional hurdles they faced.

One night, after a late shift waitressing, Arden arrived to find the two of them halfway through a second bottle of red wine, arguing about politics. She hadn't seen Kirish drink before, except that one time at the graduate student's party where he'd snubbed her, and even then, he had seemed cold sober. He did not seem entirely sober now. He welcomed her with a hug, their first ever, and ransacked his kitchen looking for a third glass for her, making jokes about his Spartan living arrangements. He was actually funny, and so different from his usual stiff self. She could see that Ophelia was enjoying the change too, and was surprised to feel a twinge of jealously at the two of them laughing and finishing each other's sentences, both buzzed.

Arden poured herself some wine and stretched out across the couch, putting her bare feet up on its ratty arm. Her feet were sore from waiting tables, running French fries and burgers to the loud families piling in, one after another, at the Applebee's. She smelled of Fryolater grease. She laid her head back on the other arm of the couch for a moment, savoring the taste of the wine, closing her eyes. After a moment, she realized the conversation had stopped and opened her eyes. Ophelia was sprawled on the only other chair in the room, and Kirish was sitting at her feet, his fingers frozen on a paperback he was pulling from the brimming bookshelf. Both were gazing at her. She felt her legs stretched out long, and knew they were tan and strong from the summer. She could feel that her uniform had hiked up, showing the side of her thigh.

Ophelia cleared her throat dramatically, to break the silence and maybe also to make a joke of the fact that both she and Kirish had been ogling her.

"Well, well." Ophelia looked from one of them to the other, smiling. "Is it getting warm in here? Perhaps we should get more comfortable. Arden, I can't imagine you'd want to wear that uniform for a moment longer." Her voice was teasing, but dead serious.

Arden laughed, unbelievingly. She knew her friend lusted after both men and women, but she had never before found herself in the crossfire. The idea was titillating, in part because she couldn't imagine that Kirish would let it happen. She decided to test that proposition.

"I did forget a change of clothes . . . and this uniform is awful. The polyester *itches*," she paused for effect, watching Kirish's eyes widen, "and it smells like French fries." That would put a damper on things, she thought.

Ophelia grinned and rose from her chair, sinuously, if a bit unsteadily. "Here, love, let me help you."

Kirish was on his feet in a flash, yanking the glass out of Arden's hand. "Out!" he hollered.

Arden was shocked at the ferocity of his response. Even though she'd been joking, mostly, it still felt like rejection. Ophelia, though, seemed to think this was hilarious, cackling and snorting as she collected her shoes and purse as Kirish hustled them to the door, repeating, "Time for bed, girls. Out."

"Jeez, Kirish," Arden protested, "get a sense of humor, why don't you?"

"Please don't fuck with me, Arden," he implored, his voice husky. "And make sure she gets home safe." He shut the door in their faces.

Ophelia was howling with laughter, standing with her arms full of her jacket and purse and a novel she'd snatched off the coffee table, one shoe on, one shoe off.

"I want my wine, you wuss-bag!" She banged on the door.

When he opened the door, all trace of emotion in his face was gone. "The wine is all gone, Ophelia. I'm sorry, I shouldn't have let things go this far," his voice was smooth, as if they were having a normal conversation in a room full of people.

Ophelia made a "Harrumpf" sound to show what she thought about the wine being gone and the apology. "Oh, you're going to regret this one, Justin Kirish," she taunted him.

"I'd regret it either way," he responded, closing the door one more time.

After that, Kirish was all business. For the rest of the summer, he would only meet them in public, and he reverted to the formal chilly manner he'd used when he was their teacher. A few times, Ophelia had tried to tease him about turning down a threesome, and he made them endure long, disapproving lectures about the importance of keeping things professional. For some reason, things were more awkward between Arden and Kirish than between him and Ophelia, which Arden felt was unfair, since the whole thing had been Ophelia's stupid idea.

CHAPTER 4 / LAUNCH

THE CROWD AT THE SPINE WAS LARGER than Arden had expected, and she was sweating. Had she remembered to put on deodorant? She sure hoped so. They had gathered all the friends and volunteers who were going to help with the signature gathering, which had to be completed in a tight two-month window. Arden was supposed to make a speech to rally the coverts, as they were calling themselves, to explain the reasoning behind the initiative and get them charged up to canvass. They had decided to call their little army "coverts" late one night, from the Shakespeare play someone was reading. Ben, the English major, had explained that the word used to mean *offering protection*. They liked thinking of themselves as protectors. Also, it sounded top secret, which it had been for a while. Now that it was out in the open, Arden was terrified. Volunteers jostled for space, and The Spine's owner, Ken, looked irritated that they were blocking the pickup line for coffee.

In the previous weeks, she had tried to get both Ophelia and Kirish to make the address, but they had refused. *You are the leader.* After a terrible night's sleep, Arden felt queasy and shaky, and had momentarily considered calling in sick for the whole thing. But here she was. From what she could see, scanning the crowd, Kirish hadn't even showed up. She was frustrated that he would miss this milestone, after all their work. Was he purposefully staying away, or had something happened?

It took Arden a while to get the group's attention, saying "Excuse me," feebly in a tone that didn't begin to cut through the din. Finally she had to stand up on a chair and, mercifully, Ophelia let rip one of those piercing two-fingered whistles she was so good at. Silence. All eyes on Arden, quaking on her chair as she began to climb down. "Stay up there so we can see you, Arden!" someone hollered from the back.

"Okay, if you insist, but this feels like I'm about to do a trust fall," Arden complained, only half-joking.

"We'll catch you!" someone else yelled. Everybody laughed. That made it easier. This was a friendly crowd. They would catch her.

"Okay! Here's the deal. We need to collect fourteen thousand signatures of registered South Dakota voters, which means we probably need eighteen thousand, since there are always some percentage that are illegible or not registered voters. That's a lot in a spread-out state like ours, so we'll be focusing on places like cities or shopping centers, where we can get at lots of people. Under the ballot initiative rules, we've only got sixty days to collect all the signatures we need, and the filing is due by December, so we've got to start on Tuesday."

Arden took a deep breath and tried to get back to the way she felt on that first day she and Ophelia were explaining their idea to Kirish, when they told her she'd found her stump speech.

"Why are we doing this?" she posed the question to the crowd. "Here's our message in the simplest terms: We think it is the right thing for South Dakota voters to get rid of corporations in our state. For too long, our politicians have been doing the bidding of corporations, rather than that of the voters."

People in the crowd nodded their heads in agreement; someone said, "Yeah!" Arden pressed on.

"Corporations profit because they exploit the labor and ideas of individuals. They are skimming off the top, for the benefit of faraway investors, who are shielded from responsibility for the human impacts of decisions made purely for profit. Corporate profits are achieved by layoffs or outsourcing, or squeezing more and more out of their workers. And because their employees aren't seeing the full value of their work, many have no choice but to rely on welfare."

Arden was starting to feel more confident, and the words came to her more easily.

"Corporations measure their success by growth. They convince people to consume, consume, consume. This has massive environmental consequences, and growth for growth's sake doesn't benefit any of us. Most South Dakotans have begun to see through the lie that corporate growth will ever 'trickle down' to create real prosperity for people.

"Most South Dakotans also don't have any meaningful savings in the stock market, so we don't benefit from Wall Street bailouts or profits. Most of us *do* stand to gain if the profits corporations have been making off our state are redistributed to individuals." Arden surveyed the crowded back room of the café, trying to gauge whether she was connecting with the group. "Damn straight, girl," someone said. "We've got your back!" someone else said. Ophelia prompted her, "Arden, can you talk about the distribution process?"

Arden swallowed a gulp of water from a glass someone had handed her and continued. "What we are proposing is to dismantle corporations, distribute their assets to people, and repurpose them as individually owned businesses or worker-owner cooperatives. The idea is that the land, property, and assets owned by corporations in the state would be forfeited, once the legal fiction of corporations is ended. After corporations no longer exist, there will be farmland, apartment buildings, grocery stores—all sorts of land and assets that will no longer be owned by anyone or anything. All of this property will be distributed to individuals and cooperatives. The idea is that we move from an economy of workers to an economy of owners and makers."

One of the coverts raised a hand with a question. "But . . . how will it be decided who gets what, Arden?"

"The plan is that each town, each community, will look at its land and assets owned by corporations and develop a distribution plan. Every town already has a town planner or a land use board, which we think are probably the entities best positioned to develop this plan. People with an interest in owning a particular business or building can put in an application. Corporate-owned farmland will be put back in the hands of South Dakotans. Chain restaurants will become independently owned neighborhood diners."

"What about family-owned businesses?" one of the newer coverts, Ellen, asked.

"Our plan will protect family ownership or sole proprietors. The corporations will be dissolved, but folks will be able to keep their businesses and assets in an individual capacity," Arden answered.

Someone in the back raised a hand. "For many people, the only grocery store within sixty miles is a Walmart. Are we really asking those folks to sign on to ban their only grocery store? That seems like a hard sell."

Arden nodded. "Agreed, for some, it will be a hard sell. I guess I'd offer a couple thoughts. First, what did people do before Walmart? There were small grocery stores and general stores, nearer to people, before Walmart and the other corporate chains drove them out of business. This will create the space for them to return. Second," Arden ticked off on her finger, "the distribution plan will convert those stores to worker-owned cooperatives. We see successful grocery store co-ops in some urban areas that will be the model. And lastly," Arden felt herself going a bit off script here but decided to go with it, "and this won't get traction with a lot of people, but it does for me—think about what stores like Walmart provide. Cheap crap from China, every possible type of fruit and vegetable you might want, no matter what the season. These things are nice to have—convenient, affordable—but is it worth any cost to have that kind of convenience? Is it worth worker exploitation? Environmental destruction? Species going extinct? Global warming? Not for me," Arden declared.

There was silence in the room, shuffling of feet. Was she being too preachy? Had she lost them? Apparently, people weren't all clamoring to give up their cheap crap from China. Arden was disappointed, and continued with less enthusiasm.

"What did people do before Walmart? Ordered things from the Sears catalog that they couldn't find in town, right? Well, like it or not, Amazon is the new Sears catalog.

Even if we won't have corporations here, Amazon could still ship to South Dakota via the US mail, just like they do now."

There was a pause in the room as people considered this. Was it a contradiction? It felt like a slimy compromise to Arden, something she had to say to get people to support the idea. Arden wanted to wrap things up.

"So I think about our campaign in three phases. First, the ballot initiative. We get our proposal on the ballot and then passed next November. Next, the war. We fight it out in the courts while preventing the land and assets from being bled away. Third, the distribution. Corporate property and assets will revert to the people."

There was nodding, but one of the guys in the front let out a low whistle. "For real, eh? Communism, isn't it? Redistribution of wealth? You're going to be burned at the stake, Arden."

She laughed with more confidence than she felt. "Maybe. But it's not communism if the state doesn't keep the assets. Private property still exists. That's key." Arden paused, checking the crowd for reactions.

"But I will say one thing: the idea about taking back the means of production and returning it to the ninety-nine percenters—we are all about that, and a lot of people *will* brand that communism." She was surprised to see the discomfort in the faces of some of the coverts. She'd gone too far.

"But really it's nothing like communism," Arden backtracked. "After the assets are redistributed, the government is out of the equation. There's less government than there was before." She was thinking of what Kirish had said about regulation of corporations going away, but this went over their heads. There was a stiffening in the crowd she could feel, a disapproval.

Ophelia stepped forward, taking the spotlight off Arden, who could feel a droplet of sweat sliding down her side. "Yeah, well, we've got a bit of work to do on the message in that last bit there, *comrade*"—Ophelia rolled her eyes comically—"or this does go up in smoke. But we think we can find consensus with the right and left that the system is rigged in favor of those in power, and that politicians now work for corporate interests. The corporate/political power structure is screwing people. We've got to find a better way to talk about it."

Arden nodded, stung but accepting the criticism. She would have to be careful about how she spoke.

Ophelia turned back to the crowd, now starting to murmur.

"This is your chance to make a fundamental change. Don't get caught up in buzzwords. Are you in?"

Cheers erupted at Ophelia's words. Arden was hanging back, envying O's ease with the crowd, when Kirish stepped toward her from the back of the room. When had he gotten there? She saw the disappointment in his face.

She was about to apologize when he hissed at her, "Arden, that was a real misstep. Some of those people aren't coming back. You've got to get your messaging together, or stick to the script, if you're going to be the spokesperson for this initiative."

Arden couldn't believe it. "You guys were the ones insisting that it be me giving this speech, so back off!" she glared at him, livid.

"We *all* have agreed that it has to be you as the spokesperson, as the only native South Dakotan among the three of us," he told her sternly. This was true, but it didn't mean he got to tell her what to do.

"Listen, Kirish, you may be doing this because you want something interesting on your resumé, but I'm doing it because I really believe in it. It *matters* to me."

For a moment they stood glaring at each other. Arden waited for him to say it mattered to him too. He said nothing.

"So," she spat, "who gets to say what the message should be? You?" Arden's voice was rising, and she knew they were making a scene. There were folks lingering to talk with her after the speech, who were now watching them argue.

Again, Ophelia stepped in, putting an arm around both their shoulders and leaning in so they could talk quietly. "Arden," she said, "get a hold of yourself. It wasn't *that* bad. Don't freak out."

Arden glared at them both, pissed at the insinuation that she was angry because she had flubbed the speech. It *wasn't* that bad, was it? Not great, but not sinking-the-ship bad. No, what she was angry about was Kirish lecturing her.

"Arden," he spoke slowly, as if to a child, "no one is trying to tell you what you can and cannot say. We are merely trying to help you be *effective*. And please don't assume you know what matters to me."

"I'm sure I have no idea," Arden seethed, and walked out.

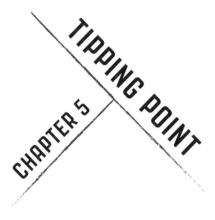

CHAPTER 5 · TIPPING POINT

ARDEN CUT THE ENGINE OF HER CAR after wedging it into the parking spot in front of the state capitol building in Pierre. As she sat, marshaling her courage, she had a flash of that moment in poli-sci nine months before, when she was so frustrated and thought, *someone should do something*. She looked at the box on the passenger seat with rueful pride: this was her anger in solid form. The air around her seemed to be vibrating. She thought of what Emma had said at Easter, that South Dakota had been the first state to give voters the power to pass laws through ballot initiatives, back in 1898. She felt the tendrils of history swirling around her ankles as she carried the box up the stone steps of the capitol building, worn concave by generations of feet.

Still humming, she pushed through the doors to the secretary of state's office. Her hands trembled as she handed to the clerk behind the glass the sheaf of petitions capturing the eighteen thousand signatures they had collected. The grueling hours of knocking on doors and loitering outside of grocery stores, colleges, and community centers had borne fruit. They had painstakingly checked the signatures against the voter rolls, and enough had checked out. After two months of working harder than she ever had in her life, she figured they should have enough signatures to get on the ballot for next November's election.

The clerk eyed her warily, flipping through the paperwork. They had been expecting her, since the signature-collection campaign had been reported by the college papers in Vermillion and Brookings. Social media and local news had picked it up too, with the news anchors ridiculing the campaign as naïve and radical. The clerk examined the materials Arden had dumped on the counter and read the title of their petition.

"Voter Initiative Abolishing the Corporation and Associated Distribution of Assets, eh? That's a mouthful. Well, if the signatures check out, it will be Ballot Initiative Number 99." She marked the petition with an official looking ink stamp. "If you'd waited one more, you could have been 100," the clerk said smugly.

Initiative 99 suited Arden just fine. It was a tipping point, and both the number of income inequality and the power of the many.

After the papers were filed and the forms were signed, Arden left the capitol building and made the three-hour drive back to Vermillion. She headed to The Spine, which had become the movement's de facto home base. Most of the team was there, waiting for her return. They had been promising its owner, Ken, that they'd find another space that fit their growing numbers, but for now, she smiled gratefully when she walked past the counter.

As she headed to the back tables surrounded by bookshelves, the team fell silent, eyes on her, waiting to hear the story. She flashed to her kickoff speech, where at the end she had fumbled the communism question, and for the thousandth time, wished there were someone else to be in the spotlight. Kirish was nowhere to been seen, and Ophelia was looking expectantly at her, gesturing for her to get started. Arden knew the moment warranted celebration, and although she had been for hours, alone in her car, truly triumphant, she was at a loss for how to convey that to a crowd.

"It is done!" she intoned, feeling like an actor but forcing herself to speak in a loud expansive voice. She raised her hands up in imitation of a small-town preacher, feeling ridiculous. "Give yourselves a hand, because we've done it! As long as the signatures check out, we will be on the ballot next November!" Cheers erupted.

When they quieted down, she went on. "This is just the opening battle. To win the war, we need to win next November. In order to get there, we are going to have to get our message out to a lot of people, and you are all essential to that work. So everyone take a break for finals and the holidays, and then come back in January ready to work!" More cheers.

Leave them wanting more, she told herself, and began to shake hands with the people around her. She was so relieved to stop talking, fearing another blunder or difficult question, that she blocked out the confusion in the faces around her that she wasn't saying more. She caught a glimpse of Ophelia standing with Kirish, both carefully masking their expressions.

Later, when all the coverts walked over to the Corner Pocket to celebrate, Arden felt a tinge of regret. Although she'd been relieved to cut her comments short, if she were honest, she was disappointed with herself. She knew she had to make the most of each opportunity she had to reach people. She couldn't get hung up on fear or misgivings; she couldn't let her own self-consciousness undermine their chances. She was quiet as they got beers and found a spot, wedging their group into the big area between the pool tables and the bathrooms. Arden sat on the outskirts of the group and checked her phone, wanting some distance. One of the guys playing pool approached her, and she looked up grudgingly.

"You're those corporation ban people, aren't you?" he asked her. He was wearing a baseball cap, drinking Budweiser. "I heard about you on the news."

Ophelia stepped forward and introduced herself, shooting Arden a look—*I'll take care of this*—and walked with the guy back over to his group of friends. Was Ophelia throwing her a bone? Arden listened with one ear as O easily rolled out the talking points, interspersed with her own raunchy brand of barroom humor. The guys were receptive. If only it were that easy for Arden to connect. She felt alone in the crowd.

Carson, Kirish's friend, asked him about the possibility that 99 could be overturned by the courts. The rest of the group quieted, wanting to hear his answer. He explained, "After the initiative passes, there will be lawsuits filed by corporate interests claiming it would be unconstitutional for South Dakota to abolish corporations. Our defense is simple, as it applies to South Dakota domiciled corporations—since they are created as a function of state law authority, then the state must also have the power to abolish them. However, the rub will be whether this requires paying 'just compensation' for any property rights lost, and if so, who exactly is entitled to what kind of compensation."

People nodded. They had heard of eminent domain cases, where the government took land for public use but had to pay just compensation.

Kirish continued, "Likewise, our initiative calls for the state to cease recognition of out-of-state corporations and for their real estate and any in-state assets to revert to the people. There will likely be challenges under both the South Dakota and the US constitutions."

"Will we win?" someone asked.

Kirish smiled. "I think we could. I've spent a lot of time researching it, and I think that I can make persuasive arguments as to why we should. I've been talking with law professors and lawyers who argue cases before the US Supreme Court, to try to refine those arguments and build support. Many of them think it is an intriguing question. So, there's definitely no guarantee that we would win, and you better believe that corporate America will be throwing all its resources at defeating us, but I believe that it *should be* constitutional. We have a fighting chance."

Carson asked a follow-up, "What's to stop corporations from just taking their assets—money and stuff, right?—out of town, if we win?"

Kirish nodded, expecting this question. He and Arden and Ophelia had hashed this out months ago. "We're building in a lockdown period where, after Initiative 99 passes, South Dakota corporations can't just move to another state, or dissolve, or sell their real estate or other assets, before the legal challenges are worked out."

He didn't tell them that there was a chance the courts might not uphold that lockdown period. Arden knew this was a risk, but Kirish believed they had strong legal arguments why the lockdown period should hold. When new laws are challenged, often courts put in place a holding period, to preserve the status quo, until legal challenges were litigated. The lockdown period built the preservation of the status quo into the structure of the bill. Moreover, the legal argument went, it was so important to the premise of 99 that there be corporate assets to spread around, that the prospects of success of the law would be irreparably harmed if the lockdown were not enforced.

It occurred to her that he also didn't mention the possibility of the state legislature chipping away at the voter-initiated law, like it had with her grandmother's anti-corporate farming law. He had downplayed the possibility the few times she'd brought it up. Arden again wondered whether they should have tried for a constitutional amendment. But thinking back over the last two months, she knew there was no way they could have gotten twice the number of signatures they just did for the ballot initiative to pass their proposed law, as would have been required for an amendment.

Arden wasn't sure she was comfortable with the fact that Kirish didn't explain these risks to the group. True, they were complicated and technical, and they were in a bar, but didn't they owe it to their team to tell them the truth? Or was it part of being a leader to motivate people by focusing on the positive and accepting some of the risk?

One of the new coverts, a young woman with a mop of curly brown hair, raised her beer as if raising her hand with a question. "So, I get the income-inequality arguments, that corporations concentrate wealth and profit off the time and labor of others. I agree that we would be better off with fifty different independently owned diners or coffee shops than fifty Starbucks or Pizza Huts. I mean, of course there are efficiencies in owning multiple restaurants, and consistent experience that customers like, I won't deny that. . . ." She trailed off, apparently afraid her admission would be met with umbrage, but others nodded in agreement. "I mean, you're likely not going to have fifty well-run, profitable independent diners that pop up in their place, employing the same dishwashers and cashiers, without corporate efficiency."

"Yeah, well, there will be a certain falling away of commerce," Arden conceded, stepping into the discussion. "But is that any great shame? Will those dishwashers and cashiers miss working those crappy minimum wage jobs with no benefits when they still can't afford to make ends meet? What if, instead, they now have their own building in town, which they can spend their time improving? What if they have some land to farm, or a storefront for a shop, or workshop, or a car repair place? What if people can spend their time on work that actually improves their community?"

One of the newer converts, Peter Bassford, laughed. "Are you living in some kind of ivory tower, Arden? *A falling away of commerce?*" he mimicked her. She blushed deeply. She shouldn't have used those lofty words, but she had heard Kirish use them last week (to describe her idea—she hadn't entirely stolen it) and thought they sounded good.

"These are people's livelihoods, you know. Just because you think they're crappy jobs doesn't mean people need them any less," he scolded. Peter had a harder edge, and was not one of the idealistic college students. Compared to the rest of them, he'd seen the world. He'd spent time in South America, working as a "roughneck" on an offshore oil rig owned by one of the big multinational oil companies. Arden had heard him tell a story about another worker, a local man, becoming injured on the rig one night, his leg crushed in the equipment. Peter had seen the accident, and had heard the man screaming through the night. In the morning, the man was gone, and Peter was assured by the foreman that they had taken him to the hospital. But Peter hadn't heard the outboard motor of the dinghy, either coming or going, and it was just as it had been the day before, lashed to the side of the rig, covered. After he challenged the foreman, demanding to know where the injured man was, the last thing he remembered was the searing blow to the back of his head. He woke up in jail without any money or passport. After living through something like that, he had just as much reason as any of them to hate corporations, but that didn't make him any easier to deal with.

Arden struggled to recover. "I get it—I've depended on these jobs too. I mean, shit, I work at Applebee's now. But the reason people are stuck in those crappy jobs is because our system doesn't offer them anything better. After 99, they won't be trapped selling their time to corporations just to pay the bills to make other corporations rich. They'll be able to start fresh, with housing of their own rent-free, to get on their feet."

"Why no rent?" Carson asked, surprised.

Kirish replied, "We believe there are enough corporate-owned apartment buildings in most communities, once forfeited, to provide housing for most South Dakotans who now rent. Likewise, lots of mortgages in the state are from corporate banks, which would be forgiven, under 99."

Bassford whistled. "Free housing, eh? Doled out by the state? Or by us? I heard you, Arden, in The Spine go out of your way to say this wasn't communism, but it sure sounds like it to me. Why not embrace it? Lots of you millennials believe in socialism, I thought." He was grinning, and looking around at the group. "What do you all think that means?" he said, rounding on Arden. "Socialism equals communism."

She froze. This was the third rail, the topic that she had botched last time. How was she supposed to handle this? She couldn't remember. After a beat, in which she felt O and Kirish waiting to see if she would step up to Peter's challenge, Kirish spoke up.

"Hold on, Peter." Kirish held up his hands, *whoa*. "There will be a state distribution of property, but only the one time, when corporations are dissolved. It's still a system of private property, not state or communal ownership. There are lots of instances of state distribution of property in our country's history, and as far as I know, we've never been communists. Land grants, to encourage settlement. Entitlements, like welfare, which dole out but don't ever make people self-sufficient."

"Yeah, maybe." Bassford swigged his beer, still smiling. "I'm thinking from a marketing perspective, though, just embrace it."

Forgetting herself, Arden jumped in. "No, Peter! Our movement is nonpartisan and apolitical. That's the only way we build consensus. We've got liberals and conservatives, Tea Party folks, centrists, Libertarians, just in this room! From a *marketing perspective*," she scoffed, "that would be suicide!" She was starting to worry about having Peter involved with 99. He was a loose cannon.

"Calm down, honey," he laughed. "I'm kidding." He took another drink, and eyed Ophelia appraisingly as she returned to their group.

"Anyway," said Ophelia, flopping back on to her high stool in the middle of the dozen people listening in, "those dishwasher and cashier jobs that Arden thinks are crappy are going away anyway. You put your credit card in the slot, and hit a button, and out comes your coffee and your hamburger. There's no more dishes in these corporate chains—just throw it away. If you get one or two successful diners and a coffee shop to replace those fifty fast food joints, where people can eat real food and come together, and maybe a simple neighborhood market where people can trade the things they've grown or made in exchange for what they need, or trade skilled work, that's a better quality of life."

"There will be chaos," Peter said darkly. It was hard to tell if he was looking forward to this outcome or just being pragmatic. "How do you make that transition from fifty Pizza Huts back to functioning neighborhoods? If all those corporate jobs go away, where is the money to buy food coming from? And how 'bout a grocery store to buy food? There will be complete chaos."

Arden and Ophelia's friend Jessica, from their freshman dorm hall, had recently joined the coverts. She tentatively raised a hand. "What do you say to critics who might suggest that there are less drastic ways to fight corruption and get money out of politics? I mean, not all corporations are bad actors."

Arden shook her head. "I don't see a way. Now that corporations' rights are sacrosanct under federal law, the only way forward is to dismantle corporations where they're created." She thought of the anti-corporate farming bill, and the loopholes eroding its protections over the years, under intense lobbying efforts by agricultural business interests. As long as those forces were at play, the soybean company would keep trying to edge out Emma and her neighbors. The source of the problem had to be eradicated.

"Listen," Ophelia said, "these questions and challenges are so important. Thank you." She made a specific point of meeting Jessica's and Peter's eyes, and then giving Arden a warning look. *Dogmatic much?* Arden could imagine Ophelia saying.

Kirish interjected, "Peter, you worry there will be chaos, and to some extent, you're right. We have plans to make sure the transition after 99 is not a humanitarian crisis. It is our belief that the corporate assets will include plenty of land and other valuable assets to set people up on a stable footing, to have enough to become functioning contributors to the community, and to feed and care for themselves. But we know there's a risk, and we take it seriously."

Arden nodded. "Yeah, there is risk, but it's a chance to give all South Dakotans, even those cashiers and dishwashers, a shot at true independence."

Peter nodded, looking somewhat persuaded, but retorted, "Yeah, well, the question will be, do they really want it?"

That question rang in Arden's ears as she lay in bed that night. Would people grab their shot at independence? She wasn't sure whether others valued the idea of self-sufficiency as she did. It was one thing to sign a petition outside a grocery store: *Sure, why not?* So many people had laughed at the idea of banning corporations. But would people actually vote to make 99 law?

And if Arden couldn't even answer the coverts' questions, how was she ever going to convince the average voter?

CHAPTER 6 — THE MESSENGER

ARDEN HAD DELAYED GOING HOME to Emma's for Christmas until the last possible moment, to the point where she had to pack in a rush and was barely on time for dinner on Christmas Eve. This served to make Emma even angrier at Arden, still fixated on her dropping out of school. During dinner, they fought about Arden registering for spring semester classes, and Emma wouldn't hear anything about the successful launch of Initiative 99. Her grandmother had been the inspiration for their campaign, Arden thought bitterly, but she didn't even know it.

Over the course of the four days that Arden stayed in Badger, their interactions slowly warmed. Emma apologized for being short-tempered over something small, and Arden decided to treat it like a broader apology, covering their fight about 99 and Emma's uncharacteristic insults last June. Emma seemed older and jumpy. This year the Christmas presents, always lean, were spartan: socks, a sweater that did not seem new, and a random book, also not new. She noticed her grandmother sitting at her desk more than usual, sighing as she looked through bills and made notes in a black notebook.

"What's going on, Emma? Please tell me what's happening," Arden begged, after Emma had brushed off her questions repeatedly. "Are you losing the farm?"

Emma slouched in her chair and looked out the window, although the night was black and nothing could be seen.

"I told you," she said quietly, "there's been a foreclosure notice on the mortgage. More than one."

"What about the AGM lease money? I thought that covered the loan?"

"Not anymore," Emma replied. "They've been paying late, and I'm behind, so there's fees and penalties. And the whole loan has been called, since I defaulted, they say. I'm trying to negotiate a payment plan, but I just end up sitting on hold for hours when I call."

"But this is your home. They can't take that, can they?"

"I don't know, Arden. Seems like they can. I gotta be in court on February fifteenth, and if I don't have the money plus the fines by then, I think it's all over."

Arden felt so helpless, so angry that Emma had been backed into the corner like this. It wasn't her fault that she'd gotten cancer, that her medical bills had been so high and she hadn't had good insurance, that AGM was late on the rent, and that the bank was ripping her off with fines and penalties. The whole system seemed like it was conspiring to take away her farm.

And then it hit Arden: if 99 passed, Emma would be free. The mortgage would be eliminated, as a debt owed to a corporate bank. 99 would also release other South Dakota farmers from the crippling debt they'd had to take on to compete with Big Ag. Corporate-owned farmland would be returned to South Dakotans, and the promise of the anti-corporate farming act that Emma had worked for would finally be realized. If they could just hold on until November, it would be okay. But November was almost a year away, and the court date was in just two months. Maybe she could talk to Kirish about whether there was a way to slow things down.

AT THE AGREED TIME AFTER HIS AFTERNOON seminar, the first of the semester after Christmas break, Arden met Kirish at The Spine. She came in the back, grabbing a coffee and joining him where he sat, absorbed in his laptop. Arden was surprised to find she was happy to see him, that she was finally over their argument about her staying on message at the kickoff speech. She fought back a smile. He was tired and rumpled, as usual, though he looked healthier, not as thin as when she'd seen him last. His mother must have been feeding him. As she sat down in the chair next to his, he smelled good, like minerals and water.

Although they'd emailed almost every day on various planning issues, she hadn't seen him in person since mid-December, almost a month ago, before they'd both gone home for the holidays. He'd spent the two weeks after Christmas in DC, meeting with potential supporters, returning to Vermillion only once classes started January 10. But he acted as if he'd seen her yesterday.

"It's been five weeks since we submitted the signatures," he said, without any preliminaries. "Are we on track with the plans? Get out the vote? Media events and outreach?"

Arden sipped her coffee. No matter how accustomed she had become to his habit of drilling her about the status of the effort, she still resented his disinterest in even the bare minimum of friendly small talk. It was especially galling after having not seen him for so long. Couldn't he at least give her the courtesy of a civilized hello? *He's on the spectrum, man,* she heard Ophelia's joke in her head, but Arden knew that was not the case. She had seen him be more than effective with social niceties when it suited him.

"How are you, Kirish?" she asked, instead of answering his campaign questions. "How were your holidays? Sleeping any better?" Asking about his sleeping was sarcasm, because of course he wouldn't talk about such a thing. His gaze was unreadable, but finally he cracked smile at her, laughing at himself a little bit.

"Okay," he relented, "it was fine. We stuffed ourselves. My mother tormented me about my grades. My dad tried to get me to smoke a cigar. The weather was terrible. How about you? How's your grandmother?"

Arden appreciated this tiny window into his life, this once. Despite their working together on 99 for almost six months now, Kirish still kept his distance. He seemed to feel very strongly about keeping things professional. Sometimes, though, even after the scene at his house where Ophelia propositioned him, Arden got the feeling that Kirish found her *interesting*. Sometimes he would forget himself and look at her with that warm look in his eye that she could still remember so clearly from when she first explained her idea for 99 to him. But more often these days, he was the cold law student again. He was only twenty-seven, six years older than Arden, but he acted like it was more.

Happy she had cracked his façade even just a bit, Arden launched into a download of all that had been going on while he'd been away. Soon they were laughing at her tales of the new covert team leaders. While the core team was mostly grad students like Kirish, they were starting

to build out a more varied network of community organizers, malcontents, angry housewives, and even a new,
rare breed—the donor. Ophelia's work as the campaign
manager corralling and training volunteers invariably led
to some ruffled feathers, but her tactics were effective
and time was short. Folks offering services and equipment
and media access, as well as financial supporters, were all
rolling in. Ophelia had completed the state filing process
to declare the coverts as the sponsoring ballot committee,
which could accept donations. Arden had been persuaded
to take a tiny salary from the committee so she could quit
her job waitressing, and the committee funds would pay
for Kirish's recent trip to DC.

"Tell me about your trip," she finally asked, after his
questions had abated.

He'd met with the American Civil Liberties Union
legal defense team to rally advance support for the legal
challenges they were likely to face in the event they won.
The ACLU was leery of entering into the private property
debate, however, with their focus on personal civil liberties.
There were fringe groups on the left and the right that
were interested in what was happening in South Dakota,
but Kirish was still evaluating the landscape, unsure which
organizations to enlist as partners. Several law professors
had agreed to meet with him, at American University and
George Washington University. There had been a suggestion of an offer of an adjunct position at GW Law School,
he mentioned casually—unheard of for someone just out
of law school. He had declined, of course, he said, but she
could see he was pleased that his prospects as a professor
seemed to be improving. He'd agreed to speak on a panel
at a conference at the law school about Initiative 99.

Arden sat back a moment and tried to imagine what
went on in Justin Kirish's mind. She knew he wanted to

be a law professor, and it wasn't lost on her that he was parlaying their work on 99 to make useful connections. She wondered for a moment if that had been the only real point of the DC trip—but no, she didn't think he was *that* calculating.

"I need to go back to DC in a few months for the panel at the law school. We've also been invited to give a talk at the Legacy Foundation. I want you to come and do it."

"What?" Arden was alarmed, sitting up in her chair. "Why me? This is clearly your area of expertise. Isn't that a constitutional law organization? It doesn't make any sense that I would give the talk."

"This can't be an academic talk. And yes, it is a think tank. I've thought a lot about this, Arden," he said sharply, demanding her attention. "It needs to be an inspiring message that reaches back to the founding principles of this country."

"That sounds like exactly what you should do!" Arden protested. "You're just afraid of jeopardizing your inside track for a cushy professor job!" She was desperate.

He did not deign to acknowledge the last point with an answer, instead responding, "It can't be a lawyer delivering it. This is not a dry academic point. And it absolutely cannot be an East Coast, out-of-state lawyer—it has to be a South Dakotan. You're the one who needs to do it."

"We can bring it up at the next steering committee meeting, I suppose, but I think that—"

He interrupted, leaning forward and speaking intensely. "This isn't a decision to be made by committee. This is a question about the success or failure of 99."

Arden leaned back and looked at him, the gravity of his tone cutting through her anxiety at the thought of speaking in front of a formal conference. It was rare that Kirish would get exercised about anything—when he did, she took him seriously. If he felt it was this important, maybe she had to put aside her fears. It was selfish, really, she told herself, to be afraid. What's the worst that could happen? She swallowed, sitting up straighter as he stared her down. She would do it.

"Arden, you don't realize how compelling a leader you are." His expression softened into an almost quizzical half smile. Arden was shocked when he reached across the table and gently took her hand. "You don't know how compelling you are. When this is all over . . ." he said meaningfully, trailing off but looking at her wistfully. After a long moment he gave her hand a squeeze and let go. He looked studiously out the window, avoiding her gaze. *When this is all over, what?* He was going to ravish her? Ask her on a date? Write her a glowing professional recommendation? What? Arden was so stunned that she didn't push for the answer—and anyway, her imagination was probably better than any answer she would get.

When he turned back to her, though, he was all business.

"This message has to be delivered by you. And you need to practice."

A FEW WEEKS LATER, ARDEN FOUND herself standing alone on the stage in a small rehearsal theater in the USD arts building. She broke off speaking as some drama majors stuck their heads in the door at the back of the theater.

"This facility is in use!" Kirish hollered in a menacing voice, standing from his seat in the third row, center, as the students backed out of the room. Next to him slouched Ophelia, who initially had found the venue hilarious, yelling "Cut!" and "Quiet on the set!" but had gone silent once she'd realized Kirish's plan for the Legacy Foundation speech. The week before, Kirish had asked Ophelia some probing questions about Arden's past. When Arden heard, she'd been flattered that he was curious about her, but she could see now that he had been doing research for the speech. It was becoming clear to Arden that Ophelia had betrayed her confidence on many personal topics. Arden herself never told Kirish anything about her mother, and he had never asked. She imagined his childhood to be as privileged as his perfect East Coast diction, and had been ashamed to talk about her own.

She glared at Ophelia. "There's no fucking way I am talking about my mother."

"Arden, I know this is hard but people need to understand the human context," Kirish responded pedantically. "Your story delivers that."

She shook her head, unable to speak, shooting Ophelia another look—*I can't believe you told him all this!*

"Start again," he ordered. "Talk about the layoffs and the workplace injury. Talk about her addiction."

Arden closed her eyes and shook her head. *No.* How could she describe her childhood? She tried not to think of herself at all, but rather of her grandmother's farm. Beginning again, she talked about how her first memories of work were picking apples. She would measure her day's work by how many bushels of apples she could collect, then sorting them to feed animals or make pies with Emma to sell at the diner in town. The grace of seeing the results of her effort in a growing row of plants. The immediacy of food coming from the rabbits her grandmother raised or the venison she'd take in trade from the hunters whom they allowed to hunt the back forty. The emotion of it, of taking life for food, that was so strangely divorced from meat wrapped in plastic in the supermarket.

"This stuff is too abstract, Arden, you need to be more focused," Kirish interjected as she paused. "You're going to lose people if you spend time on that. Start with having to drop out of college. Or with your mom getting laid off from Sears."

Arden clenched her teeth and shook her head.

"Talk about Emma's foreclosure."

Kirish had helped connect Emma to the free legal clinic at the law school, and had helped them work through the mind-boggling paperwork that was required to claim a homestead exemption, in an attempt to stave off foreclosure. Did Arden owe him? It seemed like maybe he was suggesting she did, in the flat way he was now looking at her.

"Listen, I disagree with your approach here, and I'm not just going to lay myself out like some kind of pathetic homeless orphan at their feet. These people are not going to get behind our ideas because they feel sorry for me." Arden took a ragged breath and clenched her fists. "And if you haven't noticed, these aren't things I make a habit of talking about, and I sure as hell don't plan to start talking about them by public speaking, which I already hate! Why on earth am I going to DC at all? Isn't this the land of influence peddling and legislators with votes for sale to the best-funded interest group? What is the point of me telling them anything about our plans, never mind my personal life?" She was pacing across the stage now.

"Because we'll explode after this. This is the spring-board." Something about this speech had Kirish strangely keyed up. He stood up and put his hands on the back of the seat in front of him, leaning toward her across the room. "Please, Arden, just trust me. I know it seems crazy, but unless you show who you are and what we are trying to recapture with 99, we'll just be a bunch of fringe radicals. Voters need to understand why their own problems are the fault of corporate America." He paused, Arden had stopped pacing and was listening to him, captured by the passion in his voice.

"Arden, we're asking them to question a foundational American idea. This idea that nothing else values personal responsibility and hard work except for a capitalist corporate democracy is so ingrained in us. So is the idea that there's nothing else—that the only other alternative is a socialist or communist regime. You need to show them there is another option. A third way."

Arden thought of their argument months ago in The Spine, where she had accused him of 99 not mattering to him. She could see now that it did matter to him, deeply. She took a deep breath and looked at her feet, seeing the merit in his arguments, thinking about how her story would become the story of 99. Was she ready for that? Still looking down, she nodded to herself. She would try.

Seeing a shift in her, Kirish grinned at her and kicked his feet up on the theatre seats in front of him.

"Listen," he said, "let's take a break for now on the personal stuff and run through the talking points around the voter-initiative process and legal challenge if we win."

Some break, she muttered under her breath, but obliged.

CHAPTER 7 / REPARATIONS

ARDEN, OPHELIA, AND KIRISH ARRIVED early to their new headquarters, across town from the university in an empty storefront that had once been a department store, before the big Walmart Supercenter moved in. Kirish had signed the lease last week, and they had scoured thrift shops and used furniture stores to cobble together a working space of rickety banquet tables, mismatched desks and chairs, couches, and an old refrigerator. They made coffee and prepared to meet with their new advisors: a political organizer from Massachusetts and a local millionaire who wanted to support the initiative.

Andrew Nassert was the political director for Government for the People, an anti-corruption group that specialized in voter initiatives. He had run a successful campaign in Florida limiting gifts from lobbyists and political donations from corporations and special interests. They had contacted him several months before for advice on the signature-gathering campaign. Kirish had previously met Nassert, but not the millionaire, Jeremy Hatch. According to Nassert, Hatch was a retired banking executive who had a guilty conscience and a vendetta against his former employer.

The two men arrived exactly at ten o'clock, parking a sleek black SUV on the street in front of the office. Nassert was compact, in his mid-thirties, with wiry brown hair and tortoiseshell glasses, a low voice, and unwavering eye contact that made Arden feel shifty by comparison. Hatch looked to be in about his early fifties, tall and fit, expensively dressed, with a patrician air. Nassert was enthusiastic about the new headquarters, proclaiming it a great multipurpose space for organizing. Hatch, perhaps used to nicer digs, was polite, but Arden got the feeling he was reserving judgment.

"Andrew, I want to thank you again for your support in getting us to where we are today," Kirish started warmly. "We wouldn't have been able to get the signatures we needed without you sharing Government for the People's playbook on voter initiatives." Arden noted Kirish's ability to turn on the charm when it suited him.

Ophelia jumped in. "And Jennifer's help on the media issues was huge. We weren't really prepared to deal with the misinformation campaigns starting so early, and it was so helpful to be able to work through a response with her." During the signature gathering, Ophelia'd had several video chats with Jennifer Walton, Government for the People's media director, on how to respond to misleading stories being spread about 99.

"We're really impressed by what you've been able to accomplish as an all-volunteer grassroots effort," Nassert replied. "Many voter initiatives never get this far, and you should be really proud of where you are."

Arden, Ophelia, and Kirish exchanged smiles. They had already achieved more with this campaign than virtually anyone had expected them to, and they knew it. Kirish turned to the millionaire.

"Mr. Hatch," he said, "perhaps you could tell us about your interest in the initiative. From what I understand, you are a bit of an unexpected supporter of 99." Kirish smiled mildly at the older man.

Arden noted that Hatch seemed unusually fit for his age, and could have easily passed for younger but for something in his bearing. He was almost eerily appealing—not because he was especially handsome, but because he was so utterly sure of himself. His expensive golf shirt fit perfectly over his lean torso. He was a golden tan with clear blue eyes that he fixed on Kirish, Ophelia, and Arden each in turn. Arden found his alpha poise off-putting, but she could see Ophelia and Kirish both respond to it by leaning toward him and smiling. Clearly, climbing the corporate ladder would have been easy for him.

"I moved to Sioux Falls twenty-five years ago from Wall Street," he said, "after my former employer offered me a management role in their new consumer credit division. The South Dakota legislature had just decided to do away with any limits on interest rates on credit cards." He turned his high-intensity blue eyes on Kirish, "You'll know this from law school, Kirish: until South Dakota did this, all states in the country had *usury* laws against charging exorbitant interest, which was viewed as immoral. We'd been running the operation out of Delaware, but once we incorporated our consumer finance unit as a South Dakota banking corporation, we could charge upwards of twenty percent interest. After that, all our credit cards were issued out of South Dakota and governed by South Dakota law. Even if fifteen percent of our customers ended up in bankruptcy, we were still making money hand over fist." Hatch paused for effect. Arden glanced at Kirish and O in surprise, she hadn't realized that credit cards hadn't always been that way. She'd stayed away from using plastic but had friends who'd gotten in trouble with consumer debt.

Hatch continued, "Over time, I was given more and more responsibility, and I was well compensated. After 9/11, and again after the financial crisis in 2008, I led the restructuring of the customer service and operational support teams in Sioux Falls, which cut our US workforces by thirty percent, boosting our efficiency and reducing costs. Each time, I prided myself on being honest about the layoffs, and treating our employees fairly. I told myself, my obligation was to the shareholders, and outsourcing jobs to India was what you had to do to compete in the global economy. Plus, a rising tide lifts all boats, right?"

Ophelia was shaking her head. *More like spreads the environmental harm around*, Arden imagined O thinking.

"The second round of layoffs was harder, in 2009, to send jobs overseas," Hatch mused. "We'd just taken billions in TARP money, where the feds bailed the company out of the commercial mortgage-backed securities disaster, and it felt wrong to me to pay our bills with taxpayer money, while at the same time cutting jobs. And those US workers, we had them train their replacements. But still, it was just business." He watched Arden and Ophelia, apparently gauging their reaction.

"Most recently, up until last year, I was charged with replacing another forty percent of jobs with automated process or AI, artificial intelligence. With my previous success in outsourcing, I was the perfect executive to spearhead this initiative. It was supposed to be the pinnacle of my career, to bring my company into the digital era. Fintech, the technological revolution in financial services, was the next big thing, together with big data. It was a plum job, super interesting, with lots of upside for me." He sat back, remembering, and gazed out the big shop window of the former department store.

"The only problem was," he continued, more quietly, "I stopped being able to sleep. Drank more. Started thinking a lot about a woman who'd worked for me back in 2009, who was responsible for outsourcing her team. She did it, but in the course of the eighteen months it took, she got liver cancer and was dead six months later." He paused, closing his eyes for a long moment. "I couldn't shake the idea that it had poisoned her . . . the assignment to outsource her team. I started having dreams that she was visiting me, to talk things over, from the grave. That she was unable to pass on. That I was being poisoned too."

Ophelia snickered, and the others looked at her in horror. She raised her hands, "No, no, I'm not laughing at the liver-cancer lady ghost. That's just sad. It's just that, well, you didn't get religion because you felt guilty about all those people losing their jobs. It was that you were afraid doing the dirty work would make *you* sick."

Kirish shot her a look, angry she would be this rude to their guest and possible donor.

"I'm sorry, man," she said. "I'm out of line. Please go on." Ophelia's tone, warm as if to say that this was just teasing among friends, took a bit of the sting out of her words.

Hatch nodded, smiling lightly, still perfectly composed. "You like to think, at twenty, that you would never do such a thing. I would have thought the same. But you learn, with age, to compromise. Sometimes too well."

Kirish nodded knowingly, as if he too were already making such compromises. Momentarily distracted from the drama at hand, Arden wondered what it was that Kirish had compromised—he seemed so unyielding to her.

"So, for whatever reason," Hatch continued, "indeed, I got religion. And when I started asking questions about the endgame with AI, and about holding ourselves responsible for the human and community impacts, I was quickly sidelined. Early retirement is waiting for every executive— someone less expensive, younger, and hungrier, is always ready to push you out when you no longer buy into the party line." He pursed his lips, still bitter. "But I didn't go quietly or cheaply. It's a touchy topic, AI, a public relations nightmare, in fact. So here I am. I want to make reparations for my sins. I want to become detoxified."

There was a long awkward silence. Arden felt like she had to acknowledge his honesty, especially after Ophelia's snarky comment. "Thank you for telling us your story. We welcome your support and hope that together we can be a force for good." Ophelia made an infinitesimal, possibly involuntary eye roll that called into question whether Arden was speaking for her, but she kept quiet, to Arden's relief.

Andrew Nassert began to speak, gently changing direction. "So, you guys have made it this far. You've gotten 99 on the ballot, which is further than most voter initiatives get. Because you've been successful, you have attracted national attention, both ours and that of your opponents, who are marshaling their forces. This is one of the areas where we think we can help." Kirish and Nassert exchanged a look of understanding; they had discussed this already.

He continued, "We understand from our contacts in the state capitol that a political action committee has been created to oppose your ballot initiative, and they will be well funded. While we've gotten support from Americans for Values before on other anti-corruption campaigns, this time around they're against us. They're a formidable adversary—media savvy, well connected, and pretty much a bottomless deep pocket." This was a shock to Arden that there were national groups involved already for the opposition. "And unfortunately, they don't fight fair."

Hatch sat forward, and said, "I'm willing to help you, but I don't want to waste my money." He laid his hands flat on the table, looking at each of them in turn. "Even though I've got religion"—he flashed a smile at Ophelia—"I'm still a businessman. Andrew and his team have learned lessons the hard way about how to get initiatives passed, and I want you to learn from their mistakes. I want us to win." There was nodding all around the table at this easy point of consensus, but Arden suspected that more difficult concessions were to come.

Nassert spoke again, saying, "This phase of the process—really, the last phase—is about controlling the message and the media, and about being systematic, data driven, and well organized in getting out the vote." He smiled gently. "With all due respect, you guys are babes in the woods here. We'd like Jennifer Walton, on loan from our organization, to lead media strategy for Initiative 99."

Both Arden and Kirish immediately looked to Ophelia, who had been the de facto lead of media to date. This proposition was a surprise. They'd been expecting operational and financial support, but perhaps foolishly, hadn't foreseen this. Ophelia tipped her head to the side, considering.

Kirish leaned back in his chair with a wry smile.

"We've done pretty well with the press so far," he countered. Arden suspected he felt slighted being called babes in the woods, which was rather insulting. She could tell he was making an effort not to sound defensive. "And I think I've told you about our upcoming DC media tour. But undoubtedly, we need your help on outreach and organizing. And Jennifer has been great so far. My take is that we'd be lucky to have her on the team," he said carefully, shooting another glance at Ophelia.

Nassert responded, "The DC trip is interesting, and we will definitely talk about that. Whether national attention at this phase of the process will help or hurt is a jump ball. It could go either way."

At that, Arden had a moment of wild hope that the DC trip would be cancelled and she would be released from her speaking engagement, but Kirish interjected.

"For better or worse," he said, "that trip is happening. We've made commitments at the law school that we have to keep." Kirish cleared his throat. "But we're all ears. We want to understand what you're proposing and what you see as the path to winning for 99." Arden admired how he moved the meeting forward without answering the question on the new media lead, buying them some time.

Over the next two hours, Kirish, Ophelia, and Arden got a crash course in ballot campaign organizing, with Ophelia breaking out pen and paper and taking furious notes. It was clear that Nassert and his organization had a depth of expertise that would be invaluable. And slowly, delicately, it became clear that embracing that expertise was a condition of Hatch's continued support. Again, Hatch laid his palms flat on the table, in what Arden was now recognizing as his signature negotiating move.

"I will feel comfortable supporting this work if I know that you are running the best campaign possible," he said.

Ophelia finally weighed in on handing over media to Jennifer Walton. "I'd love to work more closely with Jennifer. I feel like I have a lot to learn from her, and there's plenty of other work for me to do." Arden exhaled in relief.

"Fantastic," Hatch spoke quietly. "But actually what

I'm saying is a bit more than that. We get it that this movement is yours. Policy, we work for you. Strategy, we have a strong vote and a seat at the table."

Ophelia's body language said she wanted to wrap up the meeting and think about it, but Arden felt that if they didn't get commitments from the two men today, and give commitments in turn, this opportunity could slip away. Hatch seemed mercurial, like he might get over being fired and decide to move to a tropical island tomorrow. She was willing to take the strings attached. Frankly, she felt they needed guidance on strategy more than Kirish let on—especially now, against the opposition PAC funded with out-of-state money. She and Kirish exchanged a look and he gave her a small nod.

"We welcome you to the table, and we are prepared to take your counsel on matters of strategy," Arden responded, feeling some formality was fitting. Ophelia looked annoyed, but Kirish nodded again.

"Sometimes the line between policy and strategy isn't entirely clear," he warned them, laying down a marker, "but I am confident that we can work together. Our interests are aligned, and we want your help."

"And your money," Ophelia grumbled, and they all laughed.

The meeting broke up shortly after that, with the two visitors and Kirish climbing into the black SUV and making the drive to the state capitol to meet with a sympathetic legislator, and later heading to Rapid City, another two and a half hours west. Nassert had explained that Rapid City was the other major media market in the state, and they needed to start building a network of credible local supporters and spokespersons. They had meetings scheduled with the editor of the *Rapid City Journal*, and after that, a radio interview.

The strategic maneuvering was beginning already. To Arden, it felt like the smart thing to do, absolutely necessary, but dangerous too, somehow. Their work so far had been pure, homegrown. They were now facing a corrupt and faceless foe. What would they have to do to win?

CHAPTER 8

DISTANCE

ARDEN DIDN'T MENTION TO KIRISH that it was her first time on a plane. On the descent into DC, she was amazed by the size and sprawl of the city. The honeycomb of lives, of dwellings and pavement, the awareness of such staggering multitudes shocked her. She wondered, what was the organizing principle of all those lives? Was it government? Commerce? They were packed together like a hive around a queen. Thinking of them all, each with their own stories, dramas, disappointments, and dreams, she felt the vastness of the country. The world. How could there possibly be so many people? It made her queasy.

Despite Arden's various attempts to get out of this trip, here she was. She had spoken to Jennifer Walton, the new press lead, on her first day in the office, trying to get her support to cancel the DC trip. Didn't Jennifer think it would be better now to avoid national attention, as Nassert had suggested during their meeting? Jennifer was unhelpful, although it seemed like she agreed; Arden suspected she was just unwilling to oppose Kirish at this early stage.

Arden and Kirish landed at Dulles International after ten at night and took a taxi to a motel on the outskirts of the capital. In the cab, Arden started panicking as the prospect of delivering her Legacy Foundation speech became real, just two days away.

She turned off the video screen in front of her in the cab, with its flashing neon advertisements, feeling bombarded by sights and sounds. She turned to Kirish. "I'm not sure you really understand what you're asking me to do, Kirish. I hate public speaking, and maybe you've noticed, I don't talk about my mother willingly." She realized with a nauseous jolt that she was close to tears. Kirish looked at her strangely, as if he wanted to console her, but couldn't, or wouldn't. He raised his hand, as if to reach out and touch her, but then dropped it back to his lap, staying silent.

"I mean, fuck, you are about the least forthcoming person I've ever met," Arden continued, "so I don't know where you get off asking me to bare my soul to a room full of conservative lawyers."

He responded quietly, looking away from her now, gazing out the window at the bleak neighborhood they rode through. "I know it's unorthodox, but I believe that many of the people 99 would help, who would vote for 99, won't be comfortable with the policy details. They distrust government and the legislative process. They hate lawyers. They are not well educated, and they don't read in-depth news about policy. We need a way to reach those people. I think if you give this speech, in this room, we'll have a national audience based on issues, not policy. I think your story gives a narrative to 99 that we're missing otherwise."

They both paused as the cab stopped at a light in front of a homeless person, sitting crumpled on the median between the divided highway, holding a sign reading, *PTSD Veteran, anything you can spare will help, god bless.* "Why do you think this will give us a national audience?" she asked.

"Just trust me," he told her. "I know it seems weird, especially considering the venue, but this is the best way to get our message out there. If we do it this way, it won't be confined to this stupid conservative think tank full of old guys, it'll be prime time—but it has to be personal. And it has to be a South Dakotan delivering it, or it just looks like out-of-state interests manipulating the process."

Kirish turned to face her, making eye contact for the first time since they left South Dakota. "You'll be fine. Better than fine."

Some pep talk. She had to do her duty, is what he meant. When the cab dropped them at the hotel lobby, she felt a chill toward him and silently chastised herself. This was nothing new; he didn't really care about her feelings. She should not feel surprised or disappointed. He'd never suggested otherwise. She should be grateful for his partnership in 99. They didn't need to be friends.

Unfortunately, they were booked to share a room with two double beds in order to save money since the accommodations in DC were so expensive. The hotel was a grimy replica of the shiny rooms she'd seen in commercials, with a purple-and-orange color scheme to match the flashy company logo. The dissonance between the advertised glamour and the real thing was jarring.

As they walked into the room and looked awkwardly at the two beds, Arden deeply regretted agreeing to share a room. What had she been thinking? Kirish whipped out his laptop immediately after they walked in, sitting silently at the desk and leaving her to pick a bed. She could tell he wasn't happy with it either. They'd both argued against it, but Ophelia, who'd booked the trip, had insisted.

She wanted to take a bath but had a creepy feeling that unholy things had happened in that tub. Instead, she just splashed water on her face and pits and got her pajamas on, climbing into one of the beds. After a while, when she had turned her light out and pulled the covers over her head against his desk lamp, she heard his computer *whirr* more loudly and then click off. He unzipped his suitcase and rifled through it, closing the bathroom door softly. Arden felt raw, like she wanted to yell at him, but she knew she had no right to expect anything of him. She heard him come back into the room, and heard a dull thud as he placed something on her bedside table, near her head. A glass of water, she saw as she peeked out from under the covers. He held a second in his hand, for himself, and he turned to his bed, shutting off the light quickly.

Sleep did not come easily. The rustling of his sheets sounded so close, but in the blackness of the room, Kirish also seemed a great distance away. After settling in, he was practically motionless, although it did not feel to Arden that he was asleep. It was cold, and agony not to toss and turn amidst waves of emotion.

The next morning, Kirish was up, showered, and dressed before Arden woke, and he vacated the room immediately—to give her privacy, Arden supposed. Arden found him in the hotel lobby, and they took a subway to the George Washington University Law School. After they exited the subway car, Arden couldn't wait to get out of the tunnel, dark and close, smelling of piss. It dumped them out on a busy road, with strip malls and bars, which was a three-block walk to the campus. Kirish's panel discussion at the conference didn't start until eleven, but he had promised a reporter they would meet her for breakfast. She was working on a big story about 99, and though she'd already interviewed Kirish several times, she wanted to meet Arden. They grabbed a table at the university cafeteria, and Kirish promptly immersed himself in his phone, checking emails and reading the news. Soon the reporter was standing expectantly beside their table looking Arden up and down. She was in her mid-forties, lean, with a friendly smile but a greedy look in her eye.

"Janet, wonderful to see you!" Kirish got up and embraced her, kissing her cheek. "Janet, this is Arden Firth."

Arden stood dumbly looking at the two of them, thrown off by Kirish's uncharacteristic warmth toward the woman.

"Arden," Kirish prompted, touching her back with a little shove, "meet Janet Dowin from *The New Republic*."

Finally she stuck out her hand and the two women shook.

"Hi, Justin! Hi, Arden, so good to meet you. We're so interested in learning more about the young people behind this movement. Really very impressive, such momentum and . . . not naïveté. . . ." She laughed, as if she weren't insulting them. "What's the word I'm looking for . . . idealism!"

"What's the position of your paper on 99?" Arden asked bluntly, taking an immediate dislike to the reporter.

Janet Dowin chuckled, as though Arden had made a joke, shaking her short glossy black hair. "Well, we're still getting the whole picture, and of course we must report objectively, but I for one think it's fascinating! Reminds me of the sit-ins in college!"

Kirish steered the conversation toward some recent campaign updates. "We've got an official headquarters now in downtown Vermillion, which is where the state university is located. We're teaming up with Government for the People, the anti-corruption group, for logistical and strategic support. One thing we're working on is firming up the details for the distribution of former corporate assets. We've reached out to Ken Feingold as a possible special master. We think he's got lots of similar experience, you know, doling out assets fairly in the World Trade Center victims' relief fund and the opioid victims' settlement. The initial distribution work would be done by local town planners and then rolled up to the special master for final sign off." His tone was warm, almost conspiratorial, as if he were bringing her into the inner circle, and he was comfortable that he had her full support in this mission.

"You trust her?" Arden whispered, when Dowin stepped into the foyer to take a call.

Kirish smiled indulgently, instantly pissing her off. "No," he pronounced slowly, so she could keep up, "but with the press you act like you do. And don't be fooled by her breezy act. She's as sharp as a knife. Don't screw this up. She *is* our national stage."

Arden rolled her eyes and grabbed the newspaper Dowin had brought with her, not wanting to talk to him. The paper was almost a relic these days; it was unusual for Arden to see someone with a real one, but as a journalist, Janet Dowin was probably required to buy them. Arden flipped through the pages, struggling with the size of it and the old-fashioned folding, and gasped as she saw the page nine article entitled, "South Dakota Anti-Corporation Ballot Initiative Gaining Steam." She flipped back to the front of the newspaper to check which publication she was holding: *The Washington Post*, a real newspaper!

Dowin returned in a fluster. "So sorry, I had to take that call and haven't gotten to know you, Arden! Can we chat while we walk over to the conference hall?" It was getting close to eleven o'clock. She made a show of paying the tab with her company Amex.

"So, Arden," Dowin said, as they gathered up their things to head to the conference, "I'm dying to hear, how did you come up with the idea? Why do you hate corporations so much? So revolutionary, yet also so reductionist, sweeping away the building blocks of our economy?" Her questions were light and playful, but again, her gaze was shrewd, measuring.

Kirish nodded at Arden: *Go on, do your thing.* She took a deep breath and tried to match his previous open tone.

"Yes, well, *Justin,*" she lingered on his name for an extra second to make fun of him, because no one was permitted to call him Justin, except apparently, this reporter, "Ophelia Brooks and I really came up with the plan together. And it's not a question of hate, but rather that the idea that the corporate model has served its purpose. Corporations as a tool for fast investment and protection from personal liability have their place in a developing economy. For corporations, the measure of success is growth. Growth for growth's sake is no longer serving a social purpose. It causes environmental carnage and perpetuates consumerism and a service economy that's keeping people poor, no matter how hard they work," Arden explained to Janet as they walked slowly toward the conference hall. These were the talking points that Ophelia, Jennifer, and Kirish had vetted. Dowin nodded, looking at Arden levelly, clearly not getting exactly what she wanted.

Kirish looked on anxiously, which just made Arden nervous.

"The fairytale of perpetual growth is a lie," she blurted out, which felt a bit dramatic and was not part of the script, but it seemed to get Dowin's attention. The reporter took out a tiny notebook and pencil and jotted that down. Arden saw that she needed to give Dowin something different from what she'd already heard from Kirish.

For Arden, one of the important components of 99 was food—where it came from, giving people land to grow their own food, to be self-sufficient, and to make sure there was enough for everyone. Ophelia and Jennifer thought this was a dangerous topic that could be divisive or alienate people, and encouraged her to stay off it, but Arden saw a way to weave it in that she thought would work.

"I grew up on a farm," Arden said, "and I know what it feels like to have the fruits of your labor benefit you. You grow a garden and eat the food. You feed your animals, and they sustain you. You hunt a deer, and have meat. Most people now are so far from that—their own work benefitting them. Much of the US workforce is in service jobs, which don't even pay a living wage." She struggled to maintain eye contact with Dowin as they walked.

"There are benefits from corporations, of course, but mainly they are those of convenience. And people in South Dakota are increasingly realizing what we've given up. We've given up all these small businesses that were replaced by Walmart or Amazon: the shoe store, the pharmacy, the five and dime, all those jobs where people owned businesses, where their work benefitted *them*, rather than a faceless corporation and out-of-state shareholders. Yes, you can get cheap disposable goods at Walmart, made in China. Those manufacturing jobs making those things here in the US, things that would last, those are gone."

As they rounded a corner and continued walking across the manicured campus, Arden continued, again, departing from the script. "Some in my generation are turning back to making things by hand, back to farming, back to craftsmanship. But can those craftspeople compete with crap from China made in sweatshops? Will they be able to compete with automation, which cuts human work out entirely?" Dowin was watching Arden closely as they walked, nodding thoughtfully.

Arden rolled on, intentionally not making eye contact with Kirish. "There's something elemental to humanity about making things by hand, growing food, sustaining yourself with your own labor." Arden had been counselled by Kirish and O against making statements like these, so lofty and broad, in her stump speeches, but it felt right.

"We've all been hearing all our lives, yeah, capitalism is brutal, but it's the best system there is. We think the dominance of the corporation has perverted the goal of capitalism, which was to allow people to benefit from their own efforts. Corporations are not a required element for capitalism. We think we can do better without them. We think that people in South Dakota are ready to find another way."

Arden looked at Dowin as they walked along the bluestone walkway between university buildings. She had fixed Arden with a glittering gaze, thoughtful, perhaps mocking, perhaps moved. Arden pressed on.

"The choice between communism and a corporate capitalist democracy is a false choice. We think there is a third way." Arden could hardly believe that she'd ended this way, as gun-shy as she was about the word *communism*, but she saw with a sudden clarity that this went to the heart of why the idea of 99 seemed so radical. And that was a lie, that democracy needed corporations, or that corporations were a necessary part of the American identity.

Dowin scribbled in her little book.

They had arrived at the academic hall where the conference was taking place. As they waited in line outside the door for a moment to register, Kirish slipped a hand around her upper arm and pulled gently, making her finally meet his gaze. Arden was relieved to see he wasn't angry, but wasn't sure what to make of his intensity.

"That was good," he whispered. "Reckless, but really good."

CHAPTER 9
BELLY OF THE BEAST

THEY FILED INTO THE IVY-COVERED STONE hall of the law school, into a large foyer filled with lawyers and law students. Arden was surprised at how many people were there and craned her neck over the business-suited crowd to read the conference title, "Innovative Legal Structures—Law and Politics." Kirish's panel was the keynote on the agenda. Once inside the hall, they were whisked to the front and seated in the first row.

"I can see what you mean about her, Justin," Dowin said to him as they settled in. "She's a true believer." She flashed Arden a teasing smile, which she was forced to return, although she didn't like the idea that Kirish had been telling this journalist something about her. Arden tried to catch his eye, wondering what it had been, but his thoughts were elsewhere.

Kirish was invited up to the front to have a small wireless microphone pinned to his jacket lapel. He looked energized, rested, and utterly natural in a well-cut blue blazer. He stood loosely on the balls of his feet, like he was about to take off at a run. The speaker at the podium was introducing the panel: a constitutional law professor from George Washington, a corporate general counsel, and a proponent of small government. She got to Kirish last.

"Our last panelist is a bit unusual, in that he's not actually a lawyer yet." Some of the audience tittered. "Justin Kirish will soon graduate from the University of South Dakota School of Law and will be sitting for the bar this summer. He's here not in his august capacity as a Juris Doctor"—more tittering—"but rather as one of the driving forces behind South Dakota Voter Initiative 99, the much-discussed and controversial *Voter Initiative Abolishing the Corporation and Associated Distribution of Assets.* Please join me in welcoming Mr. Kirish." There was broad applause, especially from the law students at the back of the room.

"Let's start with you, Mr. Kirish. For those of our audience who aren't familiar with Voter Initiative 99, two months ago, South Dakota voters put an initiative on the ballot for November to change South Dakota law so that it would no longer recognize the legal structure of a corporation. Can you tell us what is motivating South Dakota voters to change the economic structure of the state, and why you think voters are venturing into a dusty area of corporate law largely untouched for centuries?"

Arden was impressed that Kirish looked perfectly comfortable sitting at the long table with the other panelists, all in their fifties at least. She would have been terrified.

"Of course. First, let me thank the law school for inviting me here and for convening this panel to discuss Initiative 99," he began. "Setting aside for a moment your statement that corporate law has been largely unchanged for centuries, because I'm not sure that's true," he said with a bit of a rueful smile for having to contradict the moderator, "I think there is broad popular consensus that the role of corporations in our culture has changed over time, and not for the better. The role of corporate money and influence in politics has increased since our country's founding, to the point now where most Americans recognize it as corrosive and corrupting. The US Supreme Court's 2010 ruling in *Citizens United*, holding that a corporation had the same constitutional right to free speech as a natural person, and could therefore spend unlimited money to influence elections, was repugnant to most Americans."

Kirish paused, took a sip of water, and continued in an unhurried fashion. "But make no mistake, most voters drawn to our cause are not constitutional scholars. They have personally experienced the negative repercussions of the US economy's domination by corporate interests. They have been casualties in the corporate drive for growth for its own sake, casualties of efficiency and profit over fair working conditions and meaningful work. Many people have lost their jobs due to automation, outsourcing overseas, exported manufacturing, and corporate takeovers. Many exist in economic ecosystems where their skills only equip them to perform repetitive, low-paying work, where they have little autonomy, are fungible and undervalued, and where they are unable to earn enough to attain even a cramped version of the increasingly elusive American dream. Each of these casualties has a vote."

Kirish sat back and looked at the audience with a challenge in his gaze, and Arden felt proud of him for his confidence in the face of the established academic crowd. She knew he admired these lawyers and professors, but he was not cowed. Arden was reminded of how much she'd liked to watch him lecture back in poli-sci. But her enjoyment was tinged by the fear that her own performance as a spokesperson would never measure up. When the moderator didn't step in, Kirish continued.

"Voters all across the political spectrum feel that we've embraced globalization too quickly, in a way that has hurt the American worker. The guiding idea of globalization, that a rising tide lifts all boats, has not borne out. Only a small and perhaps diminishing percentage of Americans are better off than their parents. Almost ninety percent of corporate stocks are held by the richest twenty percent of Americans, with the majority of US citizens having little or no investment in the stock market. Less than half of US citizens have *any* holdings in the stock market. That number drops down to less than one quarter when you look at South Dakotans. Most Americans have not benefitted from the vast accumulations of wealth that the corporate structure has created. Rather, the profits have been made at their expense." He nodded to the moderator, indicating he was done, and she slowly nodded.

"Mr. Rothsheild"—the woman turned to the corporate general counsel of a major US-based home goods conglomerate—"you've spoken publicly about the obligation of corporations to take the public interest into account when making business decisions. Is this a moral obligation or just good business?"

"Yes, I have previously said, and firmly believe, that corporations must act in a way that improves their communities and recognizes an obligation to be a good corporate citizen. Corporations exist at the will of the people, and the people, as Mr. Kirish and his Proposition 99 so clearly illustrate, can both giveth and taketh away. Whether it is constitutional to abolish corporations, as Mr. Kirish has proposed, is a big 'if'; however, it is clear that governments can and do curtail the rights of corporations through regulations and tariffs and disincentives. But really, my view is that corporations that have sustainable practices, both environmentally and socially, perform better. They are better able to recruit and retain the talent needed to drive innovation and success in the marketplace. Better corporate citizenship drives more successful corporations."

The moderator had a follow-up for the sandy-haired general counsel. "But what about the shareholder model of corporate governance, espoused in the 1970s by the economist Milton Friedman, that managers of corporations have an absolute duty to maximize the financial value of the stock of a company, often for short-term gain at the expense of other stakeholders, such as employees and communities?"

Rothsheild responded, with a troubled nod, "Yes, unfortunately, these ideas have been aggressively advanced by activist investors, pushing at annual shareholder meetings for company executives to take actions that maximize shareholder value, like making layoffs or selling off company assets. In the last two decades, these incentives have been built into executives' pay, making their compensation contingent on short-term profit and stock performance. These changes have institutionalized the shareholder model of corporate governance. But I've advocated for a return to the philosophy that charges managers with taking into account all stakeholders, including employees, the community, and the environment."

The moderator next turned to the law professor at the end of the dais.

"Professor Becker, Mr. Rothsheild questions whether Proposition 99 is constitutional. As our resident constitutional scholar, what say you?"

The professor, in his sixties with a tweed jacket and scraggly eyebrows, spoke in a condescending rasp. "Ahem, yes, well, it's an interesting question. I believe that the rights of corporations to hold property would be constitutionally protected, based on long-standing Supreme Court precedent. The Court's recent decision in *Citizens United*, as Mr. Kirish mentioned, did strengthen jurisprudential recognition of the corporate entity as one entitled to free speech protection. I believe this would likely inform the Court's evaluation of the South Dakota initiative, in the unlikely event that it is ratified by the broader electorate. Even more problematic is the Dormant Commerce Clause in Article I of the Constitution, where states are prevented from burdening interstate commerce, and by extension, it is considered the exclusive purview of the federal government to regulate."

Arden started to glaze over at the professor's arch legalese. He droned on, saying something about the Full Faith and Credit clause requiring states to honor the laws of other states. She'd previously heard from Kirish that this could mean that even if South Dakota doesn't recognize corporations as legal entities, the fact that they still validly exist in other states could require that South Dakota *has* to recognize out-of-state corps under Full Faith and Credit. She was jolted back to reality when Kirish jumped in.

"Neither the US Constitution nor any of its twenty-seven amendments makes any mention of corporations," he argued. "The corporation is entirely a creation of state law. The judicial recognition of a corporation as a 'person' entitled to legal status in the US has always been derived from its creation under state law. If state law has the legal authority to create something, it must also have the legal authority to dismantle it."

Kirish's delivery was perfect, passionate but measured. "Moreover, the Full Faith and Credit Clause also requires other states to uphold South Dakota's laws and cannot prevent the state from regulating a matter of elemental governance within its boundaries."

Professor Becker smirked, "Ah well, Justin, my dear boy, you may not have yet had Advanced Constitutional Law in school . . ." There were guffaws and laughter from the audience, punctuated by a few boos from the back. "But that's actually not how the Full Faith and Credit Clause works. Rather . . ."

Kirish jumped back in, angrily this time: "There is precedent—though old, I do not believe it has been overturned—that no state needs admit a foreign corporation to do local business, except on terms dictated by that state, in the case of *Selig v. Hamilton* . . . moreover, there is a public policy exception to the Full Faith and Credit Clause, which permits a state to disregard laws of other states where they violate the public policy of the first state."

Arden was starting to sweat. She knew from previous long and confusing discussions with Kirish that this was a key weak spot in their argument.

The constitutional law professor, whom she was beginning to hate, interjected again, overriding the start of a new question by the moderator. "Apologies, Professor Willas, but I must say that Mr. Kirish's arguments, while creative, hang on rather a thin thread. Isn't *Selig v. Hamilton* from 1914? Hardly a strong legal footing. . . ."

Kirish smiled graciously, but Arden could see he was controlling his anger. "With all due respect, Professor Becker, there isn't recent case law on the question of whether states can entirely exclude corporations, since none of the states have tried to do so for a hundred years. As I said, my research indicates that these cases still stand as binding precedent. Moreover, there is a long history in the Midwestern states of anti-corporate farming laws, as a way to preserve and protect family farms. Nine states have statutes or constitutional provisions that restrict corporations from engaging in farming or owning agricultural land, including South Dakota. Many state and federal courts, including the United States Supreme Court, consistently upheld the constitutionality of these anti-corporate statutes during the twentieth century."

Arden loved that this had become a pillar of their legal argument, since it was the inspiration for 99. She knew it wasn't a perfect argument, however, since the damn lobbyists had chipped away at the law. Kirish had to address this head on, and he leaned forward and quickly continued.

"Of course, the South Dakota voter initiative in 2003 to extend the corporate farm ban was successfully challenged in the 8th Circuit in *South Dakota Farm Bureau v. Hazeltine* as a violation of Interstate Commerce, but there is a split among the circuits with other appellate courts upholding identical language. The US Supreme Court has, to date, declined to take up the issue, but we believe the Court would resolve the split in favor of states' rights to protect family farming."

Professor Becker started clearing his throat pompously, but the moderator jumped in. "Well, this is getting exciting!" she exclaimed, leaning forward and making stern eye contact with both Kirish and the con law prof. "But I don't want to forget our last panelist, who joins us from the Federalist Society, which has graciously sponsored this conference and our upcoming luncheon. Mr. Tengrau has recently written a book in which he argues . . ."

Arden exhaled as Kirish sought her out among the crowd with a tiny nod, as if to say, *Don't worry, that was the worst of it,* and she nodded back. Arden saw Janet Dowin scribbling notes and watching the two of them exchange looks. She felt an almost irresistible urge to flee the room, as if a fire alarm were going off but only she could hear it. Considering the fact that she was at the very front of a crowded hall, she controlled herself, rooting in her purse for anything soothing, a Tic Tac, a Kleenex, breathing in through the nose, out through the mouth . . . *what in the hell are we doing?*

After a while, the panic passed, and she sat back and watched Kirish outmaneuver the law professor and the apologetic corporate lawyer. The latter came close several times to admitting that he sympathized with Initiative 99, much to Arden's delight. Soon, the talk was over and they were herded into an adjoining room for a lunch. Dowin joined them, but their conversation was repeatedly interrupted by a procession of students approaching them with offers of assistance with the legal challenge, should they be successful. Kirish handed out card after card with the initiative website and gave each of the students his full attention as they explained their ideas for legal arguments in support of 99.

After an eternity, or so it seemed to Arden, the luncheon was over. They were back out on the street, laughing and shaking their heads: *Can you believe that all just happened? That was incredible!* Kirish steered Arden into a pub, and though it was only three thirty, they both had a beer. After the initial elation that Kirish's law school talk had gone so well, she remembered that it was her turn tomorrow, and that she was angry at Kirish for making her give the speech and for being unsympathetic last night. Sure, he'd done a good job; these things were easy for him.

If he noticed the sudden shift in her mood, he didn't press her.

"It's about two miles back to the hotel. I think a walk will do us both good. Okay?" he asked. She shrugged, but rose and walked out ahead of him.

They walked for a long time, each lost in their own thoughts. The car and foot traffic got heavy as offices let out; the light softened as evening arrived, and the sun shone gold on the tops of the trees. They walked through neighborhoods with the cherry trees that Arden had heard DC was famous for in the spring, not in blossom anymore, but some had sickly sweet remains rotting on the ground. They emerged onto the National Mall and trudged down the long lawn, the grass rough and flattened from all the visitors and tourists coming day after day. They were both drawn to the Lincoln Memorial, walking slowly through the columns and staring up at the enormous white figure. Kirish remarked here and there on bits of history, pointing out where Martin Luther King Jr. stood when he delivered his "I Have a Dream" speech, but mostly they were silent.

Kirish turned to her. "There's a quote I learned in law school about the power of the state structure of the US. It was Justice Brandeis in the 1930s. He said that the states are the laboratories of democracy that can try novel social and economic experiments without risk to the rest of the country."

Arden liked that idea. Like Colorado voters who had first legalized marijuana, even though it was illegal under federal law. South Dakota would be an experiment, seeking a new way of organizing its society, one that would be perhaps truer to the ideals on which the country was founded. In many ways, the history of the country had not lived up to its idealistic aspirations. But that didn't mean its future couldn't.

The walk helped to shake her out of her brooding about the speech tomorrow. It was important for 99, and she would do her best.

CHAPTER 10

NATIONAL STAGE

WHEN ARDEN WOKE THE NEXT MORNING, legs sore from all that walking, she told herself that in twelve hours it would be over, and she would be on a plane home. She'd been through tough stretches before, and time always passed, no matter what.

Her speech was a blur, and after it was over, Arden tried not to think about it. She had taken a small blue pill, a beta-blocker, which one of the coverts had given her back in Vermillion. A cellist with terrible stage fright, Julie, had promised her it wasn't a narcotic but rather tamped down the fight-or-flight impulse that made her shake so hard she couldn't play her instrument on stage. Arden had felt otherworldly, like an impartial observer, speaking quietly into the microphone about her mother's layoffs, her injury, her struggles with addiction, and her eventual death by drug overdose her first night home after a month in rehab.

Arden's description of Jill's last morning was clinical, like a death report. Arden did not recount how Emma had tried the bathroom door when she awoke in the morning, then jimmied the lock, and let out a small shriek as she discovered Jill slumped on the floor. Arden, fourteen, had not risen to help, instead staying in bed with the covers over her head as Emma called the police. "Jill's dead, Carl." Emma had spoken to the sheriff flatly, unsurprised. "No, not an emergency at this point." The ambulance had arrived thirty minutes later, quietly. Arden didn't say, from the podium, that she had roused herself only in time to see her mother's sheet-draped body being loaded into the back of the ambulance.

Did she feel guilty for not getting up? For not crying? She had been too numb to cry then, having seen her mother when she was using drugs too many times—that slack face, the fluttering eyelids, rolling eyes. Did she feel guilty for being relieved that Jill was gone? She could tell herself she was glad Jill was out of her misery, but a part of her was glad she was dead. She'd hated Jill even harder for making her the kind of person who would be glad her mother was dead.

What she did say was, "When the ambulance arrived, she could not be revived." The audience was immobilized. No one met Arden's gaze as she looked out across the room. When she turned to the policy arguments, everything felt weightless and inevitable.

She'd been unsettled to see the reporter Janet Dowin there in the audience, again with her notepad busy, especially during Arden's opening, talking about her past. Arden wondered what the newspaper article would be like, whether it would do what Kirish believed it would. Dowin had wanted to take them to lunch afterward, but Kirish had assessed Arden's state after the speech with a glance and lied to Dowin about their flight being hours earlier than it really was.

Now they slowly made their exit, with fewer people approaching them than after Kirish's panel yesterday at the law school. Arden felt people eying her but keeping their distance. The audience had not been enthusiastic in its polite applause when her speech concluded, and she heard embarrassed throat clearings as she moved through the crowd. She suspected Kirish had been wrong about how appealing her human element really was. Kirish, too, seemed circumspect in the cab on the way to the airport and reluctant to meet her eye. She felt emptied out.

The flight home was quick. She had a glass of wine and fell asleep, wanting to put the day behind her. On the drive back to Vermillion from the airport, Kirish was more animated. The trip had been a success, and he was sure it would propel them into the next phase of the campaign. They had laid the foundation to compete with South Dakotans for Prosperity, the well-funded opposition committee, for media attention.

Arden had begun to doze again when he mentioned meeting a well-known Supreme Court attorney at the Legacy Foundation talk named Nick Karbal. She'd noticed the two of them in close conference after her talk, after a rest she'd taken in the ladies room, sitting on the toilet with her head down. The way Kirish was talking about him afterward, the guy was some kind of legal rock star.

"That con law professor on the panel worried me, to be honest."

"Why?" Arden was surprised out of her dozing. It was unlike Kirish to admit concern.

"The Dormant Commerce Clause. A regulatory taking."

This meant nothing to Arden. "Well, what does this Karbal guy think? Is that his name? Is he part of the Legacy Foundation group?"

"No, he just came to hear you."

"Ugh," Arden groaned.

"He thought it was powerful. He said he'd argue the case for us before the US Supreme Court, if we end up there."

"Wow. Does that mean he thinks we'll win?"

"I don't know. First we have to win at the polls."

Arden had drifted off to sleep until they arrived at her apartment. Kirish had carried in her suitcase; other times, she'd have insisted on carrying her own bag, but tonight she didn't object. She opened the door, and he made a quick lap around the apartment, before circling back to her in the hall.

"What are you checking for?" she asked, surprised.

He spoke cautiously, as if he didn't want to scare her. "You need to be careful now. Things are going to start getting weird." Arden's eyebrows raised, and Kirish lifted a palm. "No, don't worry about it tonight, but soon, we'll need to think about security. I'm not sure this place is the best, with you being here alone. There's an apartment in my building opening up. You should come look at it."

She nodded, feeling a strange mix of emotions at his concern. Was he worried about her personally, or was it because he'd finally been able to position her as the figurehead of 99, so she had become strategically valuable to him? There was a long pause while they stood looking at each other. Was this like when she'd been flattered that he was asking Ophelia questions about her, only to find out he'd been looking for material for the speech? Arden was never sure of his motives.

"You're going to have to step it up and be more dynamic, now," he said, moving back from her toward the door. Arden was confused. What was he talking about? He couldn't still be talking about her not living alone. It definitely did not feel like a compliment.

When she was silent, shocked, he explained. "The talk today was good for Dowin, for the newspaper article. That was the point of it. But you'll have to be more interesting for TV and rallies. More animated, less droning." He checked his watch, and turned to walk out.

"Fuck you," she said to the door, clicking shut behind him.

CHAPTER 11

GRADUATION

AFTER DC, VERMILLION WAS WELCOMINGLY familiar. The coverts' headquarters was humming with the new phone bank set up for calling voters, brimming with volunteers. There were paid organizers and media interns, hired by Jenifer Walton from Government for the People to push content. The new coverts spoke to Arden in hushed tones, thanking her for her leadership and vision. Arden tried to be gracious and to hide how awkward she felt at the praise. She'd stayed away from Kirish since the trip, which was fine with him, apparently.

A cool drizzle fell the morning of graduation. Arden told herself she was going to watch Carson walk, and Jessica, but she and Ophelia both waited for the graduate student ceremony, after the hoorays and stomping of the undergrads. They watched Kirish bend to receive the mustard-colored hood signifying law, a large sash lifted over his head and laid across his shoulders. He was awarded cum laude, high honors. This accomplishment surprised Arden—that he'd been able to do so well while waging a disruptive political campaign.

Ophelia went running across the stadium to catch a friend. Arden sat alone, watching Kirish file out with the new Juris Doctors. He was so infuriating. Despite her still fresh anger at him, she was shaken by a feeling that he had thrown away his future. He had just done such a hard thing, graduating cum laude from law school, but who would hire him now? What if the professor jobs never materialized? If 99 were to fail, would he be an untouchable? Would she?

After the ceremony, Arden had pushed her way through the crowds to find him. She saw him as she came around the corner to the back of Old Main, standing with two well-dressed adults who must have been his parents. He didn't see Arden as she approached slowly, not wanting to interrupt them, as it became evident that his mother was very upset. She was fashion model thin, with expensive leather riding boots and a trim chalky-blue tweed blazer. Her voice was shrill and furious, as if being twisted from her frail frame.

"Ever since your last year of Williams, you've been acting strangely! And now this . . . this insanity! What on earth are you doing, Justin? Why would you work so hard in law school, just to throw it away?" His mother shared the same concern about Kirish, apparently.

Kirish was stiff in his blue suit, hands wringing in frustration. His eyes showed agony. "Mom, please," he begged, "this is important to me. Please just listen to me and try to understand."

Kirish's father, portly with a graying beard and wire glasses, looking exhausted, echoed Kirish. "Ellen. Please."

Kirish looked over and saw Arden, who was backing away from their trio hoping to escape notice. He hung his head for a moment, as if this were the last straw, and Arden was mortified at intruding. She was surprised when he lifted his head and reached toward her with a welcoming gesture.

"Mom, Dad, I want to you meet someone. This is Arden Firth." Kirish paused, as his mother looked Arden over. She then looked heavenward, and closed her eyes.

"Arden, this is my mother, Ellen, and my father, Joseph." Kirish's father stepped forward to shake her hand, saying, as if by rote, "Good to meet you."

Kirish's mother finally opened her eyes, which were again trained on Kirish. She ignored Arden and the introduction entirely.

"I don't know how this happened, but you've become radicalized!" she said loudly, not caring if people heard. She and Kirish stood glaring at each other.

"Ellen, this is Arden, Justin's friend," his father prompted his wife.

She finally turned to Arden, eyes narrowing. Perhaps Arden was to blame? Arden flinched; perhaps she was. Ellen dismissed her silently, something in her appraisal of Arden's clothes or demeanor convincing her that Arden couldn't have been the corrupting influence.

"Was there a professor at this school who put these ideas in your head? Because I didn't pay good money to have you brainwashed by a bunch of socialist college professors!" His mother's fists were clenched and her voice carried across the quad.

"Mom, these are our own ideas," he began. "Can we please go somewhere and talk about this calmly?"

"I will listen to your *ideas*," she spat, "if we can also have a serious discussion about you getting in the car and coming back to Philadelphia with us. You'll sit for the bar there, and your father's partners at the firm will put in a good word for you, if you renounce this craziness."

He shook his head. "That's not going to happen, Mom."

"You know what's not going to happen, Justin?" She was yelling now. "We're not going to foot the bill for this school, just to have you throw it away! Unless you get in the car now, you can consider the tuition a loan from us, which must be repaid."

"Now, Ellen, we talked about this." Joseph approached her, tentatively taking her arm. Arden could hear him say quietly to her, "Please calm down, honey, you're worrying me." He put an arm around her shoulders and began steering her toward the parking lot, looking backward at his son with sadness in his tired face.

Ellen Kirish turned and glared back at them. "With interest!" she yelled.

Kirish turned on his heel and walked into Old Main, pushing the door open with such force that the paned glass rattled in its frame.

ARDEN DIDN'T SEE KIRISH UNTIL LATER that night, at the graduation party for him and Carson and the other graduating coverts, at the Church Street headquarters. The storefront was crowded with people spilling out onto the street, laughing and drinking beer out of plastic cups. The Greek restaurant across the street sent over several large trays of food at ten o'clock, after they were closing down, and the coverts, quite drunk at this point, had a feast.

When they finished eating, Carson got up and made a funny speech about how he hadn't imagined that he'd be running field ops for a subversive anti-corporate movement when he arrived on campus four years ago, planning to major in business, like his dad. He talked about taking poli-sci as a sophomore, and it being like a light going on for him, what he would major in and what mattered to him. He thanked Kirish for being his teacher.

Ophelia congratulated them both, stepping into the spotlight with a smile. "What you may not know is that on top of Kirish keeping everyone in line here at head-quarters, he also graduated cum laude with his Juris Doctor!" She lowered her voice playfully at the Latin accolades, and the room laughed and applauded. Kirish shook his fist at her and smiled.

Next, Andrew Nassert from Government for the People stood up, clearing his throat dramatically. Andrew had become a fixture in the Church Street headquarters, working closely with Ophelia and Carson on strategy. He was ruddy with drinking, and Arden hoped he'd be brief.

"Now, I've only known you guys since February, but I feel like there's been a lot of water under the bridge. When we first got here, well, to be honest, we expected a bunch of amateurs. But in the last few months working with the coverts, we've become so excited about this team. So let's all raise our drinks for a toast to the graduates! To Carson, who could organize a circus of cats! To Kirish, the architect of 99! With your talents, we know you will both go far!" Andrew raised his beer can to Carson and Kirish.

Arden knew that both she and Kirish were thinking of his mother at Andrew's last proclamation. Kirish raised his glass back at Andrew, and the rowdy partygoers broke into chants of, "Speech! Speech!" Kirish shook his head, trying to beg off, but the coverts weren't having it.

"Okay! Okay!" Kirish quieted the crowd. "No speech, but I do have a toast." He paused, flashing a look at Arden. "May everyone get what they deserve," he intoned, with a sardonic wink at her. Arden had no idea what the wink was supposed to mean, and was equally baffled by the toast. Did they deserve something good or something bad? There was silence for a beat, and Arden heard someone say "jeez" in the back of the room, before the party together decided to treat this as a cheerful proclamation rather than an ominous one. People began to clap robustly, calling out, "Hear, hear!"

ARDEN FINALLY CORNERED KIRISH TO congratulate him around eleven. She couldn't remember ever having seem him so loose, other than perhaps at his apartment that summer night with Ophelia. She wanted to be angry, and still was, but this felt like a different person. He was funny and warm, telling her stories about his recent trip to New York to meet with donors.

"You should have been there, I went to this cocktail party someone threw to fundraise for us, and it was full of all these Yale alumni, old families that made their money a hundred years ago in the early corporations, and still have so much it just keeps growing in the stock market, but they see how fucked up everything is." He was leaning heavily on the wall behind him.

"I bet you loved being in the middle of all those fancy academics," Arden smiled.

"They're just looking for some way to relieve their guilty consciences. Just like Jeremy." He laughed and leaned down to whisper in her ear. "One of them felt so guilty she offered to take me to bed."

"You think that was guilt?" Arden teased him. "I doubt that." She wondered if he took her up on the offer.

"No?" he said, looking in her eyes. "What was it?"

"Are you fishing for some kind of compliment here, Kirish?" She shook her head. "You're a piece of work."

Arden was struck by how much more handsome he was when he relaxed, without the pinched look around his mouth she only noticed in its absence.

He told her that while in New York, he had received a call from a law firm wanting to meet with him on behalf of an undisclosed client, and when Kirish had gone to the meeting, it had been a job offer. The law firm, a "white shoe" firm, was the kind of evil Wall Street shop he despised—working there would be the most vile form of selling out, as he saw it. She smiled at the irony. This was just the kind of opportunity she had worried, during the graduation ceremony, that he would be missing out on.

"Are you serious? Why on earth would they hire you, Kirish? No offense."

"Don't you see? It would discredit us, to have one of us sell out." He grabbed her arm and pulled her toward him, laughing somewhat maniacally. "We cannot falter!"

"Well, no one is offering me cushy jobs, so no risk here." She laughed, surreptitiously inhaling his vaporous scotch breath.

"They will try to get to you," he told her. "Offer you the thing you can't refuse, or pressure you to embarrass the movement."

She wanted to keep teasing him, to call him paranoid, but she felt it could be true.

"I'm not sure how they can. I've already told all my embarrassing secrets." For the first time, she saw what freedom this was, to have been laid bare.

He nodded darkly and looked out the window into the night. She followed his gaze, which lingered on a white van parked across the street from headquarters. Did he suspect the van? Did he think he was being followed? Arden wanted to scoff at the idea, but it gave her a chill.

"You should kiss me."

"What?" Arden exclaimed, reeling at his sudden change. "Why?"

He laughed hard, that a reason would not be self-evident. "Just do it. It will be good for morale." His eyes were a challenge. She looked around at the now thinning gathering. Indeed, several people were watching them, either furtively or overtly. She became aware that she and Kirish were standing close to each other, leaning in.

"Is that really why?"

"There's never only one reason why. But yes. Rumor is that you don't like me." His smile was mocking.

Because it felt like a dare, she leaned forward slowly, and planted a firm kiss on his mouth, lingering just a beat or two longer than a hello kiss. Both of them kept their eyes open. When she pulled away, he nodded, no longer smiling. They stood looking at each other for a minute, then Arden shook her head, told him he was drunk, and headed for the ladies' room.

Forty-five minutes later, she slipped away, catching a ride home with Ophelia.

"So. . . ." O immediately said as she started the car, "You and Kirish? What was that? I thought you were pissed at him."

"I was. I am," Arden corrected. She wasn't sure now. "That was nothing. Rallying the troops or something."

Ophelia looked at her in disbelief. "Well there's always been speculation about you guys. He's trying to fan the rumors. Is that what he told you? Not sure I buy that."

Speculation? That was news to Arden.

"He was drunk."

"Kinda looked like *you* kissed *him*. . . ." Ophelia shot her an appraising glance.

"Yeah." Arden wasn't sure how to explain that. "Yeah, I was just saying congratulations," she said lamely, knowing it sounded ridiculous. O was silent for a minute and then clicked on the radio, to protest being fed half-truths. Arden was embarrassed that she couldn't be honest. What would she say? It was a dare maybe, not sure?

Later in her bed, Arden kept thinking about Kirish and their strange encounter. She thought of his criticism of the Legacy Foundation speech, that she had not been "dynamic." Arden turned this over in her mind, trying to be objective. Either it was tough constructive criticism, or he had been trying to hurt her. She couldn't decide which it had been. She remembered the moment before "dynamic," when he'd been concerned about her, and even suggested she move to his apartment building. And then the insult, maybe he just had been pushing her away. But it was true, too, she wasn't dynamic, she'd barely limped through the speech in a beta-blocker haze.

When she replayed the kiss in her mind, it became a real kiss, eyes closed and intense. Had he really wanted to improve morale? Or had he just wanted to kiss her?

CHAPTER 12 GRANGE

THE NEXT EVENING, ARDEN RECEIVED a desperate call from Emma. The forms they'd filled out to claim the homesteading exception had been rejected by the court, and the date for the foreclosure by sale had been set. Emma was close to hysterical, imagining being turned out of her home. Even in the days following Jill's death, Arden hadn't seen her grandmother so distraught.

Arden was scheduled to speak at several Grange Hall meetings in small towns across the state over the next week, but promised to head to Badger first to see Emma in the morning. When she arrived, she was alarmed to find Emma still in bed at ten o'clock, unheard of for her hardy grandmother. She clearly wasn't taking things well.

"Em, have you talked to Jim Bouchard to see if the soybean people can work out some kind of deal here? Maybe sell them some of the land to pay off the loan?" Arden asked gently once she'd brewed a pot of coffee for them both.

"Oh, you better believe they've been sniffing around," Emma growled. "They won't talk to me at this point because they'll be the first one lined up at the auction sale." Arden imagined the humiliation of an auction sale, with Emma's neighbors sorting through her things.

"Listen, Gram, give me the papers, and I'll take them back to the law school clinic, and we'll figure out what went wrong." Arden flipped through the court papers and was shocked to see the court date to finalize the fore-closure and eviction was just two weeks away. She paged through them more carefully, trying to decipher anything else meaningful, and was surprised to see AGM, the soy-bean company, listed as a party receiving notice. Why would they be getting copies of the documents? Maybe Emma wasn't just being paranoid.

"I'll call you tomorrow night when I get back to Ver-million and can go over these with Kirish. He'll know what to do," Arden promised—*I hope*, she added silently. "I'm sorry, Emma, I've got to go up to Garden City for a Grange meeting at noon. I've got to leave right now or I'll be late." Arden couldn't understand what had happened with the homestead exemption and had a sinking feeling that the cards were stacked against them somehow.

THE NEWS ABOUT THE FORECLOSURE made Arden even more nervous than she already was about the Grange meetings. Even though she knew that Grange folks were good people, the idea of being in front of them ratcheted up her social anxiety because of her history with them. Andrew Nassert's strategic plan for 99 hinged on getting the Grange to endorse the initiative. "Arden should be the one to bring them in," Ophelia had said, waving her hand vaguely to the west. "She's got all the farm-y stuff she knows about."

"Yeah," Arden had agreed, "my grandmother is a member of her local Grange. I know some about how they work." It had been Emma's fellow Grangers who'd taken care of her when she'd been sick, who had dropped off an endless train of casseroles.

"We've got to get their support," Kirish warned her before she left. "Without it, we won't have credibility with rural farm voters. They are a must-have endorsement."

"I get it," Arden had responded, annoyed that he had to make this a high-pressure proposition. "I think they will be open to it."

Arden knew from Emma that the Grangers had been activists, when they began. The Granger Movement, in the 1890s, had centered on new regulation for railroads, which had disrupted crop markets after the Civil War. The Grange was not partisan, in that it didn't side with a particular political party, but it was no stranger to controversial legislative initiatives. After railroad regulation, the Grangers had pushed through progressive reform measures on education and anti-corruption in the early 1900s. Moreover, farmers understood that voter mobilization is power, even over a corrupt or incumbent elite.

Arden was hopeful that the Grangers, although now much less political, would be receptive to 99, but the prospect of talking to them made her anxious. She remembered the chicken pie suppers and Fourth of July celebrations, which she'd loved as a child but learned to dread as she got older. Emma would always drag Jill and Arden along, hoping that their staid community would straighten Jill out. As Arden watched her mother's boozy, overly friendly interactions with the conservative farmers, she felt the first of many hot prickles of shame about her mother. She overheard one gray-haired matron telling her teenage sons, "On no account are you to fraternize with that woman." At nine, Arden didn't understand what that meant, but clearly it wasn't good. Jill, herself only twenty-six at the time, should have been able to be her loud, brassy self and flirt with the farm boys. Instead, she grew bitter about spending time with the "Husband-fuckers," as she called them, mocking the reference to animal husbandry in the Grange's official name, to infuriate Emma. The Grangers, which would have forgiven a teenage pregnancy, turned their righteous scorn on Jill as she became increasingly dissolute. All agreed she was no longer welcome at Grange picnics by the time Arden was twelve, at that point painfully embarrassed and worried about her mother, whose presence in Arden's life now was modulated by her addictions. Two months in rehab. Two months out. A month in jail. Repeat.

Arden had repressed as much of that time as she could, stuffing it away with all her memories of her mother in a place in her mind she did not visit, unless forced to. Even for the Legacy Foundation talk, she had told Jill's story, not her own. Although Arden had been told that addiction was a disease, not a choice, she was still furious.

The first couple Grange hall talks were not easy. She became enraged at imagined slights that, upon reflection, were simply rural folks being reserved or respecting her space. In bits and pieces, scenes from the picnics returned to her, flashes of her mother stumbling, women laughing behind their hands. She digested it, this time as an adult, slowly working it into her feelings about Jill like water into a lump of hard clay. The Grange embarrassments were more forgivable than those that came later, but of course, it all must be forgiven, she thought angrily, because you can't hold a grudge against a dead woman. *Wet grudge*, she remembered Emma's angry words. At some point was Arden supposed to be totally fine with Jill giving up on life and leaving her fourteen-year-old daughter for her mother to deal with? And them together to deal with Emma's cancer? Arden didn't see the point of forgiveness. But she had to admit that talking about 99 in the Grange halls was therapeutic. After her fourth appearance, with the quiet South Dakota farmers with their flannel shirts and chapped hands, Arden let go of some of her anger over Jill.

Most of the Grangers owned their farms, so their first question was always whether their properties were at risk. "Family farms, even if you have incorporated for tax or liability purposes, would not be subject to the law. The corporation would be dissolved, but the land would revert to individual ownership by the family," Arden assured them.

Most of their farms were mortgaged and often under water, so their second question was about what would happen to their mortgage notes. Almost all had equity lines against their farms that they used to buy farm equipment, seed stock, or other necessities.

"Mortgages and second loans to corporate banks will be eliminated under 99 as corporate assets," Arden explained, praying silently that Emma could hold onto the farm until November and that Election Day would bring a landslide for 99.

"Well, that sounds great, as long as your loan is with a commercial bank, but what about when you need a loan the next year?" she was asked by a skeptical farmer in an old plaid flannel and John Deere hat.

Arden was happy that she had thought this through with Kirish. "We understand the need for credit to keep a farm afloat. We think that need will be less, once the economy is no longer dominated by corporations, but we know that people, especially farmers, will still need access to loans and working capital. The initiative doesn't abolish mutual organizations, like credit unions, savings and loan institutions, and mutual insurance companies, which are owned and run for the benefit of their members, not for profit. In the short term, it may feel unfair that mortgages owed to corporate banks will be forgiven, while those to credit unions or S&Ls would not. But it's essential that we maintain the stability of those mutual organizations, as they'll be our financial support system under the new law."

The Grangers understood that legislation was a complex undertaking that had to be handled right. The farm bill, their legislative holy grail, had created winners and losers, as well as enshrined some bad policy that was almost impossible to undo. They also knew that politics could create lousy bedfellows, and they wanted to know who they were getting in bed with, if they supported 99.

"Our supporters don't break down on party lines. Many of us have felt for a long time, that something was rotten in politics. We are independent voters, Tea Partiers, some registered with each of the major two parties, some Green Party people, and many who haven't previously been politically active or even bothered to vote. I personally know several people who registered as voters for the first time in their lives so they could sign the ballot petition. We've even got a key funder who made his money in corporate America and now wants to make amends."

Arden paused, not sure how this fact would fly with the farmers. She looked around the room at the twenty or so older folks sitting in folding chairs before her, seeing them thinking about who was funding the movement. She pressed on.

"I think our support is stronger in farm country, but some city folks in Sioux Falls see real possibility here, too—though perhaps it's harder for them to imagine their lives without corporations than it is for rural folks. But there is a new breed of city folks who seek a return to honest work with their hands, and who see craft in making and growing things. These are the same folks who go out of their way to buy food grown here in the state, who push for a return to US manufacturing, who are entrepreneurs building businesses on their own that don't rely on the global corporate complex. They have buying power but don't want the crap made in China. These are the hipsters returning to their grandparents to learn how to can tomatoes and pickle things!" This got a chuckle out of the Grangers.

Arden had done so much preparing and canning fruits and vegetables every August and September with Emma as a teenager that she still recoiled when she saw home-canned preserves or pickles. But these homemade emblems were selling fast at urban farmers' markets, and increasingly, the folks hawking them were people her age. It seemed to Arden that there was a new kind of back-to-the-land movement, more practical than the one in the 1970s her grandmother had talked about. Rather than utopians, they were craftspeople: chefs, cheesemakers, brewers, and educators.

Arden thought about how the Grangers and the farmers' market hipsters might fit together post-99. She was reminded of something she had learned about from some middle-aged Unitarians who hung around to talk after a rally. They were the "three acres and a cow" people, as she had come to think of them. Invented by Catholic scholars in the 1800s, "distributism" was a social governance idea billed as an alternative to capitalism and socialism, where the means of production are spread as widely as possible. They believed that property ownership is a fundamental right. Land or other property should be spread among the population in a way that encouraged self-sufficiency and independence.

In distributism, trade guilds and associations, like the Grange, had a key role in coordinating and combining forces to organize markets and trade. Opponents of welfare protections, distributivists believed instead that all people should be afforded the dignity and the means to support themselves. Resources should be distributed throughout a population, rather than concentrated. Like three acres and a cow. They admitted, yes, that it was less efficient for a subsistence farmer to grow all the food he and his family needed on a three-acre farm, when you looked at the pure output from that land compared to factory farming. But efficiency was not a high-order ideal in their view.

For Arden too, efficiency was not a high-order ideal. She liked the idea of slowing things down. Was efficiency required in order to feed the world, to serve global markets? Or was that just what the corporations wanted you to think? She thought of DC from the air, the hive of tiny millions, and wondered if there would be enough to go around. In South Dakota, at least, she thought there could be.

After her last Grange meeting, Arden found herself dragging her feet, making a slow return to Vermillion. She'd called Kirish the first night after leaving Emma's, and he'd promised to set up a meeting with the law school clinic lawyers and figure out what had gone wrong with the homestead exemption. She knew she had to get back to deal with that—after all, the court date was now only ten days away. But she was not looking forward to going back to covert headquarters.

Arden felt awkward about the graduation party kiss, both with Kirish but also with the rest of the coverts, who would have all heard the gossip by now. And with Ophelia, whom she'd been less than honest with. But it was more than that, Arden realized. It felt easier to talk to strangers, somehow, than to be back at coverts headquarters, always having to think about being a leader. She was uncomfortable in that role, though she should be used to it by now. She still side-stepped things she should have done, like making the final call on ending a relationship with a politician they distrusted, or resolving a dispute between two volunteers. Telling herself that others knew more about the politics, or whatever the issue was, made it easy to step back. But time and again, she felt that twinge of disappointment in herself. And perversely, she was irritated to see Andrew stepping more and more into the role of the movement's leader, though it was often into the void she created by holding back.

Ophelia hadn't said anything to her about it, but Arden imagined that she too was disappointed. There had been an odd distance between them lately, even before the kiss. Arden wasn't sure why. Ophelia also had been spending a lot of time with her new girlfriend, Jody. Of course, Arden understood, but the fact was that she was lonely, even when surrounded by people. Maybe more so when surrounded by people. Why was that? She wished she didn't always feel so uncomfortable at headquarters lately. It was so draining. Maybe it didn't sit well with her to be in charge because it made her feel apart.

She wondered how Kirish would act when she saw him, after the graduation party. His being friendly that one night, out of so many—Arden didn't dare expect anything more from him. But she wished she could talk to someone about whether she was doing a good job, someone who wouldn't hold her misgivings against her as evidence of her failing, like she thought he would.

CHAPTER 13 NOTORIETY

ARDEN WAS LATE TO THE WEEKLY leadership meeting, because she'd met beforehand with the law school clinic lawyers about the foreclosure. Her heart was beating too hard as she sat down at the head of the table, the only seat left, and met Kirish's inquiring look. She shook her head, indicating that the news wasn't good. There had been a hearing on the homestead exemption application, usually a formality, which is why the clinic lawyers hadn't bothered to attend or to have Emma show up. But there had been a last-minute objection made at the hearing, something about how the homestead exemption could not be granted if the land was leased, as hers was to AGM. This was unheard of, the lawyers had apologized, they had never seen anything like it. It was an obscure rule none of them had seen enforced before. Their only option now was to reargue the issue at the foreclosure hearing, which sounded like an uphill battle.

As Arden caught her breath, she realized that Jennifer Walton was looking at her with a self-satisfied smile that reminded her of Emma's old saying, "like the cat with the canary." *Oh, Emma,* Arden thought, her heart sinking, thinking of telling her grandmother the news. Where would she go? Arden had tried last week to broach the subject of her grandmother perhaps moving into her apartment in Vermillion, which had made Emma hang up on her in a fit of tears.

"What?" Arden asked, realizing everyone was looking at her, with that same smug look. Jennifer slid the *New Republic* article toward her. Jennifer had printed out copies of the online article and passed them around. The lead photo was a picture of Arden and Kirish on the steps of the Lincoln Memorial, on the walk after the law school conference. It shook Arden, since there hadn't been a photographer there, at least as far as she knew. In the photo, Kirish was talking, gesturing, and she imagined it was the moment he was telling her about states being the laboratories of the US, with their experiments in governance. Had he known they were being photographed?

"The article is fantastic, I've read it twice." Jennifer brought the meeting to order by banging her coffee mug on the table like a gavel. "You can all read it at your leisure, but let me read you some of my favorite parts. It's called 'South Dakota's Challenge to our Corporatocracy—Revolution or Delusion?' by Janet Dowin, *The New Republic*," Jennifer read. She continued reading in a dramatic tone, like a newscaster.

In November, eighteen thousand South Dakota voters signed on to place the question of whether corporations should be abolished in the state on next year's ballot. The initiative, called *South Dakota Initiative 99, Voter Initiative Abolishing the Corporation and Associated Distribution of Assets,* provides both that existing South Dakota corporations are invalidated, and also that corporations created under the laws of other states are not recognized as having legal status. This would lead to the seizure of property and assets held in the state by corporations, which would then be redistributed to individuals under a yet-to-be-established process.

While the proposal is rife with probably unconstitutional elements, the South Dakota electorate may not care. The initiative is gathering momentum in the state and, although voter initiatives are notoriously hard to poll, appears as if it actually could become the law of the Mount Rushmore state.

"I don't love that *probably unconstitutional* part," Kirish said under his breath. "And this isn't so great either." He read,

The planners of "99," as it is fondly called, are working earnestly to address the widespread disruption that would occur in the unlikely case that the initiative survived legal challenge. They admit, however, that there will be social and economic upheaval, which economists worry would have lasting impacts on the economy of the state and its ability to fund statewide programs like education and social services.

"I don't recall admitting any such thing," he scowled. Neither did Arden, although it was all true. She read on the next piece in her head, which she liked since it laid out the history.

South Dakota was the first state in the union to permit voter-initiated ballot referenda, in 1898. Part of the Populist movement of that time, the first modern ballot initiative process was a home-grown idea, the work of a South Dakota Catholic clergyman and a socialist newspaperman with support from fraternal organizations like the Grange. Voter-initiated ballot measures became one of the signature reforms of the Progressive Era (1890s–1920s), with 24 mostly Western states subsequently adopting similar measures. Direct democracy measures like South Dakota's have created what are widely agreed to be important legislative reforms in our country's history, but have also been criticized as mob rule that results in bad, unconsidered policy. Recent examples include marijuana legalization, anti-gerry-mandering measures, and bans on gay marriage, the latter of which the Supreme Court has found unconstitutional.

"Okay, wait, here's a good part about Arden and Kirish's trip to DC," Ophelia jumped in and read aloud,

On May 14, the two young people behind Initiative 99 traveled to Washington, DC, to participate in a panel at George Washington Law School and to give an unconventional keynote at the Legacy Foundation's annual meeting. While Justin Kirish and Arden Firth are careful to give credit to the team of well-organized activists headquartered in Vermillion, the two of them alone came up with the idea for the initiative and sketched out the initial blueprint together.

"Huh, what about me?" Ophelia protested. "I seem to recall being in your grandmother's living room when *we* came up with this idea, well before *Justin* got involved." She shot Arden a dirty look, which Arden couldn't tell whether was real or messing around.

There was some background on Kirish, describing his upbringing in middle-class suburbs of Philadelphia, the only child of a psychiatrist and a chemist, which was news to Arden. It noted that he "attended Williams, a prestigious East Coast private college, before the markedly less prestigious University of South Dakota School of Law, from which he recently graduated." She could hear Dowin's voice in the line, "About his personal history, he is circumspect, pushing Firth's story to the fore." *That's for sure*, Arden thought. When Arden reached the background on herself, she froze, blood creeping into her checks.

> If Justin Kirish is the brains of Initiative 99, then Arden Firth is either its heart or its social media personality. Firth, 20, is a born and bred South Dakotan, with the Scandinavian coloring of the region and a Midwestern "roll up your sleeves and get it done" manner. This was her first trip to our nation's capital. Unused to business attire and uncomfortable at the podium, she seemed deeply ambivalent about having agreed to speak at the conservative think-tank, the Legacy Foundation (and they seemed equally confused as to why she was there).

She hated that reporter for being so smug that she needed to point out that Arden was uncomfortable and not dressed correctly, making her sound like some kind of hick. She read on, keenly aware that the others in the room, which had fallen silent, were reading it too.

> Ms Firth's keynote speech shocked the staid crowd as she unsparingly laid out the brutality and humiliation of working-class life, following her mother's struggles to be gainfully employed, pay the rent and bills, and resist the promise of escape through prescription (and later street) drugs, which plagues so many disadvantaged communities.

Arden thought of Emma reading this, aware for the first time that telling her story publicly was also telling Emma's story, and she should have warned her. She forced herself to read on.

> Although Firth defers to Kirish on points of law and policy, she is searing in her proclamations that this is not the country our founders intended. She firmly believes that her mother would have fared better in a different America, one where the fruits of her labor benefitted her, rather than her employer.
>
> Hers is a troubled story, from which she has arisen as the figurehead of the movement. Born to a teenage, unwed mother in rural northeast South Dakota, she spent her childhood bouncing between her maternal grandmother's farm in dairy country and her mother's string of apartments around the state. After her mother died when Firth was fourteen years old, she was raised by her grandmother, who nearly lost her farm during an uninsured bout with cancer.

A thin, sad tale, laid out here in print. And about to get sadder, Arden imagined, thinking again of Emma's foreclosure. She quickly skimmed forward, the article moved on to her losing her scholarship and refusing to borrow the almost $70,000 after interest for the rest of college. She liked the line, "Firth sees student debt as a societal trap that locks people onto the 'gerbil wheel' of working for others and lining the pockets of corporations." She skimmed on through the discussion of how the idea for 99 was an extension of the anti-corporate farming law which Emma had worked on.

Ophelia chimed in again, reading from the same section Arden was. "... *much of Firth's passion relates to land and property ownership as a fundamental right, which she believes empowers people in controlling their own destiny.* That's really good," she said. Arden cringed as Ophelia continued reading aloud the next section, smirking as she read the last line.

Kirish and Firth met while he was the teaching assistant in her political science class at USD. After dropping out of school, she sought him out to discuss her idea to abolish corporations, as he explains it, *careful to note that they did not socialize while he was her student teacher.*

"What's that about?" she asked, and then continued,

After a month of research, Kirish came back to her with the conviction that it could be done. Corporations are a legal fiction, granted "personhood" and legal existence in each state under state law. Such that the state giveth, it must be able to take away, Kirish reckons. Whether this idea can be squared with established US Supreme Court jurisprudence that corporations are legal persons entitled to free speech and other protections remains to be seen, but Justin Kirish believes that there is a path toward a constitutional termination of South Dakota corporations. Whether Kirish, a freshly minted Juris Doctor yet to pass the bar, has a realistic view of the law remains to be seen.

Ophelia paused here and looked at Kirish to gauge his reaction, skipping the article's sharp questioning of the Fifth Amendment due process and just compensation issues. He had a bemused look on his face, sitting back and listening.

"Now don't worry," Jennifer jumped in, "some controversy here is a good thing. Wait till we get to the end." Everyone started to read the last paragraph, and with a sinking feeling, Arden realized what Jennifer meant.

While Kirish dismisses suggestions that he and Firth are any more than a team of like-minded activists, there is a certain intensity between the two that begs the question. Ms. Firth was more equivocal on the subject, and follows him like a compass. She admits they have no time for romantic entanglements, somewhat wistfully, as they count down to Election Day. Time will tell, however, come November, whether South Dakota Voter Initiative 99 is a new populist revolution or merely collegiate naïveté.

There was a long pause in the room, longer than it could have taken everyone to finish the article. Arden looked at the last picture on the printout, of her and

Kirish over coffee, eyes locked in an intense gaze. She remembered the moment in the George Washington University cafeteria. They'd been arguing. But the photo looked like something else.

Andrew cleared his throat. "Yes, well, as Jennifer said, controversy can be a good thing, and there's lots of that here. Overall, I think it is a strong article. Not all complimentary, but balanced, and the cover story. Jennifer, will the cover of the magazine be this picture at the Lincoln Memorial?" he asked.

She nodded. "I haven't seen it yet, but I think so."

"Kirish, did you know they were taking this picture at the Mall?" Arden asked him.

"I knew the photographer was there," he said, looking her in the eye as if to challenge her to say more. Why hadn't he told her that they were meeting a photographer? She thought they had just accidentally stumbled upon the National Mall as they walked to the hotel. She didn't like the feeling that she was being managed by him, it felt like manipulation.

"So long as it's not this other pic," Ophelia exclaimed, "what's up with that?"

"This soap opera stuff, it is a way to sell papers," Kirish exclaimed. "It makes the whole thing more interesting." Arden narrowed her eyes, wondering if he'd done something to plant the narrative of a romance between them.

He continued. "They basically have to say that, just because we're young and the opposite sex. It's insulting, really, that because you're female and I'm male then there must be something going on," he snorted dismissively. Arden and Ophelia exchanged a look, both thinking of the graduation party.

AFTER THE PUBLICATION, ARDEN FELT THE coverts treat her differently. Most of them hadn't heard the story of her past. Although Arden had lived it all, until the Legacy Foundation speech, she hadn't necessarily seen her own family history as an argument for 99. But she had to admit it made for a more interesting backstory.

The "soap opera" stuff, as Kirish had called it, was beyond embarrassing. And because a few coverts had seen them kiss at the graduation party, the rumor had traction, and she felt people watching when she and Kirish were together. Peter Bassford, the former oil rig roughneck, took to making lewd comments whenever they were around, and liked quoting the article, which someone had posted on the wall in the media room.

"No time for romantic entanglements, Arden Firth sighed," he pretended to read verbatim.

"She follows him like a compass. . . ." he intoned breathlessly, making a pumping motion with his pelvis. Arden wished she could fire him. Kirish took to avoiding Bassford entirely.

Despite these embarrassments, Arden saw the power of the *New Republic* article; it became their national stage, as Kirish had predicted. Jennifer used it as a springboard to book television interviews for Arden and Kirish; there were follow-up interviews and reprints and radio spots. She encouraged all the coverts to send the article to their friends and families, and the article was widely shared and reshared on social media. It was picked up by both the right and the left, each of which pulled out pieces of the policy discussion that aligned with their viewpoints. However sensationalist the article had been in describing Arden and Kirish personally, it was disciplined in laying out the policy strengths and weaknesses, making for sound bites both sides could get behind. Of course, when it was reposted, it was radicalized in the retelling. Several well-known Tea Party activists came out in favor of 99, and just as many left-leaning pundits declared their support. The nation was abuzz with talk of Initiative 99. Did the voters of South Dakota really understand what they were doing? Would mass chaos result? Food and gas shortages? What about banks and hospitals? There was talk about the state economy being destabilized, and even suggestions that it was already happening. A few South Dakota corporations threatened publicly to pull out of the state and were beginning to see stock devaluation. There were reports of corporate-owned property being quietly sold to individuals in bargain sales to avoid property loss.

But most corporations, especially the out-of-state ones, were vocal that Initiative 99 was unconstitutional and any loss of corporate property would require just compensation by the state. The banking giants, like Jeremy Hatch's former employer Unibank, were mobilizing with op-eds in the local papers, lobbyists, and paid economists making ominous warnings about what would happen if 99 passed.

The "Vote No on 99" committee—calling themselves South Dakotans for Prosperity, or SDP for short—flush with corporate support, was able to blanket the state with TV commercials. Arden had seen several, all variations on a theme. In one, black-and-white footage of Depression Era unemployment lines. In another, Dust Bowl images of parched farmland, as if 99 might bring about drought and pestilence. In a third, actors sat cross-legged in gray uniforms in a classroom setting under the caption, "Communist Reeducation Camp." To Arden, the intentional misinformation seemed obvious, but she wasn't sure if the voters would see it that way.

Jennifer had set up a series of phony profiles to follow SDP, so she could monitor their social media outreach. SDP used the *New Republic* article liberally, misquoting it and linking to it with misleading headlines ("Left-Wing Media Proclaims 99 to be Anarchist–Socialist Dangerous Experiment" and "Teen Leaders of 99 in Sex Ring"). Jennifer warned them all to watch out for moles from SDP trying to invade their ranks.

"You mean like a spy?" Arden asked incredulously. "There are hundreds of volunteers coming in and out of 99 headquarters in any given week. How are we supposed to spot a mole for SDP?"

"Well, just be careful who you let under the tent," Jennifer replied. "I've seen operatives from opposition campaigns infiltrate ballot initiatives before. Just watch out you guys don't do anything stupid." She eyed Arden and Ophelia speculatively.

Over the course of the days that followed, Arden began to realize what Kirish had meant, upon their return from DC, about things getting weird. She was now recognized almost everywhere she went. That wasn't entirely new in the town where she'd gone to college for the last two years, but the kinds of people who recognized her had changed, and the attention was not all friendly. There were actually photographers hanging around outside headquarters one day, trying to get a shot of her. She didn't like the feeling of being a celebrity.

AT LEAST THEY'D BEEN ABLE TO BUY SOME time on Emma's foreclosure. Arden and one of the clinic lawyers had driven out to the circuit court hearing on the appointed day, meeting a pale and drawn Emma on the courtroom steps of the Kingsbury County Courthouse. The clinic lawyer had been able to convince the court that the homestead exemption should apply at least for the three-acre parcel containing Emma's home, barns, and orchard. Though the Unibank lawyer in his expensive suit had argued that the foreclosure should still be finalized that day, they'd been able to delay the final decision, convincing the court that a land survey was needed to establish the new lot.

While the homestead ruling had provided the delay that Arden was hoping for, at least until September, and meant Emma wouldn't need to move out of Badger, Arden was worried by the look on her grandmother's face. Though she was silent in the courtroom, when they got to the parking lot, she unleashed her fury on the clinic lawyer and Arden.

"You told me that my land was protected as my home under the law. And then AGM and the bank get up to something funny when you're not around, and now I get three measly acres? This is what they wanted—don't you get it? This is what they wanted all along."

For the clinic lawyer's sake, Arden was relieved when Emma slammed the door of her old pickup and drove away. But she wondered what Emma was talking about, that AGM was involved. Wasn't the issue simply that leasing the land to AGM made it ineligible for the homestead exemption, since if you are leasing something out, you are not using it as your homestead, as the lawyer had explained? It was troubling that Emma saw it as a conspiracy, but no wonder that she was furious. All that she had worked for, farming that land over the years, and working on the anti-corporate farming initiative, and now, to have this happen to her. Arden thought about Unibank, ruthlessly pressing this foreclosure, and their funding of the opposition to 99. They were Jeremy's former employer, the one he wanted to make pay. Was it possible that Emma was getting singled out as retribution for Arden's activism? Perhaps they'd never know. But it made Arden want to roll right into Sioux City and burn down Unibank's corporate headquarters.

The next time she saw Jeremy, she asked him if he through his former employer might be going after Emma's farm because of 99.

"Maybe," he responded. "I've already been contacted by their lawyers, trying to say that what I'm doing is a violation of my noncompete in the early retirement settlement. Which I told them is bullshit. But they are definitely exploring all legal angles."

A FEW NIGHTS LATER, ARDEN WAS followed home from headquarters by two men, only to have them run off by Peter Bassford, 99's resident roughneck, at the last minute. But this meant that Peter might have been following her too, which Arden didn't like either. He was creepy. The next morning, Arden signed a month-to-month lease for the apartment above Kirish's, which was just a few blocks from 99 headquarters. Ophelia was so upset about what had happened that she made Arden promise not to walk alone at night anymore, and gave her some pepper spray. Arden shared the picture she had snapped with her cell phone of the two men with the Vermillion police, who dutifully put a copy of the photo on file but warned her to take better precautions. She didn't mention Peter, in part because she wasn't sure that the black gun he'd flashed, tucked into his pants, was legal. Although Kirish had been the one to suggest she move to his building, he now feigned surprise that she was in the process of doing so. He was nowhere to be found on move-in day; nevertheless, she was glad to be there. The apartment was homey and small, and it was much closer to their Church Street headquarters.

After that, she would try to walk home after dark with Jess and Carson, her new neighbors, or with Kirish, although he rarely seemed to be on the same schedule as she was. He never did invite her back into his apartment, apparently still freaked out about the incident with Ophelia and the red wine. Still, there was some comfort in knowing it was his footsteps creaking the floorboards below her, not a stranger's.

CHAPTER 14
EXECUTIVE PRESENCE

WITH FIVE MONTHS LEFT UNTIL NOVEMBER, Kirish and Arden were traveling the state to talk at town halls and community centers about Initiative 99, to increasingly large crowds. From what Arden could tell, the climate was shifting and people were starting to think 99 could be a reality. She could feel the momentum building. Sometimes crowds laughed at the idea of 99, sometimes they seemed angry or frightened, and sometimes they were gleeful in their support. Sometimes the crowds that were the most enthusiastic made her uncomfortable. There was an anarchy to some of them that reminded her that 99 was something entirely new—a roll of the dice. There would be massive disruption, and she worried that vulnerable people, the poor and elderly, would be unable to adjust. Although the coverts were working hard to plan for these risks, it frightened her that she was leading a charge that could actually make things worse for some people, especially in the short term.

Arden was becoming more comfortable speaking to the crowds, however, and felt that she actually had answers to people's questions. At a town hall in Monroe on a Wednesday night, Arden was at the front of a room of thirty people, mostly friendly. She'd just run through her standard talk, which she could do in her sleep by then. The forty-something guy in jeans and work boots raised his hand. "I work at the Meineke muffler shop in town. What will happen to my job if 99 passes?" He stood up to ask the question, removing his worn baseball cap, and then sat back down.

Arden nodded; she'd seen the place on the way into town. "Because the shop is owned by a corporation, it would be forfeited and available for redistribution. The town planner would evaluate the business, and match it with people who had the skills and drive to take it over, either through individual ownership, or with a partner, or through a worker co-op—you would have the opportunity to be owner of the shop, or one of them."

The man looked skeptical. "How does a worker co-op work?" he asked.

She asked the man if he was familiar with Cabot Cheese and he nodded.

"Great." Arden was relieved, this was hard to explain otherwise. "So there, the farmers own the individual farms, but together, they own and operate the cheese-making operation, the marketing, and the advertising. They share profits according to what each member contributes in milk and time invested. But the business is owned by the members jointly." People looked suspicious of this.

"Muffler shops could fall under this business model. For example, the shops might be individually owned, but there's a co-operative business that deals with ordering parts, bookkeeping, payroll, those kinds of things. The folks who own the individual shop can decide whether they want to be in the co-op. It's kind of like having a franchise, but it is worker owned." Arden was happy to see the man nodding. He liked this idea.

"Now, what about your residential situation," Arden continued. "Do you own or rent?" "Rent," he responded quietly, clearly not proud that he wasn't a homeowner.

"So that could change as well. Apartment buildings owned by corporations would be forfeit under the initiative, like the Meineke. These buildings would be largely made into condominiums, where renters would have the option to take title to their homes; if your building is currently owned by a corporation, you could put in your residential application for the place you currently rent."

Arden glanced around the room trying to gauge how many others might be in the same boat. She continued, "I saw a number of vacant houses in this town, and more on the outskirts. Oftentimes these vacant properties are owned by banks, after people were no longer able to pay their mortgages. Again, under 99, these would be forfeit to the distribution pool, and would be available to all of you in this room. Perhaps you'd like to fix one of those up, or perhaps build something on your own piece of land. All of these would be possibilities. They'd require hard work, and they'd take time; Initiative 99 is not going to do that for you. But your labor will benefit you, that's the goal, rather than Meineke or your landlord or the bank."

The man nodded, and put his hat back on, seeming satisfied by her explanations.

"What about health care?" a gray-haired woman in a velour track suit asked her at a community center outside of Brookings. "Will I still be able to get my blood pressure pills? What about the hospital? What does this do to my Medicare benefits?"

"It wouldn't do anything to your Medicare," Arden responded. "And South Dakota is in a good position, in that our two major medical groups are not corporations. One is a nonprofit community hospital system and one is a religious charity, so both would be unchanged under 99."

There was murmuring in the room, and Arden could see that people were relieved to hear this. She continued, "These two groups offer the only health insurance plans on the state healthcare exchange, so that would also be unchanged. Some folks who get their insurance through their corporate jobs would have their healthcare disrupted, but they'd have the opportunity to get insurance on the exchange. Some think this would strengthen the exchange, since the pool would get bigger, and we've discussed using some of the distribution funds to temporarily cover premium subsidies for those whose income would be disrupted as a result of 99."

After each town hall or public meeting, Arden felt that she was chipping away at the veneer of the glossy doomsday television commercials aired by SDP. But she worried whether their speeches, reaching only a hundred at a shot, if they were lucky, could compete in the long term with the overfunded opposition campaign.

In late July, the coverts had organized a rally at the state capitol. Ophelia was the emcee and had the crowd cheering within five minutes. Then their donor Jeremy Hatch gave a long speech, telling the story of how he came to Initiative 99 from the corporate world, in such a compelling way that the crowd seemed to be frozen, hanging on his every word. Kirish followed with a tightly scripted description of the legislation and the implementation plan they'd drafted. This was where they often lost the audience's attention, which worried Arden. "If they aren't listening to the way it's going to work, how do they know what to vote for?" she'd asked Kirish. They both thought it was crucial to lay out the legal process in as simple and clear a summary as possible, but they were still refining those talking points. As usual, the crowd grew restless, but then the national director of Government for the People spoke, rousing the crowd with the charge to take back their government from the hands of corporate lobbyists. After that, a famous actor involved with Government for the People spoke. The young people in the crowd cheered wildly; Arden wondered how big a draw the actor had been. She had played the heroine in a dystopian action movie Arden had seen, and she'd liked how powerful the girl had been, lethal but not flashy about it.

"Because I've been lucky enough to have been successful acting in movies, I have a platform, which I want to use to help those who don't have a voice," the actor said. "The reason people don't have a voice is because politicians work for corporations, which have overpowered our economic and political systems."

Arden spoke last, after the actor left the stage to hysterical cheers. The audience started thinning out after that, and Arden struggled to hold the focus of the crowd. While she had actually gotten good at the Grange talks and town halls, she still felt awkward at a large rally like this, especially when the audience's attention was waning. In desperation, she retold the story of her mother that they had refined for the Legacy Foundation speech. It wasn't so hard the second time. In the end, thanking the audience for coming, Arden flinched as she heard an apologetic note in her voice. Why had they scheduled her last? Poor planning, she thought.

Jeremy Hatch pulled her aside later as they were standing around the capitol steps with a critique of her talk, uninvited.

"You've got to work on your voice. It's a common problem for women; really, you're all raised not to be loud. Somehow you have to be able to project without getting that freaked-out strained sound. It totally undermines your authority." He was snacking on cashews as he talked.

Arden was momentarily speechless. It was hard enough speaking in public. Now she has to worry about how her voice sounded? Easy for him to say. He had a deep, appealing voice, never faltering, and was eminently comfortable in front of a crowd. Arden thought again how much of a natural he must have been as a banking executive, hating him a little despite all the support he'd given to 99. No doubt he'd been able to make all his workers follow him loyally, until he outsourced their jobs.

"Nobody is going to tell you this because they are afraid of sounding sexist, but I think it is sexist *not* to give you the tough feedback I'd give a man. Can you take it?" His smile was encouraging, taking the edge off his words.

Arden nodded nervously.

"If you sound apologetic, people are going to think you have something to be sorry about. You need to own the role you're in. Margaret Thatcher said, 'A prime minister *should be* intimidating.' Do you know what that means?"

"No." Arden was starting to feel schooled.

"I've always believed it meant that people want their leaders to be impressive. Not apologetic. People are pack animals. If the alpha is nervous, the pack is even more nervous. You built 99. You're in charge here. You've got a big outline. Fill it out."

Arden nodded, appreciating his words but not really seeing a way to put them into practice. "Own it" was one of those platitudes she didn't really understand. *Have a deeper voice, a bigger presence, be more alpha. Aren't those just other ways of saying, be more like a man?* She thought of the dystopian heroine: lethal but not flashy. Maybe that was one way.

At USD, she'd taken a class on primate behavior, and she remembered learning that alpha chimpanzees had lower stress levels than the ones further down on the social strata. Monkeys of a lesser status perspired more, worried more. Scientists believed that alphas had lower stress levels because their social position and safety were more assured, and because they got more grooming and physical attention. Or was it the opposite, Arden wondered, thinking of Jeremy—did confidence beget authority? Arden wasn't sure she wanted to be an alpha. But she didn't want to be subservient, or just a follower, either.

Was it so essential to calibrate herself based on social standing? Perhaps it was in Jeremy's corporate world, where the leaders told you what to do. But was that even the right model for direct democracy? She wasn't telling people what to do. She was asking them to join her.

CHAPTER 15

BIG BROTHER

DESPITE THE MOMENTUM BUILDING around 99, Arden couldn't stop thinking about Emma and the farm. In just a few short weeks, the final court hearing on the foreclosure would be held. After multiple meetings with the clinic lawyers, Arden had been unable to find a way to delay the proceeding until after Election Day. The survey was now complete to define the parcel around the house that the court determined the homestead exemption would cover. Their only hope was to somehow convince the judge not to grant the foreclosure order, which the clinic lawyers were doubtful could be done. Short of some evidence of fraud or corruption by the bank, they explained, or Emma coming up with the loan amount plus fines and costs, the foreclosure was as good as complete. Arden hadn't been able to get Emma on the phone the last several times she had called and was worried. She knew she needed to get back to Badger and check on her, but it was so hard to tear herself away from the work.

The coverts' headquarters teemed with people. With fewer than three months now until November 7, Election Day, the get-out-the-vote effort was everyone's focus. Arden had been on the road so much that it was strange for her now to be there at the Church Street headquarters and see so many people there she didn't know. She felt their eyes on her every move, and everyone knew her name. She struggled to wear the mantle of leadership with ease, as Jeremy had coached her to, although the confidence felt forced. Her thoughts returned to Emma, who years ago had chaired the Grange meetings to plan the education committee activities for the year, with a gravity about her but a sense of humor and humility as well. Maybe leadership didn't need to be overconfident.

As she sat around the table with the other leaders of 99 at their weekly strategy meeting, Arden picked at a bagel and studied their various styles. Andrew Nassert, their ally from Government for the People, had a leadership style she admired. As political director, he was responsible for advising on strategy and developing a network of supporters for 99. His manner was earnest and often grave, reminding people of the weight of the political moment and their responsibility as citizens of a democracy. In private, he had a Machiavellian streak, thinking several moves ahead of his targets. His ability to build coalitions was the thing that impressed her the most, and he was able to articulate the things that united disparate groups, like unions, business chambers, student groups, Native American tribes, farmers, and environmentalists.

So far, most labor unions had been unwilling to commit, seeing their structure as too dependent on the current economic framework, but Andrew kept trying to bring them around. He worked just as hard with local chambers of commerce, and had been successful in convincing a handful that Initiative 99 would actually improve the local business climate. This was possible in towns or counties with dysfunctional relationships with absentee corporations that polluted or were bad employers. In other towns, local business people saw advantage in the redistribution process: to take back local resources and put them into the hands of residents.

Andrew was also courting environmental groups that had opposed gas pipelines, fracking, or mining. He was selling a vision of green ecotourism with a libertarian flavor, which appealed to independently owned hotels, restaurants, farmers, ranchers, sport fisherman, hunting guides, white-water rafting tours, vineyards, and campgrounds alike. Arden wasn't entirely sure how he got so many diverse constituencies moving in the same direction, but Andrew explained that many of them were industries ripe for consolidation, or at least people were receptive to the suggestion that they might be so. Prohibiting corporations from operating in the state would protect these small business owners from consolidation. If not for Home Depot and Lowes, he reminded her, the neighborhood hardware stores would still be there.

Jeremy Hatch sat at the head of the table, as usual. He was often pressed into service by Andrew to help him build coalitions. Jeremy was able to connect with people quickly, knew the language of business and commerce, and understood people's related concerns. He was a natural leader, exuding creature confidence like a pheromone. He made a point of establishing his role, as funder, expert, businessperson, and elder, at every meeting, to the point where Arden could almost cue his expected drawled comment. Was it Arden's competitive nature that made this annoying, when others were drawn to it?

Kirish sat quietly at the far end of the table, listening

with one ear to Carson's field report while marking up a document with a red pen. His authority seemed to flow in part from his legal training, or perhaps his intellect. Like Andrew, it was clear that his mind moved quickly. His insights seemed of a larger scale than Andrew's somehow, about society or history rather than social manipulation. Kirish did not seek a position of leadership, satisfied to stay in the shadow of Arden and Andrew's more public roles with the team. But in the coverts' leadership meetings, his opinions often carried the most weight. When he spoke, it was because he had something to say. He was Arden's most trusted advisor, although she disliked how he kept everyone at arm's length. Despite the distance between them, Arden felt that he understood her vision best. Even though she sometimes questioned his motives, she still felt he could be trusted to preserve the integrity of their idea. As appealing as he had been as a teacher, he could also be so in front of a crowd. He spoke often and effectively around the state, at rallies and town meetings, but seemed to be avoiding a leadership role at coverts headquarters. Again, Arden felt a guilty twinge—he was probably stepping back to make room for her to take that role. It was her own fault if she didn't fill that role, as Jeremy had challenged her to do.

Carson, Arden's neighbor with the shaggy beard and booming voice, continued his update on field operations.

"We've now got field locations in five places across the state, including this one, with close to two hundred fifty regular volunteers we can call on," he told them proudly. He was their field director, and he was a great storyteller. Carson had just graduated in May with a political science degree, and while in school, he'd run food service for the college ceremonies and football games, so he was used to organizing events and getting teams of people where they were needed. He'd often start a field operation with an anecdote about a battle, or a game, or a lesson he'd learned, which were invariably funny at his expense, but always touching and inspiring in the end. He was working with Ophelia to roll out field canvassing across the state. They had organized large rallies at the universities, where Carson quickly had huge crowds laughing at his stories, and then he handed the crowd over, as a unified tribe, to Andrew or Arden for the call to action. Arden feared that she was too self-conscious for the storytelling that came so naturally to Carson, although she loved it.

Jennifer Walton, their media director, went next with a media update. As she spoke, Arden considered Jennifer's leadership style, if you could call it that. Her update was insightful and shrewd, and she was skillful in selling her own value—perhaps less so at giving credit to her team. She often reminded them that she was a veteran of several high-profile political campaigns, which she would reference to give her ideas more weight. She ran their small crew of media specialists hard, and as a result they were super-human at churning out print, radio, social media, and internet content. From what Arden could tell, Jennifer seemed to draw her authority from her position, and the fact that she could fire and replace any of her staff that displeased her. She was dismissive and brisk with the college interns who reported to her. While they respected her and were learning under her leadership, Arden knew it was their admiration for Ophelia that made them stay late or come in early.

While Arden was appreciative of Jennifer's contributions, she disliked her. Jennifer always made it clear that this was a temporary assignment for her, on loan from her real job at Government for the People. On several occasions, Jennifer had let it be known that she was not a supporter of the anti-corporate idea.

"Listen," she'd told Arden once while they were hashing out how best to present an especially wonky policy point, "I'm here because I believe in direct democracy and de-rigging the political system. But personally, I think 99 goes too far. Or at least I wouldn't support the idea of no corporations if it were to extend beyond South Dakota." It was clear that Jennifer didn't think South Dakota mattered. "I believe in the free market, and I want to be able to go to Nordstrom, or Whole Foods, or order something up on Amazon and have it arrive the next day. Having that all go away is not an improvement to quality of life in my view. You're going to be up against a lot of people who think like me."

As Arden was mentally dismissing her as materialistic, hobbled to consumer culture, Jennifer continued, "Not all corporations are bad. Many of those jobs you cast as exploitative are good jobs. People are happy to have them. You know that, don't you?"

Arden had struggled to work with Jennifer after that, in part because her challenges were hard to answer. She thought of the people that had worked for Jeremy at Unibank, their complex tasks greasing the way to their own obsolescence. She couldn't quite shake the feeling that Jennifer couldn't be trusted, or couldn't effectively advance their message, because she wasn't a true believer. Kirish and Ophelia were less concerned. When Arden told them of her conversation with Jennifer, Ophelia shrugged, saying, "Help doesn't always come in the package you want it to. Don't be picky, Arden. Not everybody is pure of heart. Sometimes people who know how to compromise are the ones who can get things done."

Arden had to admit that Jennifer was good at her job. She landed radio interviews for Kirish and Arden, wrote op-eds that were placed in state and local papers under their names, cultivated newspaper endorsements, and fed content to news bloggers and journalists.

As Ophelia broke into Jennifer's update with a good-natured challenge, Arden realized she had been forgetting Ophelia. Ophelia didn't want to bother with being a role model, and confidently did what she pleased. Ophelia prized being able to speak her mind above anything else, which had won her a small but devoted following. Others with thinner skin avoided her. She certainly had her own style—was it too irreverent to be considered leadership? No, she stood up for what she believed and inspired people. That was what Arden aspired to. She watched Ophelia joke with Andrew in that lighthearted, deadly serious way of hers Arden loved. Sometimes the two clashed over who was the arch campaign manager, but mostly Ophelia was happy to be learning from Andrew. She always seemed to have the last laugh, somehow, even when she conceded a point.

Peter Bassford interrupted Arden's reverie. He had managed to get himself invited to the strategy meeting, convincing Andrew that security needed to be on the agenda. Arden didn't trust Bassford and wasn't sure he was the right one to be handling security. However, she didn't feel right raising that, since she was one of the "targets" he was worried about protecting.

"We need to consider a set travel schedule for Arden, Andrew, and Kirish, and notifying local police on their whereabouts. And we need to have increased security at rallies. Yesterday's was risky, especially with that fancy celebrity actress. We are seeing some concerning levels of threat chatter on the internet from the opposition camp. And everyone knows what happened to Arden a couple weeks ago. That wasn't a coincidence, it was targeted at 99."

The team looked at Arden. She didn't relish the idea of having to stick to a set schedule, but she did sometimes feel like she was being followed. Sometimes, out on the road, she worried that no one knew where she was. The idea of "threat chatter" got her attention, but something about giving Peter her travel schedule made her feel less safe, not more.

"Let me think about it," she deferred, wanting to speak with Kirish privately.

The next item on the agenda was get-out-the-vote effort, GOTV for short. Arden had seen the old-school techniques for voter mobilization—Ophelia had used them in the signature-collection phase. But with Government for the People's help, they were now much more sophisticated and high-tech. There was a phone-banking system that dialed numbers and routed only those calls that picked up to volunteers, either in 99 headquarters or to wherever they were remotely logged into the system through their phone or computer. Arden was shocked to hear that volunteers in other states were phone banking to convince South Dakota voters to support 99, because she still thought of it as a local issue.

Today, Jennifer wanted to talk about the voter database. Early in the campaign, copies of the entire voter file of all registered voters in South Dakota had been purchased from the Secretary of State (for $2,500, which had seemed an enormous sum to Arden). The voter files included the names, addresses, age, race, and political affiliation of all registered voters, as well as whether they had voted in past elections (but not for whom).

"As some of you have heard me explain before," Jennifer began in a bored tone, as though teaching the same kindergarten lesson, "the goal of GOTV is to identify those voters who are likely to vote for your candidate and then focus on encouraging those targeted voters to follow through on that vote. Traditional GOTV takes place in the week or two before the election and basically offers help finding your polling place, transportation there if needed, and help with absentee ballots. What we are doing now is classified as early phone canvassing since we are still three months out."

"What's the difference?" Ophelia asked.

"Right now we are calling any and all residents, registered voters or not, to talk to them about Initiative 99. Assistance will be offered to folks who supported 99, in getting them registered to vote. But at this stage, one of the primary goals is gathering information for Susmita's database," Jennifer answered.

For every substantive conversation, anything they learned about a voter was meticulously documented by the canvasser into a database curated by Susmita Pradesh, a data scientist and pollster from Government for the People. If the coverts learned that John Smith vehemently opposed 99 and that canvasser felt he was not likely to change his mind, that was noted in their voter database, and he was not called again. If he shared his political affiliation, that was noted, along with any other pertinent demographic, like *business owner, high school education or less, blue collar/white collar, Native American, working mother*. With this data, Susmita explained that she had begun to develop a description of their likely voters.

Arden disliked this. "People don't support 99 because they're part of a particular demographic," she said, sounding stubborn even to herself.

"To some extent, that is true," Susmita responded with a bemused smile, "but I work in the realm of large numbers, where there are always patterns. It doesn't mean people aren't making their own decisions. It's just that those decisions can be predicted."

There were other ways to inform these predictions, Susmita explained. Other avenues for getting data, in addition to what they could gather.

"We can purchase third-party data about South Dakota citizens, about what they search for on the internet—what they buy, where they go, their social media profiles and preferences—that could help us identify who to target with our outreach," Susmita explained.

"Isn't that illegal?" Ophelia was suddenly paying attention, slapping her phone down on the conference table. "Listen, that's not how we operate here."

Susmita fought back a smile. "Of course we wouldn't buy data that wasn't legally gathered. But unless you use a private anonymous browser, there are no privacy restrictions on your internet browsing. And your credit card company and your grocery store, along with most internet retailers and social medial purveyors, specify in their privacy policies that they will sell your data so that you can receive offers that appeal to you. Didn't you know that?"

Eyeing Arden warily, Jennifer added, "We're not proposing that bots will target our likely voters with inflammatory misinformation. But you better believe that the opposition campaign is doing that already. I've created a phony Instagram account with the pro-corporate demographic, and there's already an onslaught of *The sky is falling with communists* messages slamming my account. All we're talking about doing is accessing legally gathered data about voter preferences so we can deploy our limited resources more effectively."

At the mention of resources, Jeremy cleared his throat and leaned forward. "I like the idea of running a smart campaign. If you're not using the latest in data and behavioral science, you can't win the competition for hearts and minds."

"I don't know. . . ." Arden murmured, troubled. "Even if it is strictly legal, how would people feel if they knew we were studying them and compiling dossiers about their personal characteristics so we can better target them?"

Ophelia nodded. "I wouldn't like it, that's for sure. What kind of info are we talking here? It's so Big Brother . . . and really, what will people's browsing histories or shopping lists tell us about whether they will support 99?"

"The more information I have, the better my model will be able to predict what people will do," Susmita replied simply.

"But what about people's expectation of privacy?" Arden looked to Kirish. "Isn't that a legal thing?"

He looked up to meet her eye, shaking his head. "That mostly relates to unreasonable search and seizure by the government. But if data is collected legally and disclosures are clear about internet browsers and credit card companies selling consumer data, then people can't claim to have any expectation of privacy. Even if they don't read the privacy warning saying that their data will be sold, they're charged with that knowledge," Kirish answered.

"It might be legal," Arden responded, "but I'm not convinced that it's ethical."

Jennifer sighed heavily, exasperated. "Really, Arden, if people were so concerned about keeping this stuff private, they wouldn't be sacrificing their precious privacy for convenience. It's easy enough to turn your browser to private, or use cash. Nobody thinks it's worth it. It's easy enough to read those stupid privacy notices they're always bombarding us with, but none of us bother. There is no such thing as an expectation of privacy anymore."

"I'm not so sure," Arden replied stubbornly. "I think that could be changing." She struggled with how hard to push for her perspective. Even if she felt something strongly, that didn't mean she was right. But it seemed wrong to her. "What if it gets out that we're doing this? Is that something we'd be comfortable with? That's not who I want to be."

Jennifer said under her breath, "That will be a great comfort when you lose, I'm sure."

Kirish shook his head and spoke quietly. "I think this is an area where I'd be inclined to follow the lead of the professionals. As Jenn said, this isn't some kind of misinformation campaign they're proposing. It's just a way to find people who are more likely to be sympathetic to our cause. Those are the people who want to hear from us. Really, we're doing everyone a favor if we only call those people. It saves us a lot of wasted effort, and people who don't want to hear from us are saved the frustration."

Ophelia expelled her breath through pursed lips, shaking her head, but turned back to her phone, apparently mollified.

Arden considered Kirish's points and sighed. "I guess so. But . . . blechh. Keep me out of it." Arden stood up, and so did the others. She guessed this was the end of the meeting. She didn't have much appetite for any more strategy.

A WEEK LATER, ARDEN ARRIVED EARLY at 99 headquarters to find the front door hanging loosely in its frame, the latch broken. At first she thought one of the others—Ophelia or Andrew, perhaps—had arrived before her for the weekly meeting and had forced the lock. Then she pushed through the broken door and saw the destruction as she crossed the threshold. *Commies get shot* was written in black spray paint in a disturbingly controlled hand across the phone bank table. The new high-tech phone system, their largest single investment, was in a tangle on the floor, broken plastic shards scattered around it. Most troubling was the smashed computers. Arden thought of their work to identify and track voters. Would it all be lost? She didn't know their backup protocols. She couldn't tell if anything was missing. She sat at the table looking at the black paint, which looked like it could still be wet. She didn't want to touch it. Could the intruder still be there?

Moments later, Kirish was walking in the door; he called the police immediately.

The morning was a jumble of making witness statements to the authorities and speaking with reporters. Arden felt shifty when she primly declined to share with the reporter from the *Vermillion Plain Talk* the particulars of what they might have lost in their voter database, and like a bloodhound, the reporter suddenly became interested in the get-out-the-vote process. Silently cursing Jennifer, Arden walked him through the process.

Although the police had shrugged her off back in May when she reported her encounter with the two men in front of the sandwich shop, they seemed now to be taking things more seriously. They dusted the headquarters for fingerprints, which Arden thought must be futile since so many volunteers came through there each week. They took her prints and those of all the other coverts who were in the office that morning. Kirish was pale as the female plain-clothes cop rolled his fingers across the black ink pad, while a uniformed policeman had Arden email him yet another copy of the photo she had snapped of her accosters from May.

Peter gave witness statements too, having arrived a few minutes after Kirish. He was calling himself head of security for 99, which Arden didn't recall ever having been decided, but she supposed there was no one else clamoring for the job. He cornered her before she left, about to head out for an overnight to the western part of the state.

"Arden," he said gently, "please consider what we discussed at the leadership meeting. Giving state police and headquarters a set travel schedule for you and Kirish is the responsible thing to do." Knowing it sounded like she was just putting him off, Arden promised to talk to Kirish and Ophelia about it on their trip and get back to Peter next week.

"It seems like you have reservations. What are your concerns?" he pressed her.

She looked at him levelly. She wasn't sure—it was more of a feeling. She felt like something bad was going to happen, but didn't think there was anything Peter could do to help. She shrugged, ducked under his arm blocking her exit, and was gone.

CHAPTER 16 RISING

THEY WERE LATE LEAVING FOR RAPID CITY because of the break-in, and Arden had to run into her apartment and quickly pack an overnight bag while the others waited in Ophelia's idling car. They were due in the western part of the state for a big regional fair early the next morning and had planned to leave earlier for a stop midway at a rally, which they now were missing.

The Central States Fair on the outskirts of Rapid City drew more than a hundred thousand people every August, and the plan was that Arden, Ophelia, Kirish, and Jessica would take turns staffing the booth they had arranged in the fairgrounds. Carson had made a connection with a Native American musician named John Two Sight who was headlining a concert that night on the fair main stage, and he had agreed to support 99. The plan was for him to invite Ophelia up onstage during the concert, and she would say something fast, inspiring, and interesting while the drums kept time in the background.

Initially, it had been Arden who was supposed to speak, but it had been embarrassingly easy for her to convince everyone that she was too uptight for this format. Two days after the fair, they would have an audience with the Great Plains Tribal Chairmen's Association, which they hoped would pass a resolution supporting 99.

They were crowded into Ophelia's Subaru for the five-hour drive, with the air conditioning struggling against the heat. As they drove west from Vermillion, picking up Route 90 and crossing the Missouri into the West River region, Arden felt acutely aware that she was driving away from Badger, and Emma's farm, rather than toward it. She hadn't been able to tear herself away from Vermillion these last weeks, and still hadn't been able to get Emma on the phone. As soon as the trip west was done, she would go.

It was going to be a long drive. Ophelia was in a rambunctious mood, which Arden found exhausting after the long morning she'd had, and with the foreclosure weighing heavy on her mind.

"Those cowards think we're commies?" Ophelia ranted about the break-in. "Yeah, well, I'm going to go *Animal Farm* on their asses if we ever figure out who they are!"

Stuck behind the wheel, she entertained herself at their expense as she drove fast down the pin-straight highway. Jess was an easy target.

"So, Jess, is Carson, like, super organized *everywhere*?"

"Yeah, he's a bit of a neat freak," Jess replied, apparently game to play along. Arden hadn't known Jessica well in school, but she appreciated how she was willing to do anything to help. From acting as a bouncer at a rowdy college rally, to working the phone bank and licking envelopes, she was not above any task. She'd recently made a habit of walking Arden home, since the apartment she shared with Carson was just half a block from Arden's new one, above Kirish's.

"So, completely shaved, then? And does he give you a pep talk before sex? Give clear instructions?"

Now Jess got it, blushing and laughing. "Ha-ha—not necessary!"

Kirish was in no mood for Ophelia's teasing, snapping at her to leave him alone as he tapped out emails on his cell phone with his finger, still stained from fingerprint ink. Even before the break-in, he'd been tense recently, and the few times Arden had seen him in their apartment building, he'd acknowledged her presence with the barest of nods. Not that she felt that she needed his protection, but hadn't he urged her to move into the building after the *New Republic* article so they could keep an eye on each other? The way he had acted toward her since graduation made it clear that borrowing a cup of sugar was out of the question. Enduring five hours in the hot car with him seemed like an eternity.

Arden focused her attention out the window, taking in the golden grassy plains pocked by strange, singular buttes, looking like ancient dried-out volcanoes as they rose from the flat prairie. Passing Badlands National Park to the south, Jessica lobbied to stop and sightsee as dusk fell, which Kirish vetoed, citing a phone call he needed to make at the hotel, which was annoying since they had to sit through his other calls in the car. As they approached Rapid City, the terrain began to gently roll and rise. Arden knew the Black Hills rose up west of Rapid City, remembering camping trips as a kid with her mom and one of her many boyfriends. When they passed through the small city to reach the fairground, she could see the mountains silhouetted in the fading western sky.

They dumped their things at the motel and met up

again at the car, wanting to find supper before the local restaurants closed. The three women were sharing a room with two double beds, with Kirish on his own. He was late for the meet up, and Arden went knocking at his door to hurry him along. She heard him angrily protesting something, presumably on his cell phone, through the door of the motel room, and he did not come to the door when she first knocked. Arden wondered if it was his mother, but he'd said it was an important call, which they'd all presumed was about 99. He hadn't corrected them but who knows, with him, she thought. After a time he emerged, looking angry, and she stomped back to the car, sliding into the front seat and leaving him to ride in the back.

The fair the next day was crowded and dusty, and sitting at the booth was exhausting. Arden must have shaken thousands of hands and was sunburned by noon. John Two Sight's concert set didn't begin until nine o'clock, after two hours of loud country music. By the time Ophelia took the stage, with tribal drumming in the background, the crowd was thoroughly drunk. It was hard to tell whether the catcalls were friendly or menacing, but either way, the reaction fell far short of their hopes. Ophelia's attempt to summarize the goals of 99 in a quick, understandable way was valiant, but by the time she was done, no one was listening. Arden even heard a couple boos in the back.

After Ophelia was done, Arden felt a tap on her shoulder. A reporter, it looked like, with a camera slung around his neck and a small notepad out.

"Not a great reception, eh, Arden?" The reporter smiled. "I'm Jason Wendell, with the *Plains Inquirer*. Is this indicative of a drop in support for 99?"

Arden was tired, and not ready to be interviewed. She looked around for Kirish to pass this reporter off onto, but he was nowhere to be found.

"Not necessarily," was all she could come up with, rather than seizing the press opportunity. After the reporter was gone, she thought of what she should have said: there had been five hundred supporters at the recent rally at the capitol.

Not only did Ophelia's upbeat pitch get roundly ignored, but so did John Two Sight's set. The four coverts hung around for his set out of solidarity for his support, Arden drinking her third warm frothy beer and standing in the front dancing. After the set, John sought them out and invited them to come tomorrow to the *wacipi*, or powwow, at his tribe's reservation, promising a more attentive audience.

They rose early the next day, stopping for breakfast at a diner and driving southeast to the Rosebud Reservation to meet John at ten. The Rosebud Sioux Tribe, John explained, is the tribe's legal name, but the people call themselves the Sicangu Lakota, which means Burnt Thigh. They are a sub-band of the Lakota Sioux and part of the Oceti Sakowin (the Great Sioux Nation). The Rosebud Wacipi is held every August to commemorate the first tribal celebration in late summer of 1876 at Rosebud after the Lakota learned of the triumph at the Battle of Little Bighorn in June of that year, where the Lakota and Cheyenne tribes defeated General Custer and the 7th Calvary. Having grown up in South Dakota, Arden knew some Native American history and had seen enough of life on reservations to know that it was often grim. She knew that the treatment of the tribes was a blight on the story of the US, like slavery was. Much to be proud of in the founding of our country, she thought, but also so much to be ashamed of. The Battle of Little Bighorn, which ended with Custer's Last Stand, was in fact the indigenous people's last stand—one of the last armed conflicts as the tribes struggled to preserve their land and their ways.

The fairgrounds where the wacipi was held was in the town of Rosebud, on the reservation. There was a main street, which could have been any Midwestern town, anywhere. But past the four-square block center, there was the devastatingly poor dusty smattering of trailer homes, rusted cars, old dogs, and cement-block structures that Arden had seen before on reservations. Also beautiful land, wild, untamed, dotted here and there with horses, small gardens, and rolling grassland, yellow and dry in late summer. The fair, too, could have been anywhere, with the same rides shuttled around the state from place to place by the same company—the Ferris wheel, the spinning tea cups, the centrifugal tube, and Arden's favorite, the swings hanging on long chains that spun you out into the night in long breathless circles. Only the parking lot looked different from your average state fair. Beat-up, ancient pickup trucks from South Dakota and Montana, with feathers hanging from rearview mirrors and pipeline protest bumper stickers. But also common were shiny late-model cars with out-of-state plates and anonymous rental cars belonging to tourists.

John met them at the ticket gate and walked them through the fairgrounds. The celebration began with young Lakota men and women, in full celebration regalia, racing through the fairgrounds on horseback. John helped them get permission to set up a table to talk about Initiative 99 in an informational area between the food concessions, the dancing arena, and the bathrooms. Both tourists and tribespeople stopped by to learn about the Initiative 99, but Arden observed that the Lakota seemed puzzled, or rather not quite trusting the explanations they provided.

Arden and Jessica stopped by the table next to theirs, where a middle-aged man laid out dog-eared pamphlets on suicide prevention and hotlines. He quietly explained that suicide among indigenous people, especially teens, occurred at a rate several times higher than the national average. Likewise the rates of depression, alcoholism, drug addiction, hopelessness, and despair. He was courteous in his explanations, but his eyes darted through the crowd passing by, not wanting someone who needed him to slip by. He had lost a son to suicide. Arden and Jessica moved on, not wanting to keep anyone away.

There was a booth on the gas pipeline that had been built over the Oglala aquifer, crossing over sacred tribal sites and under the Missouri River in North Dakota. The tribes had been unable to stop its construction, despite fervent and widely publicized protests in 2016 and 2017. The Dakota Access Pipeline moved crude oil from the North Dakota Bakken shale oil fields, extracted by fracking, through South Dakota and Iowa to Illinois, the tall boy manning the booth explained. The pipeline route skirted the Standing Rock Sioux Reservation, which straddled North and South Dakota, to the north of Rosebud and Rapid City. For long stretches, the pipeline hugged the reservation boundary by just five hundred feet. The pipeline had been drilled under Lake Oahe and the Missouri River—one of the main objections of the Lakota, because of the risks of an oil spill in their water supply. The Standing Rock Tribe maintained that the Dakota Access Pipeline threatens their water, fishing, and hunting rights, guaranteed to the tribe by treaty. The latest of many betrayals. The information booth showed a timeline tracking the small spills that had happened so far, warning of the danger to come, and the status of activists arrested during the protests, now languishing in federal jails.

At the last table before the bathrooms, a young woman and an old grandmother laid out photocopies of pictures of dark-eyed women and girls. "Who are they?" Arden asked, touching the picture of a girl with long braids, maybe fourteen or fifteen years old.

The young woman answered nervously. "They are missing women and girls. We're here to tell people about the problem of missing and murdered indigenous women in North America. Canada recently studied it, admitting that at least six hundred indigenous women and girls had been abducted or murdered in the country since 1960, but we know it's thousands. Indigenous women are most likely to be the victims of violence, rape, abduction, and homicide, but the police response has been to ignore the problem." One of the causes, the girl explained, was so-called "man camps" that housed workers for mines or pipelines adjacent to reservations; tribal police often couldn't or wouldn't prosecute them, allowing these perpetrators to slip through loopholes in jurisdiction. Arden and Jessica took a small stack of brochures to put out at 99 headquarters and moved on, saddened.

Arden saw corporations at the heart of these problems. The gas pipeline being forced through the land. The man camps that followed, forcing themselves on women in an eerie parallel. Seeing that 99 would help the tribes, Arden felt a new resolve. She had the feeling of a grain of poison, here in the past of the Native Americans, that continued to create sickness. In order for that grain to be extracted, that splinter removed, so much would need to be undone that could never be undone, unless there were a mass annihilation of white people. *Perhaps we are doing that to ourselves,* Arden thought, thinking about climate change. *But unlike the Aztec, what we would leave behind will not be beautiful.*

Arden felt out of place with the booth on 99, which seemed like such an abstraction compared to the immediate harms of missing or murdered women, teen suicide, or polluted water. But she fervently felt that there was a connection between their work and at least some of the harms. Maybe what had been done to the indigenous people wasn't the fault of corps, but now, they were making it worse.

John Two Sight's concert at Rosebud was very different from the one at the Rapid City state fair. For one, it took place at five o'clock, and although not strictly sober, the crowd was not drunk and was anything but distracted. John sang about the idea that decisions should be made with the impact on future generations in mind, up to the seventh generation. But the song changed, becoming darker, with John singing that the seventh generation had arrived, it was his generation, come to call the past to account. They were rising. The decisions of the past had created them, and they were coming to claim what was rightfully theirs. The song ended with the audience joining in impassioned chanting, "Rising, ya! Rising, ya! Rising, ya!" Fists pumping into the air and feet stomping. Kirish looked nervous, and the tourists in the crowd melted away back to the safety of the fried dough and monster truck pull.

Later, around a firepit in the campground on the perimeter of the wapici, Arden asked John about the seventh generation song. She'd heard of the idea, from the eponymous natural laundry detergent company, but hadn't realized it was a Native American concept. He told her, "The seventh generation idea exists across tribes. It's part of Oceti Sakowin spirituality, as well as Iroquois and Ojibwe, and many others. It's part of the Iroquois Great Law of Peace. Are you familiar with it?" When Arden shook her head, he grinned wryly at her.

"Your precious United States Constitution was based on it," he explained. "The Great Law of Peace is a set of laws, a constitution, which was created six hundred years ago to bring together five warring tribes in what's now upstate New York. It's one of the earliest examples of a representative democracy, and was the only one still functioning at the time the United States was formed. It preserved the local governance of each separate tribe, just like your US Constitution does with the union of confederated states. It created three chambers of government, like your executive, legislative, and judicial branches, complete with those nifty checks and balances you all are so proud of. Freedom of religion too."

John looked off into the fire, watching the sparks loft up into the night. "When the colonists went for independence from Britain, the Iroquois were an inspiration for the Boston Tea Party. Your so-called Founding Fathers—James Madison, Ben Franklin, and John Hancock—met with Iroquois leaders. It's said that the idea *we the people, seek to form a more perfect union*, is taken from the Great Law of Peace. Still never heard of it?"

"No," Arden replied, "I never knew."

He looked back at her, not surprised. "Too bad. In the 1980s, your US Senate finally acknowledged that the Great Law of Peace served as a model for the Constitution of the United States, but they still don't teach it in schools I guess."

"The seventh generation idea is in the Great Law of Peace?" Arden asked.

He nodded. "Oh, yeah. The Iroquois constitution says that decisions made by the governing council must take into consideration the welfare of all the people, past, present and future, including those in the future generations—the seventh generation," John explained. "The other thing that's interesting is that the women chose the representatives for the governing council."

Arden agreed that would be interesting—if women chose the politicians. "But your song, it's not about deciding for the seventh generation, is it? The idea is that yours *is* the seventh generation. What does that mean?"

"My grandfather learned our native language from an elder who had been alive and who could remember the time before the white man ruled. Think of that. It hasn't been that long that Europeans have been here in the Americas, and even shorter that they have controlled this land. In the 1860s, the Lakota were still warring with the settlers, and entered into the Treaty of Fort Laramie. That's about 160 years. If you figure twenty-three years per generation, that's seven generations." John paused to let that sink in.

"My song means that our generation, yours and mine, is that seventh generation that should have been considered in the decisions of those who came before us. And also that the future generations are shaped by the decisions of the past. In this time, the selfishness and foolishness of the past has come home to roost. I'd like to say that ours is the generation of change and retribution. But maybe it's just a song." John looked at Arden closely, as if trying to see inside her. Did he see that she was part of that wave of change and retribution? Arden hoped so. She hoped it was more than a song.

JOHN HAD OFFERED TO ACCOMPANY THEM the next day to Rapid City for their meeting with the Tribal Chairmen's Association, an offer they gratefully accepted. They met up for breakfast the next morning, and he told them what he knew of the association, how it worked, and who were the key players. They piled into Ophelia's and John's cars, Arden riding with John for the short drive. The five of them stood nervously in the small lobby of the group's office, in a brick building in a nondescript neighborhood, waiting to be admitted. Arden read the plaque on the wall under the pictures of gathered leaders.

The Great Plains Tribal Chairmen's Association (GPTCA) is made up of the 16 Tribal Chairmen, Presidents, and Chairpersons in the states of North Dakota, South Dakota, and Nebraska. The Tribal Leaders of the Sovereign Indian Nations meet quarterly to take action on various matters affecting the Tribes. The primary purpose of the GPTCA is to unify to defend the Tribes' inherent rights under our Treaties, to come together in a forum to promote the welfare of the People, take up matters affecting the Tribes and to protect the Sovereignty of each Tribe.

Arden thought of the Iroquois Great Law of Peace, with its governing representatives selected by the women of the tribes. She imagined this council in its lineage, a shadow.

John, Arden, and the other coverts were ushered into the council room, which consisted of a large ring of tables. They were invited to have a representative enter the middle of the ring to address the council.

They had previously agreed that it would be Kirish to speak, but now Arden saw that this had been a mistake. She hadn't wanted to be the one to speak, thinking he would have more gravitas, imagining an intimidating room of angry tribal leaders. She now saw that she would have been the best person to address them and regretted that she had not stepped up to the task. She thought of Jeremy Hatch's admonitions about claiming her leadership role, seeing that Kirish's explanation of 99 was too lawyerly and abstract. As she had seen on the faces at the wacipi, the tribal chairs were listening, but not believing. When Kirish was done, there was nodding. No questions, which Arden took as a bad sign. She asked permission to enter the circle.

Once there, it was hard to know where to look; her back would always be to someone. She turned slowly, trying to make eye contact with the various leaders but many were looking away. They were mostly men, but some women. She thought carefully of what she would say and was glad that Kirish had laid out the particulars already.

"Part of our sickness is that we have created a parasite that now controls us," Arden began. "We created it with laws and contracts, and now those laws and contracts protect the parasite, the corporation, more than they protect the people. We are trying to kill the parasite."

Arden paused and took a deep breath, trying to imagine what her words sounded like in their ears.

"I can see why you might wonder why you should help us kill our parasite, why you might think we deserve it."

A couple of the women elders smiled at her, and they kept making eye contact after their smiles were gone.

"Corporations aren't the sole cause of our problems in the US, but they amplify and feed on all our worst impulses—greed, selfishness, consumerism, vanity."

More of them were now looking her way, if not directly at her, listening.

"Now, it is the parasite that pulls fuel from the ground and lays the pipeline."

One nodded.

"It is the parasite that puts camps of angry men on your borders, harming your sisters and daughters."

More nodding.

"It is the parasite that floods your tribes with alcohol and opiates, which lead your sons and brothers to take their own lives."

One man made a noise, saying gruffly, "*Hecetu yelo.*"

"This parasite makes us worse than we would otherwise be, makes it harder for us to be good. It answers only to our greed, and it shields us from seeing our role in the harm we do.

"And it hurts you too." Arden sensed that she had said enough, and that any more would be counterproductive. The elders were somber now.

"*Mitakuye Oyasin*," one of the women said, bowing her head graciously.

The supplicants were thanked and escorted out, without hearing from the council on their view or explanation of what would come next.

"That was good," John told Arden on the street, as they were saying goodbye. "The tribal leaders will tell their people what you said. It is a good story—your parasite. It invites the retelling." She smiled gratefully at his encouragement. He continued, "I don't know whether they will pass a resolution supporting it. It is rare that they would do that on a non-indigenous issue. But the tribes are encouraging their people to vote this year, and there has been a big push to get people registered to vote and to get more polling places. So this will definitely get talked about."

"What did she say, the woman with the gray hair?" Arden asked John.

"*Mitakuye Oyasin*. It means, literally, *all my relations*, but also means we are all connected. It means she approves of what you are doing."

As John got in his car and drove west, and the four coverts went east, Arden kept thinking of the Lakota woman and what she had said. Arden was honored that the woman would have expressed the idea that they were connected, that they were relations. Arden resolved to be worthy of that connection.

CHAPTER 17

INDIAN SUMMER

WHEN ARDEN RETURNED FROM ROSEBUD, she had planned to go to Badger, but Ophelia and Andrew had pressed her not to cancel several speaking commitments she had in Sioux Falls. Arden had still been unable to get her grandmother on the phone and was close to panic. So she called Emma's close friend Betsy, who could at least confirm spotting her out in her garden the day before. Arden checked her calendar and sent a couple emails clearing her schedule for the weekend, begging Jennifer to find anyone else from the coverts to cover for her. She had to go. Even though Emma probably wanted to be alone, with the seemingly unavoidable loss of the farm just one week away, Arden had to go. She had a dread in her gut that reminded her of how she felt when she used to see her mother Jill strung out. If she was completely honest with herself, she was afraid of seeing Emma depressed and unstable. But she couldn't put it off anymore.

Arden had felt off-kilter since the trip to Rapid City and Rosebud. She kept seeing the photocopied pictures of missing women and girls on the information table at the Rosebud Wapici. She thought about the Tribal Chairmen's Council, and felt anxious that she would let them down. She even imagined or sensed a few times that she was being followed. She never got around to talking to Kirish about Peter's suggestion about security, resolving instead to stop appearing in public alone.

All of a sudden, the rallies felt more volatile, as supporters became galvanized, and opponents seemed to fear the possibility of success for 99. The day before, at a rally organized at a local lumberyard, Arden and Ophelia could feel the electricity immediately upon stepping out of their car. Their contact explained that several carloads of union workers from the nearby factory had just arrived. Arden hadn't liked how the podium at this event was simply a microphone on a stand in the bed of a pickup truck; she felt exposed, and the gravel parking lot at dusk full of angry men didn't feel safe.

Before the microphone was even turned on, one angry middle-aged man had shouted, "This stupid idea is the last nail in the coffin for US manufacturing!"

"Man, you guys gotta give this a chance!" Ophelia's voice rose over the din. "This is going to make things better for you!"

The man responded in some way which Ophelia couldn't hear, which made her climb down out of the back of the pickup. For once, Arden cursed Ophelia's lack of fear, watching as she propelled herself out into the crowd to go talk to him before Arden's speech started, presumably to tamp down any heckling that might be in store. In a momentary hush, Ophelia's voice rose to explain that their factory could convert to a cooperatively owned worker-run facility. Even to Arden, it sounded like pure insanity in that context. As Ophelia finished her sentence, several men responded at once, and started shoving each other. Arden instinctively leapt down off the back of the truck to run to Ophelia, and they found themselves swept into the roiling, yelling crowd. "What makes you think I want to own that piece-of-shit dinosaur!" one man angrily yelled in Ophelia's face. "I just want a goddamn paycheck!"

Together with one of the rally organizers, Arden pulled Ophelia out of the crowd, and both were unceremoniously stuffed into their car. "You girls should hit the road," he had said, in a tone that felt like a threat.

In the car afterward, Arden fought to suppress the feeling, rising in her throat like a scream, that 99 had spun out of control. It was too soon to tell whether it was a revolution or a wildfire, but it had become a thing unto itself, no longer answering to its creators. In her head, in the abstract, the changes that would accompany 99 could be made in a way that minimized disruption, with people talking through any problems that might arise. She finally saw what chaos it would bring. Would it cause too much turmoil, without addressing the underlying disease? What if that underlying parasite wasn't really corporations, but something more elemental, something part of them as Americans? What if it *was them*?

THE NEXT MORNING, AS SHE QUICKLY packed an overnight bag for Emma's, Arden remembered being woken in the night by noises from Kirish's apartment below. A phone ringing, a landline, and Kirish's groggy answer, and then a low, angry conversation. Arden must have been dipping in and out of sleep, incorporating the strange sounds into her dreams, because it felt like the conversation had gone on for a long time. Who was he talking to? She dreamed that he had been abducted, or that she had, that they were missing, wandering in the desiccated plains at dusk with hundreds of indigenous women in white nightgowns. She shivered as she remembered the eerie feeling.

On the road to Emma's, Arden wracked her brain for a solution to the foreclosure. If they could not pay off the whole mortgage, the lawyer had told her, the court was sure to order the foreclosure, unless there was some evidence of wrongdoing by the bank. They had listened as Arden sketched out her idea to argue that the late fees, which had quickly compounded Emma's monthly payment so she could never catch up, amounted to wrongdoing by the bank, but the clinic lawyer just shrugged. *That's the way things are*, he seemed to say.

It was an unexpectedly warm week, the autumn fields yellow and shimmering as Arden drove by. Indian summer, as her mother used to call it. *Why is it called that?* she wondered. Was it like the old saying, *Indian giver,* to give something and take it back? Were these old slurs how we had justified what we had done?

She showed up at Emma's worried that she'd find her grandmother in bed, in a darkened room, but was relieved to find her outside, as always, working in the garden. From what Arden could tell, she was pulling up plants that were past their season, preparing for fall. Hopeful, in a way. Arden called out a hello and was warmly enfolded into her grandmother's arms; Arden surprised both of them by bursting into tears. *Some job I'm doing of checking on her,* Arden thought, wiping her eyes. She laughed it off as sleep deprivation and PMS, but the idea of having Emma lose her land, any of it, against her will, was too much to bear.

Later, they sat on the porch and watched the autumn sun set on the farm to the west, the soybeans full and green in the dusk. Somehow it felt so different to have the land be leased, but still Emma's to reclaim at any time, than to have it be gone.

"It's your inheritance," Emma said, as they sat, her voice breaking. "Your grandfather and I cleared those fields ourselves. I wish I'd never borrowed to pay those medical bills. I should have just declared bankruptcy. I was stupid. I was too proud to do it, and look at me now."

Arden reached out and held her wrinkled and calloused hand.

"Emma, if we win—Initiative 99, I mean—you might be able to get the farm back."

Arden watched her grandmother closely. Emma had held back from fully supporting 99, blaming the movement for Arden quitting school. But now she nodded, looking again out over the darkening fields.

"Well, that would be only fair, since it's being stolen by two corporations," Emma said, scowling.

"Two?" Arden asked.

"Yes, two," Emma snapped. "I told you AGM was behind this."

Arden wondered. Of course, Emma was angry with Unibank; their late fees and penalties put her deeper and deeper in the hole, and she could never get a person on the phone there to help her. But AGM? Arden recalled being surprised that AGM was getting notice of the court papers. And the foreclosure was happening because Emma couldn't pay her mortgage payments, in part because AGM was late on their rent. Was it possible the two were connected? She hadn't really taken Emma seriously when she'd claimed AGM was to blame, but as they sat there in the dusk, the soybeans seemed dark with gathering malice.

ARDEN WOKE LATE THE NEXT MORNING to an empty house. She remembered Emma saying something last night before they'd gone to sleep about taking a friend to the doctor in the morning. Arden lingered on the porch with multiple cups of coffee, looking out over the deep-green fields of soybeans. She picked up a basket from the screened porch, which smelled of fermented apples. The root cellar below the porch had stored decades of apple bushels. She walked out to the small orchard, bringing the rickety wooden ladder from the shed. Not yet the middle of September, it was before the prime of apple harvest, but she was still able to fill the basket twice with early apples, maneuvering the ladder around the old trees. She felt the pull of the harvest, the deeply centered, almost thoughtless focus on collecting, gathering for winter. After she picked all the apples that were ready, she visited the garden behind the house, finding green beans, kale, scallions, and carrots.

Heading back to the house, she heard a low nicker from the old barn. Emma's boarder was restless; Arden could hear Nick moving in his stall. The air in the below-grade livestock keep was warm and moist with the earthy smell of horse and manure. She'd always liked the smell of horse and cow manure, so much more vegetal than the rotting smell of pig or human waste, with their stench of meat. Leaving her gatherings at the barn door, she went in with the carrot tops, feeding them to him slowly to prolong their contact. When the tops were gone, she gave him the carrots themselves, although she knew she should have saved them for Emma, who had grown them. She then retreated to the house and returned with apples, leading the horse out of the stall and cross-tying him in the center aisle of the barn, finding brushes and a hoof pick and spending the better part of an hour brushing the caked mud from his shaggy coat and cleaning his unshod hooves.

When the horse was spotless, she turned her attention to the saddle and bridle in the adjacent stall, rifling through a tack box to find saddle soap and an old cloth. She filled up a bucket of warm water at the house and set to soaking and saddle soaping the cracked leather. She then oiled it and rubbed it with the soft cloth for a long time. When she was done, there was nothing else to do but put the tack on the horse and lead him out into the sunshine. He followed her willingly, nosing the pockets of her flannel pajama bottoms, hoping for more apples. She put a foot in the stirrup and hoisted herself into the old saddle, pushing aside thoughts that she should not be taking the horse without permission, telling herself that the horse clearly hadn't been ridden in weeks and she was doing Jimmy Bouchard a favor. She wondered what he knew about Emma's foreclosure.

The bay was frisky, trotting quickly and spooking at a chipmunk, and heading into the fields across the road where he was used to being ridden. They explored the fields she'd known so well as a child, then hayfields, now deep-green correct rows of soybeans. She could see that this was altered nature, genetically modified and suspiciously robust, without the weeds that accompanied any other crop she'd ever known. There was a path she'd loved as a child that was still there, narrower now, which looped through the woods around the cultivated fields. She emerged out of the cool and quiet woods into the back forty, the most remote section of Emma's land and came suddenly upon the red pickup truck parked at the edge of a field that had always been boggy, and where now the soybeans were shorter than they were elsewhere. Arden was glad to see it—that all natural obstacles hadn't been overcome by modern AgChem.

Jim Bouchard stood at the back of the truck, inspecting one of the soybean rows. He looked thinner than he had in April. It was comical to see the realization on his face that she was riding his horse, well-groomed but quite lathered from galloping, in her pajamas, without permission.

She stopped the horse in front of him, fighting back a smile that she worried might be a smirk. He was silent for several beats, looking grave, and finally cracked a wry smile.

"Uh, I can explain," Arden fumbled, having no idea what she would say next.

"You riding my horse, there?" His broad smile undercut his gruff tone. "Taking that redistribution of property to heart, eh?"

"Sorry about that. One thing led to another, and he talked me into it." She returned his smile. Luckily he didn't seem angry.

He cocked his head, looking her and the horse up and down. "Do me a favor? I'm thinking of entering him in a barrel cutting contest next summer and I'd like to see how he moves. Would you ride him around in that field for me?"

Arden put the bay through his paces in the clearing. She was suddenly self-conscious about not wearing a bra—after all, she was still in her pajamas—but hoped it wouldn't be obvious under the old flannel of Emma's she had thrown on as a jacket. The horse moved smoothly, spooking a bit in the far corner of the field but coming back in hand easily without Arden losing her seat. She trotted back over to Jim and halted in front of him where he sat on the bed of his pickup.

"He looks good. Thanks."

"Sorry for taking him without asking."

"I don't mind."

Jim was quiet, not in an awkward way but just comfortably sitting, watching her astride his horse. She looked past him into the truck bed, which held a large plastic vat of liquid—some kind of fertilizer or pesticide, she guessed.

"Can I ask you a question?" Arden started, taking a deep breath. This could get sticky. "Is there something going on with Unibank, the bank Emma owes her mortgage to, and your employer? Emma is convinced there is."

He nodded, looking serious. "Come get a drink with me later. I'll tell you what I know, but not while I'm on the clock."

Arden was taken aback, and for a moment didn't know what to say.

"C'mon, it'll be fun. We can reminisce about high school," he joked—they hadn't known each other in high school. He smiled at her, and Arden decided she liked that smile. Maybe she could use a drink. And anyway, it sounded like he knew something about the foreclosure that might be useful. She returned the smile and said yes, and they agreed he'd swing by Emma's place at eight. Arden wheeled the horse around and galloped off, smiling to herself.

Emma watched openmouthed as Arden rode out of the soybeans. Once she was assured that Jim didn't mind Arden taking the horse out, Emma was laughing at her, then whooping and snorting once Arden admitted that "they might be going on a date later." After the two of them put the horse away, they made a big breakfast and then drove out to the lake for a long hike around its shores. It was nice to be together, but it was hard to find things to say, with the foreclosure looming before them. When they got home, Arden fell asleep on the couch in Emma's sun-dappled living room.

They made an early dinner of hamburgers and a salad of the kale and vegetables from the garden. Arden left her jeans on, mostly still clean after the hike, and raided Emma's closet for a blouse, a dusty rose button-down that felt like silk. She brushed her hair, which made it puffy and reminded her why she never did that, usually just raking her fingers through to calm it down. She considered the bottles of perfume on Emma's dressing table, probably decades old, and decided it was better to smell like whatever she might smell like after the horse, the hike, and the hamburgers than like an old woman. Rifling through the drawers of her old dresser, she found the embroidered jean jacket Emma had given her at Easter. She sat on the edge of the bed, holding it for a moment. Before she had thought it was garish, as an embarrassed teenager, a younger Arden had been captivated to watch her mother create the design. When she wore it for the first time, it had seemed to Arden like magic, that Jill had conjured the flowers, so lush and vibrant. Once, she'd thought her mother was beautiful. She slipped the jacket on.

Jimmy was early by a few minutes, and Emma joined him on the porch in the twilight until Arden was ready, having trouble at the last minute finding her sneakers and then realizing they were filthy and squeezing into Emma's old cowboy boots instead. He had showered, and his short brown hair was still wet and combed back. He was in jeans as well, with a muted blue-and-gray flannel shirt smooth across his broad shoulders, tucked in, with an old leather belt. When Arden walked out onto the porch, he flashed her a smile and continued with the story he was telling Emma, which had her rapt.

". . . so they've sold the soybean futures already to a Japanese company, and locked in whatever price was being paid on the commodity market in April, so they couldn't give two shits about how this crop does. I'm having to beg for permission to treat the blight, and fix the tractor, and the thing that they don't realize is they still get paid based on volume!"

This had them both laughing cynically. After muttering something under her breath that sounded like, *"They can rot in hell,"* Emma said, more loudly, "Have fun," and the screen door slammed behind her.

The night was warm for September. Jimmy's truck smelled of diesel, earth, and an old whiff of cigarette. It also smelled of the clean smell of a man exercising outside, slightly salty and piquant, and made her take a deep breath. Neither of them spoke for a moment, suddenly shy, and he put on the radio, tuned to a country-western station playing a twangy old-fashioned bluegrass song.

Arden broke the silence. "I enjoyed the ride on Nick this morning a lot. He's a great horse."

"He keeps Emma company. I know she's had a hard go of it," he replied. Arden realized she'd been fishing for an offer to ride the horse again, but he didn't bite.

"Do you see much of her?" she asked, surprised.

"I keep an eye on her, yeah. I know that she's been getting pressured to sell. She chased my boss off her front stoop with a shotgun six months ago."

This was news to Arden. She was not entirely surprised but wished Emma had told her more about what was going on. She guessed it must have happened during their stretch of not really talking with each other, after she dropped out of school. *I should have been here*, Arden thought.

He pulled into the dirt parking lot in front of The Hall, the single eating and drinking establishment in the tiny downtown of Badger. One side was a family dining area, with one older couple having a silent meal, the other side a bar with a handful of loud men watching a basketball game. After assessing the crew in the bar—who, Arden had no doubt, Jimmy knew well—he steered her toward the restaurant side.

"Do you still live near Huron?" she asked, sliding onto the maroon vinyl booth seat. His family's farm had been there, a sizable operation. She remembered the school bus stopping there on the long rides to the regional high school. He nodded. "My dad died three years back, and my older brother's running the farm."

"Oh, Jim, I'm so sorry to hear that!" she cried, seeing the tall stern man, sitting astride the combine when the school bus picked up in the morning, and still there, hours later after the school day was done. "How come you don't work on your family farm?" she asked.

"My old man didn't believe in splitting up the operation, and my brother and I don't see eye to eye," he said shortly, flipping open the menu and glancing though it. Arden remembered Scott Bouchard, sneering at her in detention, leaving her in the lurch. Though she didn't know Scott well, she could see that the two brothers were very different.

He folded the menu. "I'm saving for my own spread, s'why I'm living there still. I've got a trailer there on the farm." He watched her to see how she reacted to that, whether she was too good for trailers after having been in the city.

"That's cold of your old man. Your brother gets it just because he's older?"

Jimmy shrugged. "I don't mind making my own way. And the farm came with its share of debt, so it's no prize."

"Speaking of farm debt," Arden said, deciding to broach the subject of AGM, "is Emma right that your employer is somehow behind her foreclosure?"

He leaned in and spoke quietly. "All I know is that there were lawyers in the headquarters a few weeks back, when I was there to pick up my paycheck, and I heard her name a few times. I thought it was weird. I know they've been after her to sell for years, but I'm not sure why they want her land so bad. Probably they need the water from her creek. Anyway, it was AGM's lawyer, Jarvis, who I've met, but also another guy, who I think was the bank's lawyer. Emma's bank. I tried to hear what they were saying, but I got hustled out. Something about a homestead exemption. They were going to try to block it because the land was leased to AGM, so it was an income stream. Does that mean anything to you?"

Finally, it made sense why her homestead exemption had been denied. Those bastards. Arden wondered how Jimmy could keep working for them. Though she guessed he had to pay the bills somehow.

As if sensing her disapproval, Jimmy said, "I told Emma right away. That's why she knows they're up to no good."

"Well, shit! I wish someone had told me, or Emma's clinic lawyers—we could have tried to stop the homestead exemption from getting blocked. Now I think we might be too late. We got stuck with this cruddy compromise of just three acres around the house. Which for some people might be okay, but not for Emma."

"AGM is going to buy the farm at auction. They already signed the papers with the bank. At least that's what I thought I heard. Emma's right. It's an inside job."

Arden sat back and looked at Jimmy. This might be enough to block the foreclosure, at least until after Election Day. But would it mean that Jimmy would have to come to court and testify against his employer? Surely if he did, he'd lose his job. Arden didn't think she could ask him to do that.

"What do people around here think of Initiative 99?" she asked, changing the subject. She knew that he knew about it—he had made the joke about redistribution of property when he found her trespassing with Nick. She smiled at the joke again, and because she appreciated his giving her the space to bring it up on her own terms.

He responded with a smile of his own. "I dunno, haven't talked to anyone about it." He waited for her to ask the next question.

"What about you?" she prodded.

He scratched his head, making a show of thinking about it. "I'm not sure. Part of me likes the idea, especially seeing all the bullshit that happens at AGM. But I'm not sure how realistic it is. I mean, it's kind of reckless, isn't it, like voting for a candidate who's totally unqualified just cause you want to run the incumbent out?"

Arden nodded slowly. While she had the same concern, she hadn't expected that to be his reaction. "But sometimes something untested is better than something corrupt. Sometimes you shake things up, so they can be fixed. And voter initiatives exist because people knew there would be times when the politicians weren't doing what the people wanted. They aren't doing what we want because they don't work for us anymore, they work for corporations. Bought and sold."

He nodded. She wanted to hear more from him but also wanted to respect his privacy. "You have a good job," she said. "Seems like you have more to lose than some. I'd understand if you had concerns."

"I don't know if you've looked at the prices lately for farmland, but they're sky high. I'd put my name in for the old Johnson farm," he said, referencing the farm north of Emma's. They'd been the first to sell out to AGM. The old farmhouse stood empty now, facing south on a sweet bluff with a nice stand of big oaks behind it.

It took Arden a moment to realize that he meant he'd apply to be awarded the farm in the distribution, if 99 passed. She was gratified that it had sparked his imagination, that he had made plans about what he would do if it was successful.

"What about you? Will you come back and farm, to help Emma?"

Arden played out that idea in her mind, not for the first time, and was surprised at how appealing it was. Emma wouldn't be able to run the farm alone forever, even if they could prevent the foreclosure or get the land back through 99. She imagined beehives, an herb-growing operation with hoop houses to extend the growing season, and a press for making cider from the apples in the orchard. The warmth that suffused her when she thought of it was so overwhelming that she closed her eyes and savored it for a moment. She knew that the reality of it was hard work, grueling and repetitive—the weeding, harvesting, and tending—but it was also deeply satisfying. After 99, she thought, things would be different for farmers, more sustainable. If there wasn't the specter of not being able to pay the bills, the bank, the seed supplier, that always seemed to haunt Emma's former life, then Arden thought it might be really peaceful. To spend her days outside, moving, rather than sitting behind a desk. If she had a partner, someone like Jimmy, to share the work with and to keep her company. It might be perfect.

"Maybe," she said. She liked the idea of Jimmy taking over the neighboring farm, of him working the land for himself, rather than the soybean operation. "I can't promise I won't put in a competing application for the Johnson farm," she teased, "because Emma, she's hard to share a bathroom with."

"Well, if it comes to that, perhaps we can work out a partnership," he drawled, laughing. "Of course, not the business kind." He waggled his eyebrows at her suggestively, grinning. She smiled back at him, enjoying the proposition, if that's what it was. She had a flash of helping him paint a bedroom in the old farmhouse.

"Worse matches have been made for farmland, I'm sure," she retorted, to which he whooped out a loud laugh.

"To be sure, darlin', to be sure."

After that they moved over to the bar side of The Hall, having a couple beers and playing pool with the remaining patrons. If the men knew who Arden was, they didn't let on, which was welcome after the long months of notoriety and speeches.

As Jimmy pulled the truck into Emma's front yard at eleven thirty that night, Arden felt a sudden electric charge in the air that almost took her breath away. With certainty, she wanted to kiss him. He cut the engine and looked at her, his eyes shining in the dark. He reached across the bench seat and took her hand in his, flipping over her palm and stroking it lightly with his calloused fingers. His touch made her shiver. Seeing that it was affecting her, Jimmy grazed his fingers up her forearm, slowly dipping his finger under the cuff of her silk shirt, slipping the button of the cuff free from its loose button hole and exposing her elbow, the tender inside of the crook of her arm, and her bicep. He watched her face as she controlled herself under the sensation, closing her eyes. It had been a long time since she'd been touched by a man, and maybe never exactly like this, so slowly and deliberately.

Arden slid across the bench seat until she was pressed up against Jimmy, slipping her left leg up under her and sitting on it, so she could face him. He wrapped his arms tightly around her, and she could feel the strong, wiry muscles in his arms and torso tensing against her. It started as a hug, with him burrowing under her hair to the side of her neck, his lips warm and stubble scratching, sending her nerves tingling. Sliding her hands around his shoulders and solid upper arms, Arden pulled back against his grip. He instantly loosened, looking for her face. She leaned in to kiss him, a kiss that quickly became urgent. Arden pulled back again, this time lying backward on the seat, wanting his weight on top of her. She felt that her silk shirt had come untucked and lifted her right arm above and behind her head to further pull it up, arching her back slightly and feeling the soft fabric slip and the cool air on her belly and hip. He paused, enjoying the sight of her in the dim light, drawing out the moment, making her wait. Just as he began to lean forward, reaching forward to grab her hips firmly and pull her toward him, they both froze, hearing Emma's front porch door slam.

"Kitty-kitty-kitty kitty! Here, kitty-kitty-kitty!" Emma trilled loudly from the step. "Sammy kitty-kitty-kitty!"

Arden closed her eyes, suppressing a laugh.

"Missing kitty?" Jimmy whispered.

"Quite. Been dead a year, at least." Arden took a breath, opening her eyes again to gauge his reaction. Amused.

"I see," he chuckled huskily. "Well, then." She nodded and slid away from him back to a sitting position, smoothing her hair and her shirt. She caught his eye as she tucked in her shirt, smiling, *next time.*

"I want to see you again, soon," he said. "When will you be here next? Or I can come to you."

Arden thought of the foreclosure hearing, and almost invited him. But she couldn't ask him to jeopardize his job, could she? She promised to call him soon and then finally he did make the standing offer that she could ride Nick whenever she wanted. "Since I know you will anyway."

She laughed and opened the truck door, shooting Emma a glare across the yard. Emma scooted into the house, the door banging behind her.

CHAPTER 18

HARD EVIDENCE

BACK IN VERMILLION, ARDEN WAS QUICKLY absorbed into the press of campaign tasks, strategy meetings, and speaking engagements. The foreclosure hearing was on her calendar for next Tuesday, and she kept meaning to find time to talk about what she had learned about AGM with the clinic lawyers. She thought of that night with Jimmy many times but was too distracted or surrounded by coverts to take the time to call him. One evening, thinking of him in his truck that night, she sent a late-night text, but he did not immediately reply. *Of course, he's a farmer, probably been asleep for hours*, she told herself. When he called the next day, she couldn't pick up. Finally, after trading calls over a few days, she sent him a text: *Can we make a date for November 8? I'm busy until Election Day, but I'm still thinking of you.* He'd replied: *Keep me posted on Emma.*

She felt somehow that she was at the beginning of something with him; whether it would be a friendship or something more, she was not concerned, but just had the sense that it would be lasting. And the attention from him had made her feel attractive. She realized that all her time around Kirish had made her lose some confidence. Despite his being a jerk most of the time, she thought about him entirely too much. There was so much about Kirish that was closed; for example, there would be no point in even asking him why he'd been getting all the strange phone calls. Whereas Jim felt more open, even in their short time together.

Ophelia, who had a nose for such things, looked Arden up and down the Monday after her trip to Badger.

"You got laid!" she'd proclaimed, indignant that Arden hadn't yet dished.

Arden laughed. "Hardly," she corrected her. "Although I did have a hot date at The Hall for pie and beer."

"The Hall!" Ophelia screeched, having been there before for breakfast and proclaimed it *too crappy*. "Tell me everything!"

THE DAY OF THE FORECLOSURE HEARING, Arden and Emma met the clinic lawyer at the county court early and went to the nearby diner to discuss their plan. Although the lawyer seemed to think it was doomed to fail, he agreed to put one of them on the stand to talk about the backroom deal between AGM and Unibank to steal the farm.

"Everything you want to say is hearsay or conjecture," the lawyer warned, "so don't be surprised if you get shut down before you even start."

They agreed that it would be Arden to take the stand, since Emma said she was *angry enough to spit*. Arden thought hard about what she would say while avoiding hearsay, which basically made everything Jimmy told her off-limits. If only he were here himself to testify.

"Miss Firth, you have something you'd like to say to the court about this proceeding?" the lawyer asked her, when she had climbed up to the stand and been sworn in. The lawyer for the bank had objected to Arden testifying, and the judge had called the two lawyers up to the bench. "Counsel, I want to allow the landowner to have her day in court, but no shenanigans here, you understand? You're on a tight leash, both of you," the judge had warned, speaking off the record to the lawyers, but Arden could hear from the witness stand. "I've got lunch plans at noon sharp." The lunch comment made Arden angry, which ended up in a funny way steeling her jittery nerves. She sat up straight, and faced the judge, making him look at her.

"I have good reason to believe that this foreclosure is the result of Unibank and AGM colluding together to force my grandmother to give up her farm. She couldn't pay her mortgage because her tenant, AGM, was intentionally late paying rent, repeatedly. The bank refused to talk to her about restructuring the loan until the late fees and fines were too much for her to ever repay. AGM has wanted her to sell the land to them for years, and now they've found a way to force her off."

"Your Honor, I object. These are wild claims with no basis in fact. This witness has no firsthand knowledge here, and appears to be testifying based on her own conspiracy theory." The Unibank lawyer was on his feet, speaking over Arden.

"I'll allow it," the judge drawled. "Miss Firth, please do tell us your good reason for believing this."

"I believe that there is already a deal between AGM and Unibank to sell the farm, which shouldn't be legal. It should go to an auction to be sold to the highest bidder, and any value over the loan amount should go to my grandmother. The deal between AGM and Unibank probably pays her nothing."

"Pure conjecture! Your honor, you can't actually be considering this as evidence, can you?" The Unibank lawyer asked the question in such a good-old-boy way, so smug and certain, it made Arden want to scream.

"Miss," the judge addressed Arden, "these are serious claims. Do you have any evidence that what you say is true?"

"Every month for nine months, AGM paid its rent late, always several days after my grandmother's mortgage was due. She got further and further behind. And then once the foreclosure happened, they stopped paying altogether, saying that they were paying the rent into escrow because it should go to the bank, even though there wasn't any court order instructing them to do so. Then, at the hearing for her homestead exemption, she was denied the farm exemption, which expressly allows three hundred acres, because supposedly it doesn't apply if the land is leased."

"Your honor, that is the law. All entirely appropriate," the Unibank lawyer interjected.

"It seems to us that the bank and AGM cooked this up together, to push her out," Arden concluded.

She was dismissed from the stand, and the bank called its own witness. A woman about Arden's age, who talked about the steps the bank took to collect the loan, their processes for loan workouts, which they claimed Emma never took advantage of, and the homestead exception. The Unibank employee looked deeply uncomfortable, and though Arden hated her, she had a moment's feeling of *there but for the grace of God go I*—after her summer temping in banks in Sioux Falls, that could have been her. *She deserves it for being a sell-out*, Arden thought, watching the woman shoot a guilty look at her. Though, if she was a sell-out, was Jimmy too?

When the clinic lawyer cross-examined her, the Unibank woman hadn't heard of AGM.

"I just get an account put in my queue in my portal, or my computer work queue, that is. Once an account is overdue, it is eligible for foreclosure, after we send out the required notices and after the cure periods have elapsed. I never know why an account goes into my queue, just that it is flagged for foreclosure. Here, all the required notices were sent, and the cure periods have elapsed."

"Is there an agreement for the sale of the farm between the bank and AGM?"

"That's not my area, but that wouldn't be something we would do. I've never seen that. The lawyers handle that, but it has to be put up for sale by auction. There are requirements for public notice, so it's fair and all that."

The judge was glancing at his wristwatch when he said, "No further witnesses?" in a way that was much more like a proclamation than a question.

"Petitioner's motion for foreclosure by sale is granted," the judge intoned, signing an order put in front of him by the Unibank lawyer. "Three-acre homestead exemption granted per this court's previous August 6 order, in accordance with the surveyor's plan submitted as respondent's Exhibit 3. All other acreage to be vacated by November 1. Foreclosure sale date to be set at November 15. Counsel for the bank, I want to see you dotting your *I*s and crossing your *T*s to make sure the foreclosure sale is publicly noticed. I don't want to hear anything more about a backroom deal."

With that, court was adjourned.

Outside, Emma was kind.

"Thanks for fighting for me, honey. Sometimes the deck is stacked. At least I keep the house and the barn. It could be worse. And who knows, maybe your 99 will turn things around."

As she walked slowly to her car and got in gingerly, Emma seemed smaller and older than she ever had before. Arden watched her go, and then headed back to Vermillion, to go back to work. She would fight like hell to stop Unibank from doing this to anyone else. And when they won, they'd get Emma's farm back.

CHAPTER 19
CRASH AND BURN

ON OCTOBER 15, KIRISH WENT MISSING.

The 99 headquarters was in an uproar. Rent was due, and Kirish was the only one who could sign checks on the bank account. He didn't show at a speaking engagement, and Arden had to drive an hour at breakneck speed to cover for him at the lakeside community gathering. The organizers had requested Kirish and were less than thrilled with Arden arriving late as his replacement. He was a favorite with the well-heeled liberals, discussing the finer policy points in his Northeastern prep-school way.

Arden was stricken, and felt terrible that she had no idea what had been going on with him. She hadn't spoken with him much in the last couple weeks, having been consumed with the foreclosure, 99, and thinking of Jimmy. Had he been dealing with some kind of personal problem, or been acting strange? Arden didn't know. Unaccountably, she felt like his disappearance was linked to the late-night phone call she'd overhead a couple weeks before, and the eerie feeling that someone had been watching them. She would have filed a missing person's report after a day or two, but for a single of line text she received from him: *I am okay—taking some time to think.* Although they had never spoken about it, and Arden had never seen his resolve waver, she wondered if he was struggling with doubts about 99, too.

After a week of his being gone, with the coverts becoming increasingly agitated, Arden and Ophelia began to worry about word leaking out that he had abandoned the movement. They suspected it had gotten out when Arden started getting strange phone calls. Normally, the coverts' media relations team handled press inquiries, fielded by either Jennifer or Ophelia. Arden was always given advance warning if they had agreed to an interview, and times would be prearranged by email. However, in the week following Kirish's disappearance, she received two phone calls outside of the normal protocols that scared her.

First, late on a Wednesday night, her cell phone rang with a Washington, DC, number. She almost didn't answer it, but did, in case it might be Kirish or somebody associated with his legal efforts.

"Ms. Firth, I am writing a piece on Justin Kirish for a nationally recognized newspaper."

"What's your name and what is the paper? Was this interview scheduled through the Initiative 99 media center?" Arden knew that it was not.

"I am not at this stage disclosing our paper or our sources, but we may publish the piece on very short notice and I wanted to give you the opportunity to comment. We have information that Mr. Kirish was expelled from Williams College for misconduct. Are you familiar with the allegations?"

Arden paused. She knew nothing about this and was suspicious. How could he have gotten into law school if he'd been expelled from Williams?

"What is your information?" she asked carefully.

"So you don't know?" The voice on the other line sounded like they were smirking.

"I'm not going to respond to this type of rumor. If you have a real story, call our media center."

"Ms. Firth, for the record, are you and Justin Kirish romantically involved?"

Arden hung up.

She texted Kirish: *Unnamed person calling with questions about you at Williams.*

There was no response.

THREE DAYS LATER, SHE RECEIVED A CALL from the *Dakota Free Press* from a sympathetic reporter that both Arden and Kirish had talked with a number of times.

"Arden, it's Kyle from the *Free Press*. I've heard from a source, not sure if it's reliable, that Justin has taken a job at a corporate law firm. Is this possible?"

Arden was floored. Was it possible? She didn't know. They had been working side by side for more than a year and he was her most trusted advisor. But she really didn't know Justin Kirish that well. She knew that firms had approached him with offers, to entice him to sell out by becoming a corporate lawyer, to discredit the movement, but he had sneered at the idea. She knew these law firms paid well, but she didn't think Kirish cared about that enough to accept such an offer, at least before November 8. She recalled his scorn for his father's law firm, for that life. Was he in some sort of trouble?

"Arden? Did you hear me?"

"I don't know," she admitted. It was not impossible.

"The source claims that he has joined Wentworth Brown's class of incoming first-year associates in their DC office. That he's being paid a salary of two hundred K a year." This was the firm that had propositioned Kirish a couple months back.

"I don't know how this could be," she repeated, knowing she should not be acting so crestfallen with a reporter, no matter how friendly.

Kyle thanked her, apologized to be the bearer of bad news, if in fact it was true, and hung up.

Arden texted Kirish: *What the fuck is going on? You work at Wentworth Brown?* No answer.

SHORTLY AFTER KYLE'S CALL THAT EVENING, Arden's phone rang again with another unfamiliar number from a South Dakota area code.

"Arden! It's Jim." The voice was familiar but Arden couldn't place it, still in shock from the call from the reporter.

"Jimmy Bouchard. . . ." he said flatly, after her pause.

"Jimmy! Of course! I'm sorry . . . I didn't recognize your number . . . I just . . . we have a lot of crazy stuff going on right now. Tonight."

"Are you okay?" His voice was concerned, reacting to her tone, which she knew was strained.

"I am, I am," she assured him. "Things to do with the initiative, but I'm okay. Rattled, I guess. I can't really get into it." She hoped he would understand.

"Okay . . . is Emma doing all right? I heard about the foreclosure."

Arden swallowed. "I wish I knew. She's not answering her phone. I'm worried she's taking the foreclosure hard.

Still a month until the auction, but I'm sure it's hell having all the neighbors know."

"Yup," he said grimly, "the November 15 auction is on the calendar at AGM. I'll go check on Emma tomorrow. Listen, Arden, you joked about being followed when we played pool, but I got the sense it wasn't really a joke. You'd tell me if it was something like that, wouldn't you?"

She assured him that she would. Before saying goodbye, she gave him the address of the Church Street headquarters. He was coming into town in the next few weeks on business and wanted to say hi. Arden hung up and called Ophelia.

THE NEXT DAY OPHELIA AND ARDEN broke the news to the coverts, telling them about the rumors. The volunteers were stunned, and after a moment or two of shock, broadly rejected them as impossible.

The following day, several online newspapers ran stories on Kirish's new job, and the next day, the print edition of the *Washington Post* showed a picture of him walking into the firm's Pennsylvania Avenue office in a suit and tie, sunglasses, head down. "South Dakota's Voter Initiative to Abolish Corporations Loses Its Founder to Corporate Law Firm," the headline declared. Few coverts came to headquarters that day. The phone banks were quiet. They were disgraced.

South Dakotans for Prosperity, the opposition group, was having a field day with Kirish's defection. They were quoted at length by the state papers calling into question the whole movement, and undertook a full social media blitz. At the same time, an "exposé" on 99 was released by a shady internet news site, full of half-truths and twisted inside information. It focused on the break-in, describing it as a data breach that impacted "hundreds of thousands" of South Dakota voters whom the coverts had been assembling dossiers about, including personal information about their voting preferences, children, education, and personal habits. The article claimed that its source was the police report, but it was clear that they had additional information about the coverts' work that had not been in that report. It seemed they had a mole.

With a dull throb, Arden knew that it was Peter Bassford. She'd suspected him but been too sheepish to act. The same article showed a picture of Ophelia apparently being booed on stage at the state fair outside Rapid City, with a quote from Arden saying, "The low turnout may not reflect low interest in 99." Is that what she'd said? Ugh.

Arden tried to organize an emergency leadership meeting to discuss how to proceed, but no one was around. Ophelia had gone to New York for an unscheduled break, and Nassert and Hatch were nowhere to be seen. Jennifer left town too, without a word. Every time Arden picked up the phone, it was a reporter looking for comment on Kirish's departure. Arden had no comment.

As she was locking up to leave the Church Street office, Peter Bassford arrived, looked extremely smug.

"Well, well, things seems to be going to shit, don't they, Arden?" He smiled.

"Can I see your keys, Peter? Mine don't seem to be working." She held out her hand.

He immediately was suspicious. "I don't have keys," he responded evenly.

Arden did not know if this was the case. She'd been hoping to confiscate his keys before telling him off.

"I don't want to see you around here again. I don't trust you. I think you set me up with those two guys after the *New Republic* article just so you could come sailing in to the rescue, and I think you leaked the information about our database to the media for this week's story. I think you might have even been behind the break-in, where we lost the things that were most important to us." Arden's voice shook as she spoke, and she had a flash of Bassford outside of the sandwich shop coming to her rescue, lifting up his shirt to expose the gun in his waistband against his bare stomach. What she was doing right now was not smart.

"You can't prove anything, girlie." His lip was lifted in a snarl, although his eyes still crinkled, showing he was amused, ever amused. "You have no idea what's in store for you, you little princess. You think this week was bad? Hah, you just wait." He left without a backward glance.

What did he know? How could things possibly get worse? She thought of Kirish with an icy jolt, hoping he was okay.

FOR A FEW DAYS, NO ONE EVEN UNLOCKED the doors to the Church Street headquarters, and Arden stayed in bed. She was too depressed to check on Emma. The thought of doing so just made her feel worse about the spectacular crash and burn that had just occurred. Not only had all they'd worked for been pissed away, but the farm would be irretrievably lost. She thought of her mom spending days in her room with the shades drawn, later explaining in a shaky voice that she'd *been down a hole*. Arden had worried that Kirish was giving up a bright, successful future as a lawyer because of his dedication to the cause. But apparently his dedication had not been what she'd thought, and perhaps his role in 99 had not been so anti-establishment as to blacklist him. Indeed, it had drawn attention to his talents, as a lawyer, public speaker, organizer and leader, and she shouldn't have been surprised that these talents had engendered job offers. What baffled her was the timing. Why now? Why this firm, which represented Exxon, Philip Morris, Monsanto—exactly what she truly believed he hated? Why not hold out and hope for a university job after the November election? Perhaps he believed 99 would fail at the ballot, or that it would not survive constitutional challenge, and that he'd best capitalize on the high point, before things started to crumble.

Indeed, it did seem that 99 was crumbling. Although there was no polling for state voter initiatives, local news was widely reporting that the public sentiment had shifted and that 99 was now considered to have been an embarrassing infatuation, from which the electorate, luckily, had been woken, just in time, by Kirish's disappearance. There were op-ed pieces on the dangers of voter initiatives in these days of increasingly uninformed and reactionary voters.

FINALLY, WHEN SHE COULDN'T IGNORE THE banging on her door anymore, Arden roused herself from bed and admitted Jessica and Carson. After the trip to Standing Rock, Jessica and Arden had been closer, often walking to and from the headquarters office to their apartments. They often invited her for dinner. She got the sense they were keeping an eye on her, which she appreciated. Kirish certainly wasn't, although he had been the one to suggest she move in the first place. A lot of good that had done, she'd thought on more than one occasion, above his now-abandoned unit.

Jessica and Carson bustled in, putting a cup of coffee in her hand and bagels on the kitchen table.

"It's been a week, Arden. It's time to come back," Carson said gently. "The coverts are ready to get back to work. But we need you. We can't lose both our leaders." "Drink that coffee and get in the shower. You stink," Jessica said, less gently. "You need to come down to the headquarters. The tide is turning again; 99 is back in the running."

"Is Kirish back?" Arden asked, with a leap of hope.

Jessica guided her toward the bathroom with a wrinkled nose and turned on the shower. "No. But we think he's being blackmailed."

CHAPTER 20

BLACKMAIL

TWENTY MINUTES LATER, ARDEN WAS sitting with Ophelia, Jessica, Carson, and a covert she didn't know well, Erik, in the headquarters office. Erik had a laptop and was pulling up chat forums, mainly conspiracy-theory stuff, that all claimed that Kirish was being blackmailed. Speculation on what kind of dirt the presumed corporate blackmailers had on him ran the gamut, ranging from his being busted for a drug lab at covert headquarters to secrets from his past. One article claimed that he had spent time in juvenile detention for an underage manslaughter charge; another that he had been expelled from prep school for sexual misconduct. It all seemed crazy, and Arden had no reason to think any of it was true. Still, she thought of the mysterious phone call about Kirish getting in trouble at Williams. About the comment in the *New Republic* article about USD Law School being "markedly less prestigious" than the exclusive Williams College. *Why* was *he in South Dakota?* Arden wondered.

The blackmail theory, although still upsetting, was at least mobilizing. She was angry, confused, suspicious, but not despairing, as she had been the week before when she'd been unable to leave the apartment. It was still a betrayal, but at least there was a reason—dark and convoluted, but it seemed possible to her in a way that the straightforward selling out for a six-figure salary had not. It was too unlike Kirish simply to opt for the big paycheck. The idea of his having secrets in his past—well, in hindsight there were other signs that pointed in that direction.

The theory seemed to have resonance for the other coverts as well, who began returning in force. Phone banks that had been silent for ten days were now buzzing, ramping up the get-out-the-vote effort, with the election just fifteen days away. Likely voters again and again raised questions about Kirish, and the team scheduled a meeting on how to respond. Several phone canvassers were expressly referencing the "apparent blackmail," while others were more circumspect, answering questions on the point with "we don't know why he left, but many of us feel that some kind of pressure was put upon him by corporate interests that he was unable to resist."

The special strategy session was convened early Tuesday morning, before the day's phone-bank volunteers were scheduled to arrive. Andrew Nassert, Jeremy Hatch, and Jennifer Walton were in whispered conversation at one end of the conference table, which they broke off when Arden walked in. Arden was irritated to see Jennifer back in the office. Hearing that she had flown back to New Hampshire, shortly after Ophelia announced her unplanned vacation last week, had been the last straw before Arden took to her bed. The "no comment" responses from the campaign belied the lack of direction from Arden, Jennifer, or others who could have stepped into the leadership void. Arden doubted Kirish's disappearance had taken the same emotional toll on Jennifer that it had on those who actually cared about the outcome of the election, or about him, so she'd merely been jumping off a sinking ship. Arden supposed that her reappearance promised 99's return to favor but found herself holding it against Jennifer as a fair-weather friend.

Jennifer kicked off the discussion. "This is a classic crisis-response situation. First rule, contain the crisis and control the message, and foremost, do no harm. As in any crisis response, we are going to have to act without a complete understanding of what happened and where this story is going to go. The 'no comments' haven't helped control the message. The story has continued to swirl and has done serious damage in discrediting the ballot initiative. The way I see it, we have two options: either we embrace the conspiracy theory, or we play it straight, move forward, and hope the ideas stand on their own despite the noise in the narrative. Either approach has risks, but I believe the conspiracy theory has more risk, though also significantly more upside as well."

Ophelia responded strongly. "It's manipulating people to suggest blackmail, unless we have some evidence that this is what has actually happened."

Arden had hoped that O would take this approach, and was proud of her for doing so. It felt principled. Arden, however, was more conflicted.

Andrew was watching her closely. "I think this discussion needs to start with what we believe to be the truth. Does anyone here have a window into what actually happened here? Arden?"

She shook her head and clutched her cooling coffee. "I guess I might know more than anyone, but I definitely don't have the whole picture. I know that he'd gotten a couple of job offers, including this one, over the past few months, but I never had any sense that he'd been tempted by the money. He'd seen it for what it was, an attempt to discredit 99. He warned me that they would come for me too, would try to get to me. I said I had no secrets. . . ."

Arden trailed off, not wanting to give voice to her suspicions about Kirish, but she pressed on. She owed it to them to tell the truth, or what she knew of it. "There were a couple weird things . . . I think we were both being followed."

There was general nodding; this was not a surprise to people. Arden continued, "Also, right after he left, I got a call one night—supposedly from a reporter, though he wouldn't identify himself. The guy said he was doing a story on Kirish getting into trouble for something at Williams, where he went for undergrad in Massachusetts. He didn't say, but I got a feeling it was tied to some kind of . . . uh . . . sexual misconduct."

Ophelia groaned and cursed under her breath. Andrew hung his head, shaking it slowly. Erik, who'd walked them through the conspiracy theory blogs, nodded, and said, "I was afraid of that. The swirl seems to be coalescing around two narratives: a sexual misconduct charge either at Williams or during high school, or some kind of criminal act as a child. I hate to say it, but the first seems more likely to me."

Jennifer Walton cleared her throat. "Anyone have any reason to think this is true? My experience with Kirish has been nothing but respectful and appropriate. Ophelia? Arden? You guys know him best."

"I've seen nothing inappropriate out of him ever," responded Ophelia. "He's too uptight for that."

"Could be in reaction," Jeremy suggested.

Arden considered this. She thought of the time that first summer in his apartment when Ophelia had propositioned him and he'd exploded, throwing them both out. She thought of their kiss at his graduation party, where he'd asked her to kiss him, rather than just kissing her, or even just asking if he could kiss her. She'd thought at the time it was a test of wills. He'd been extremely careful never to socialize with her when he was her TA. She'd ascribed it to snobbery, but maybe it was something else. Even more than just being careful at the time, Kirish kept pointing out in retrospect that he hadn't had anything to do with her while he was her TA—to the point that the reporter had noted his protestations in the *New Republic* article. It had seemed silly to her at the time. And it wasn't just her he was standoffish with. She couldn't recall him dating or flirting with anyone.

"Could be," Arden agreed. He could be uptight in reaction to something that had happened in his past, as Jeremy had suggested. They all stared at her. "He's pretty private about his past. I haven't ever heard him talk about Williams or high school at all. He rarely drinks, though I know he likes to, and then never to excess. I think alcohol is involved in a lot of incidents like that. . . ."

She thought again of the night of his graduation party, when he was loosened up with drink, asking her to kiss him with that strange look in his eye. She remembered the feeling with Kirish sometimes that he didn't like himself, although it wasn't a confidence thing, like Arden sometimes struggled with. It was more like he felt there was a bad streak in him, or something dark in his past. Maybe it was this. Was he capable of something like this? Like a date rape or something like that? If he'd been drunk? If the signals had been unclear? Arden found that she couldn't entirely rule it out.

As a freshman in college, she'd gone out one night with someone she'd considered a friend, and they'd both drunk way too much. She'd woken up in his dorm room without any memory of the final few hours of the evening. She'd been angry when she'd realized they'd had sex, and she'd confronted him about doing it when she'd been so drunk. He'd been sorry, but had maintained that he'd been hammered too and that she'd been into it. Arden had no idea whether that was true or not, and wouldn't ever know. She had dropped her friendship with him and warned friends away from him, but she hadn't considered going further with it. Whether she had provided "consent," she could never be sure. She was angry at him, but more furious with herself for being in that state and getting herself into that situation. Could such a thing have happened with Kirish? Not in her experience with him— he was way too careful for that. But maybe with a younger, less careful version of himself.

Carson came to Kirish's defense. "I've known Justin for almost three years, and I really don't think he would do something like that. He's very respectful of women. I've never seen him act inappropriately. I've never even heard him make a crude remark or any kind of comment. . . ." He trailed off. "I don't believe it. I think it's wrong to perpetuate a rumor that he did something like this unless we have hard evidence."

Andrew was more circumspect. "It's true that we don't have any evidence of misconduct, but we also can't rule anything out at this point, specifically because Kirish is not here. The fact that he bailed without a word to any of us, and did something that people who know him think is out of character—that's suspicious. That suggests he was hiding something. Even if he isn't hiding anything, his actions betrayed our efforts, and he didn't bother to give us any explanation. I don't think we owe him anything. We should do what is in the best interests of the movement."

"We could hire a private investigator to try to find out more," Jeremy suggested. "The problem is time. We have only ten days until November 7. We need a strategy to deal with this issue that gets us successfully over the finish line."

"Okay, so back to our options," Jennifer picked up again. "Option A: Get behind the blackmail narrative and paint him as a victim. Option B: Get behind the blackmail and paint him as a perp, and us as the victim. Option C: Ignore the blackmail narrative, and play it straight. Anyone see any other paths?"

Nobody volunteered anything.

"I get it that the first two are not terribly appetizing," Jennifer allowed. "My gut is that they are the most likely to turn the tide in our favor. Moreover, they are likely to gain traction anyway. It's just a question of whether they gain traction in time to make a difference on Election Day. Option A will be the most galvanizing and is probably the most appealing to the disenfranchised, pissed-off voter, who's voting for 99 because they want to throw the bastards out. Many of those voters are in backlash against the whole #MeToo movement already."

Ophelia and Arden erupted in objections simultaneously. "So we want to capitalize on morons who think sexual harassment and consent is a stupid feminist campaign that went too far? Really?" Ophelia's hollering drowned Arden out.

"I don't like using a backlash like that to our advantage," Arden began again slowly, "but I also think it's wrong just to condemn him for a mistake in college that we don't understand. Even though we don't know why Kirish left, I still feel like I owe him that. What about some middle ground, where we acknowledge what seems like blackmail, but say that we don't know the details? We think, based on the way he left, that it is possible that he was acting under some kind of duress. We say we're sorry we lost him, he was a real contributor to our work, and that we wish him the best."

"That's basically Option A," Ophelia retorted. "When it comes out that he date-raped someone in college at a frat party by dropping a roofie in her drink, we've said we wish him the best."

Arden shook her head. "No, I can't believe that's what happened. If it turns out that it is, well then, I guess we readjust our position. But is this a Hail Mary? Is it the only way we could win?" She turned to Andrew and Jennifer, watching them weigh the alternatives.

"What about Option B?" Jeremy mused. "We acknowledge the blackmail, say we haven't been given any details by Kirish, and we condemn the decision that he made to sell out. His actions have been a distraction and a harm to 99, and we regret that we were involved with him. That way, if and when the sordid details come out, our hands are clean."

"I don't like Option B," Andrew spoke up. "It looks like we're throwing him under the bus, and we lose the value of him as a martyr figure. We look disloyal. Option C, we look wishy-washy and complicit when the details come out." He seemed like he was making up his mind. He spread his palms on the table and looked around the room.

"This is a strategy decision," Andrew spoke quietly, making pointed eye contact with Ophelia, Arden, and Hatch, reminding them of that first meeting in this very room, where Jeremy and Andrew agreed to support 99 in exchange for the final word on strategy. "Unfortunately, sometimes you find yourself in these shitty situations in a campaign. You've gotta make the best call you can, and it's often a roll of the dice. As Jennifer said at the outset,

Option A has the most upside, but also the most risk. That's my vote."

Andrew was watching Arden with a warning on his face. She had the feeling he was going to try to pull rank if she moved to veto him, and she wasn't ready for a showdown. She hadn't yet made up her own mind.

"I want to try again to talk to him. Can we reconvene tomorrow?"

"If you do get him, depending on how bad the facts are, try to bring him back into the fold," Jennifer pressed. "An apology and explanation right now—that validates the blackmail theory and gives us some clarity. It would also create a lot of drama right now. It could be just the media bump that gets us back on top."

"Did you really just say 'media bump'? Ugh." Ophelia stood up quickly, shoving her chair back with a loud screech. "You're all willing to just jump into bed with a bunch of conspiracy theorists who hate women, just as a means to an end, is that it? Doesn't even matter to you what is true? I vote for Option C or whatever you're calling it. Why is taking the high road always Option C?" She stormed out of the conference room, slamming the door behind her and continuing out the front door of covert headquarters onto the street. They were quiet as they watched her get into her dented white Subaru and peel away.

Arden thought about calling Kirish, and what she would ask. Was asking him to return to 99 a compromise they shouldn't make, as Ophelia seemed to fear? Did Arden have the stomach to do what it took to win?

CHAPTER 21   RETURN

THREE DAYS LATER, KIRISH WAS ON A plane back to Sioux Falls. Two days after that, the story of his suspension at Williams was on the front page of the *Washington Post*. "Disgraced Founder of Corporation Ban Resigns Law Job Amid Reports of Sexual Misconduct," read the headline of the piece, which revealed new and seemingly credible details about the complaints against him as an undergrad. An anonymous source had provided a copy of the college's confidential records on the matter, in which then-college senior Kirish was accused of having sexual intercourse with an intoxicated freshman. He had been both her dorm residence advisor and captain of the crew team on which she was a member. Whether those roles were akin to teacher or manager was a gray area, and one that would have made the interaction clearly improper. It was unclear from the report whether the freshman had alleged lack of consent, but there was no suggestion of force.

This was all part of the plan. Option A. As Jennifer had proposed during the Tuesday-morning strategy session, Kirish's return was part of a plan to generate press attention for 99 while allowing them to control the message. Arden was disgusted that they'd found themselves in such a position, attempting these unsavory manipulations, but at the same time, she was exhilarated at the reversal of fortunes for 99. The idea of corporate blackmail had gained such traction and had galvanized so many potential voters in South Dakota, it seemed that most people didn't care what Kirish might have done. That his opponents had tried to silence him only served to make his voice louder, more vital.

AFTER THE TUESDAY LEADERSHIP MEETING, Arden had tried to call Kirish. She'd gone into a private office at covert headquarters and looked up the law firm, Wentworth Brown, on her laptop. There he was, a professional photo of him on their website, looking entirely at home in an expensive suit. He was listed as a member of their prestigious appellate advocacy litigation practice, with a direct phone extension and email address. They hadn't spoken since before he left and had exchanged only those few terse texts. Her early attempts to contact him, the pleading voicemails that had gone unanswered, had ceased upon the news of his joining the law firm, the betrayal.

She called the number and listened to his voice in the phony professional out-of-office message—"You've reached Justin Kirish at Wentworth Brown. I'm unavailable. Press one to reach my assistant, Heather, or leave a message at the tone." As she left a message, she imagined him sitting in a small modern office, high in a skyscraper, having sent the call to voicemail because he could see that it came from the familiar South Dakota number, from headquarters, from her.

She spoke into the line in a tight tone, her voice shaking. "It's Arden. I need to talk with you," she began her voicemail. "All of us, me, Ophelia, Andrew, and Jeremy, need to make a decision about how to spin your . . . situation. There are rumors that you're being blackmailed for some indiscretion in college, and we need to decide whether to get behind that angle. They think it might be the thing that saves 99. I'm not sure I even want to win that way. It depends on what you did, if you did end up at that firm because you have something to hide. It seems like it's probably going to come out anyway, so maybe you can help us come out of this in one piece. You've done a lot of damage to the movement, but the blackmail thing has kind of been a lifeline in a weird way. People are mobilized again for the first time since you left . . . things were bad here for a while. I need to talk to you. Can you call me later? Call my cell after seven. I'll be home then." She hung up.

AFTER A LONG FULL DAY AT THE COVERT headquarters making up for lost time, when Arden finally got to her apartment at seven o'clock that night, she was exhausted. She made herself a grilled cheese sandwich, took a shower, and was in bed by nine. When she fell asleep, there was still no word from Kirish. But that night, after eleven, he finally called her. It felt so strange and intimate to hear his voice again after so long while she lay in the dark in her bed, awoken from a fitful sleep.

"Justin," she mumbled when she heard his voice saying, "Hello? Arden?" There was a long pause, which she did not move to fill.

"Well?" he said finally, "What do you want to know?"

"Why did you leave?"

"The thing at Williams. I was twenty-one when it happened, so I was able to keep my parents out of it. Privacy rights, you know. You met my mother in May. She's pretty tightly wound. She's been in treatment for stage two breast cancer for the last year. I didn't want her to find out." Another long pause. "I didn't want you to find out."

"Well, I don't know what you did, but is it really worse than abandoning everything we worked for and selling out? Or was the cushy law job another enticement?" Arden was surprised at the venom that rose in her, and she struggled to keep it out of her voice, not wanting to drive him back into hiding. "I mean, was it really that bad?" she whispered.

His response was measured. "An enticement? Well, it's not working at Walmart," he replied, answering her second question but ignoring the others. "If my life had gone a different way, I'd probably be happy here, in an empty sort of way. It's interesting and challenging. And I can see how having money changes things, how it would be hard to go back. But no, it wasn't an enticement. It's prostitution." He laughed without humor. "No one would pay for my body, but my mind, that's a different story."

"Was it blackmail?"

"There were threats, yes. Of exposure, and also, of . . . other things. Then the law firm approached me on behalf of an anonymous client with an unusual offer. If I accepted the position, the details of my suspension at Williams would not be released. So yes, it was. The firm claimed they'd been able to negotiate on my behalf, to protect me, because they saw me as a promising legal talent they didn't want to see destroyed. Bullshit, I think."

"Was it so bad?" she asked, again. "What you did? Is it worth throwing away all your work just to keep it a secret?"

"No, it wasn't." He apparently wasn't going to say more. Arden rolled her head from side to side slowly on the pillow. Was he going to make her drag it out of him? She sighed, and continued wearily, "Kirish, we need to understand the allegations, so we can decide how to play the next ten days. Only ten—well, nine now—till the vote, you know."

"Oh, I know." Another long pause. "I can't bring myself to talk about it right now. Do you guys want me to come back? I think you're right, it is going to come out anyway. I might as well give up this charade."

"What about your mother?" Arden asked, thinking of Emma. When Emma had been sick, Arden would have done anything to shield her from bad news. She felt a twinge of guilt now; she hadn't talked to Emma in what felt like weeks.

"My mother is going to find out anyway. I'll tell her tomorrow. I'm ready to come back, and I only want to tell the story once. After everyone hears it, then we can, or rather you all can, decide what to do."

Arden croaked out an "okay," and after a pause, each of them waiting for the other to say more, Kirish rang off.

He was in touch with Andrew after that, making arrangements. It was decided that Kirish would resign from the law firm Wednesday and fly back to South Dakota that afternoon. As threatened, upon his resignation, the story would be released to multiple news outlets, and they expected it to run in the following days. On Thursday or Friday, after the mainstream release, Kirish would hold a news conference telling his side of the story. Someone from 99 would give a follow-up statement, warning that corporate forces worked in many invisible, insidious ways to protect their own power. They hoped that "someone" would be Arden, but she had been noncommittal. She still hadn't heard the full story from Kirish, although Andrew seemingly had (despite Kirish's claiming not to want to tell it over the phone). Andrew hadn't shared any of the details, only that it was "not so bad" and "not rape." Arden still didn't know what she believed; she needed to look Kirish in the eye and hear it for herself. She offered to pick him up at the airport, over text, but he declined, saying he would take a cab and be at their apartment building after ten o'clock. She should leave her hall light on if she wanted him to come up, or they could talk in the morning.

Ophelia wanted to stay and hear it from him that night as well, so she came by with a six-pack of hard cider for them to share while they waited. Though she couldn't really explain why, after a couple of drinks, as ten o'clock approached, Arden awkwardly asked Ophelia to leave.

"Listen," Ophelia protested, "I have just as much right as you do to get the real story. I committed almost a year of my life to this work. And I don't know about you, but I don't want to hear this story for the first time in front of an audience. If I'm not satisfied with what I hear, I'm not going along with fucking Option A, and I'm not going to hold back from telling that to anyone who asks me. You all might want to know this sooner rather than later."

"I know that you have just as much right as I do. It's just that, well, I don't know . . . I got the sense he wants to tell me alone."

"So you're just going to accommodate him on this unspoken wish?" Ophelia shook her head. "I think you are better off with me here, frankly. You'll be less likely to end up forgiving him on the spot without thinking it through. And do you really want to hear some kind of romantic confession from him tonight? Are you going to stand by him up on the podium like some kind of senator's wife after he gets caught sending dick pics to the intern?"

Arden let all that sink in. Could he possibly be looking for that, for her to stand by him in that way? She didn't think Kirish would ask her to do that, but she wouldn't put it past Jennifer. Was that, in fact, what was already being asked of her? In any event, Arden didn't want things to get too emotional. "Yeah, I guess you should stay."

When the cab dropped Kirish off on the street at ten thirty, Arden watched him trudge up the walkway to the apartment building, raising his eyes to see whether her light was on. Though she doubted that he could see her through the gauzy drape that hung across the kitchen window, she imagined that she felt a jolt as their eyes met. He let himself in the building and then into his apartment below hers. Arden and Ophelia were silent as they listened to his steps as he rolled his suitcase across the living room below and into his bedroom, then headed to the bathroom and was quiet for a while. After another ten minutes, there was a rap on the door.

"Come in," Arden said quietly, and as he pushed open the door into the small kitchen where the two women sat, she watched his face register that she was not alone.

"Ophelia. Afraid to leave me alone with her?" His voice was bitter.

"It's not like that, man. I have a right to know, too. That's why I'm here." Ophelia's voice was gentler than Arden had expected, and she appreciated her not taking the bait. He looked at them both, measuring the extent to which they'd prejudged him. Ophelia pushed him a cider, which he received as a peace offering. He opened the can and drank deeply.

"I'm sorry," he began, looking at both of them. "I'm sorry that my past mistakes hurt the movement and hurt you, and I was too much of a coward and too egotistical to face up to them. You told me once, Arden, that you were glad to have no more secrets, that there was a freedom in it. I want that now. I'll tell you what happened at Williams, and I hope at some point you'll forgive me and that I won't have completely discredited our work. It's out of my hands now."

He sat down at the kitchen table. It took him a mere twenty minutes to tell the story of Penny Nordin, his freshman entanglement. She had been seventeen, he twenty-one. She had pursued him, and he had put her off for months. They'd gotten together at a party, when they'd both been pretty drunk, a grievous lapse in judgment on his part on many levels. He was her dorm residential advisor, an older student given free board in exchange for living in the dorms with the freshmen. In addition, he was captain of the crew team, on which she was a member. She was attending Williams on a crew scholarship as the coxswain for the men's crew team. Kirish had to explain the role of the coxswain: to call and direct the rowing, keeping time and motivating rowers, all the while preferably weighing exactly 125 pounds. With their one encounter, he got her pregnant. Because she was a minor, the clinic where she went to terminate the pregnancy was required by law to notify her parents. They objected to the abortion on religious grounds, and as a result the girl was unable to proceed. The parents filed a complaint with the school against him. He had been in a position of power over her, they had argued, as her RA and captain of the sports team on which her scholarship required she play. Moreover, the age difference between them made him guilty of statutory rape, the parents claimed. In Massachusetts, the age of consent was sixteen—however, an old law on the books raised the age of consent to eighteen if the victim is "of a chaste life" and the offender induces her to have sexual intercourse.

Although the girl had refused to testify in the proceedings and would not make a statement against Kirish, the allegation of statutory rape unfortunately required inquiry into whether she had previously led a chaste life, which indeed, she had not. Kirish was cleared of the statutory rape charges but was suspended for sexual misconduct under Williams's strict code of student conduct, which required explicit consent that could not be given when under the influence of alcohol. Moreover, the differential in power between them was found to have created an environment of duress, despite the evidence that she had pursued him. He was permitted to graduate but was banned from campus for the remainder of his senior year, having to complete his remaining classwork online. The girl dropped out and gave the baby up for adoption. The adoptive parents had asked Kirish to give up all rights to the child, which he had agreed to do.

"That story sucks," Ophelia exhaled. "You had to slut shame her? Because that's what this looks like, you know. A chaste life! And crew? You were seriously her crew coach? Do you know how fucking WASPy that is? Jeesh!"

"Not her coach," he corrected her, with an edge in his voice, "merely a student who had been elected captain, for no money, in a figurehead leadership role. And yes, I am aware that the story does not paint me in a flattering light."

Arden asked, "Have you been in touch with Penny? What's her side of the story?"

"I don't know. I don't think I'm supposed to contact her. I assume that the newspapers will try. Maybe one of you could . . . just even to give her a heads up that they'll be calling," he replied, looking sad.

"You know," Ophelia mused, "under the student code of conduct, supposedly there can be no consent if someone is drunk? Well, weren't both of you drunk?"

"Yes."

"So it's a double standard? Applied only to women? Because, *Oh, we can't be trusted to speak our minds? Oh, we get swept away?*" Ophelia had applied a bad Southern accent to the last part of her rant, and laid the back of her hand across her forehead. Her rendition of *Gone with the Wind*.

"I'm sure if a man claimed lack of consent due to intoxication, or someone claimed it on his behalf, as here, that the school would apply the standard evenly. No one was asserting lack of consent on my part," he replied stiffly.

"But you could have."

"Yes, I suppose, if I wanted to make the whole thing even more ridiculous."

"Well, it might have gotten you out of the sexual misconduct stuff," Ophelia muttered. "That's not seeming so ridiculous to me at this moment."

As Kirish sat across the table from them, he sighed and hung his head. "She was a minor," his voice was muffled until he raised his head to continue, looking out the darkened window. "She was a student entrusted to my care, as her RA. She looked up to me as team captain. I didn't feel it was right to try to get out of it. I screwed up. People got hurt. I'm not going to cop to some kind of excuse. I made that decision. I put myself in the situation where that is the decision I would make. I did it, and I'm going to have to live with it. Just like she's going to have to live with it."

After that, they all sat there in silence. Arden knew that Kirish was waiting for her reaction, but she was still processing how she felt. She felt a surge of anger toward the boy she'd woken up with after her drunken night, and knew that at some stage, intoxication did cancel out the ability to give consent. Had Kirish taken advantage of the girl? How drunk was she? How drunk was he? Did that absolve both of them of their bad decisions, or only her?

If so, why the double standard? Did it absolve Arden's college assailant, if that's what he was? Arden could not resolve her conflicting emotions.

She looked up finally, meeting his eyes. "Thank you for telling me. It's still sinking in, but I can see your side of things. I can understand how something like that could happen, I guess. From the other side, I mean."

He looked horrified. "This has happened to you?"

"Not exactly," Arden answered, and said no more.

When it was clear that she wasn't planning to share that story, Kirish stood and paced around the small kitchen and then headed to the door. He stopped with his hand on the doorknob, then turned and leaned back against the door, looking bone tired.

"I came back because I want to repair whatever damage I can that this caused to 99, and because I think you asked me to, in your voicemail. But I want you to tell me—tomorrow, before I go to the office, preferably—whether that's what you want. If you say the word, I will give a press conference and own up to this. I know that Nassert has ideas about how to make this work in our favor, which I know we both . . . we all"—he added Ophelia here—"have serious reservations about. But if you want me to go, Arden"—now speaking only to her—"if this is too much, or if it taints what we've worked for too much, you tell me that, and I'm gone."

She nodded, hoping he wasn't expecting her to make up her mind at that moment. He paused, watching her, understanding that she wasn't ready. His expression twisted up; he looked angry and pained. Arden imagined he was furious with himself for this mess, but also hurt that she hadn't forgiven him yet. But this was just speculation. And then there was a flash of bitterness in his eyes as he looked at the two women, as if he felt he was being unfairly blamed, again. Though he had said he accepted responsibility, there must be some part of him that was still pissed at the girl, at his shitty luck in her having religious parents, the unwanted pregnancy, the school, the bad odds. It was this bitterness, the *poor me* look in his eye, that turned her away from him. She felt it like a hardening in her frontal lobe, the judgment forming, and she shook her head, trying to forestall having an opinion, until she was alone in the dark and could think.

Kirish turned and walked out the door without another word. Ophelia, uncharacteristically, didn't have much to say, and Arden was locking the door behind her just a few minutes later. She washed the few dirty dishes in the sink, brushed her teeth, and flipped off the lights, listening for noises from Kirish's downstairs apartment but hearing none.

When she climbed into bed, she felt a strange communion with him, there in the building below. She imagined she could feel emotional turmoil radiating from him. Did he regret coming back? He had said that he'd come back because she had asked him to, in her voicemail. She didn't remember doing that. Had he returned because she meant something to him? Or did he feel like he owed it to her, because they had created 99 together?

CHAPTER 22

THE SENATOR'S WIFE

ARDEN SLEPT BADLY THAT NIGHT, and when she was still awake at five in the morning, she texted Kirish: *I'm still processing, but I think you should stay, at least to present a united front through this storm.* She knew he was an early riser, and that he'd need an answer when he woke so he could plan his day. She didn't relish the idea of seeing him in the morning, and felt a text would buy her more time. After sending the message, she fell into a deep sleep, ended only at eleven thirty when Ophelia was banging on her door.

"People are freaking out that you're not there. Kirish is telling them you've signed off on his coming back and the group is planning a response, but they need to see you, hear it from you. Is it true? Why are you still home?" Ophelia bombarded her with words as she pushed through the door.

"Yeah, of course it's true. I needed to sleep. I was up late."

"Alone?" Ophelia eyed her.

"Yes," Arden hissed, stomping off to the shower.

Twenty minutes later, they were at covert head-quarters, walking into a tense scene. Kirish, Jennifer, Andrew, and Jeremy were behind the closed door of the conference room, but the fifteen or so volunteers at various tasks in the lobby and phone bank whipped their heads around to watch as Arden walked through the lobby and made her way to the conference room. She worked to keep her expression calm, knowing that everyone was trying to read her face for some sign of her reaction to the scandal. She herself still didn't know. Although all her instincts begged her to slip quietly into the conference room and shut the door behind her, she stopped short outside the room. She turned back to the volunteers, recognizing some of the original coverts, their earliest supporters, watching her and Ophelia walk through the office.

"Thanks to all of you for being here today," she began. Her throat was froggy; she hadn't spoken more than a few words yet this morning. She cleared her throat. "This is an important day. We hope this will be a turning point, so we can put some things behind us and refocus our work. As I know each of you is acutely aware, we have seven days until voters head to the polls. We've lost important early voting time with this distraction. We need to double down on our get-out-the-vote work and amplify our message in these final days. We"—she jerked a thumb at the conference room, as the door opened and Andrew looked out—"we are going to put our heads together about that message. Together with Kirish, who has returned. Soon, we'll be back to you with the information you need to do your work, which is truly our most important work. . . ."

She trailed off, feeling the team's attention shift. Kirish had stepped out of the conference room and was standing beside her. Arden had a flash of the senator's wife.

"Thanks, Arden," he said simply. He tilted his body toward the conference room, as if to indicate politely that she should go first, but she stayed stock still, facing the small crowd. If he wanted to stand beside her, he'd have to be part of this attempt to soothe the team. She tilted her head, looking at him. He got the cue, and addressed the coverts.

"I'm back to do whatever I can to fix the damage I caused. I need to talk with the leadership to figure out the best way to do that, but I am committed to doing it. I am truly sorry for the distraction and for undermining Voter Initiative 99, which I still believe deeply in. As Arden said, we will come back to you soon with our plan."

Again, Kirish inclined his body toward the conference room, this time with a relieved look on his face, not smiling but regarding her with warmth.

"Payback for the Legacy Foundation?" he whispered as she walked past him. Arden ignored him. *Hardly*, she thought to herself. She sat down at the table.

"What's the *proposed* plan?" Arden was in no mood to be diplomatic. She knew they'd been hashing out a plan since nine o'clock, and she wanted to establish her veto power at the outset. Kirish had given her that power last night, or maybe it was just hers to take. She didn't relish a clash with Andrew and Jeremy, but she agreed with Ophelia that the ends might not justify the means.

Jennifer Walton laid out the plan. They were expecting the story to hit the online press today, and print media tomorrow. They were set to hold a press conference, here in the headquarters, tomorrow morning, where Kirish would tell his story. This would include a closely scripted version of the Williams story, the offer of the Wentworth Brown job, which he'd first declined, then was re-offered with a threat to reveal his past. His mother's cancer. His belief that quietly leaving the campaign would be less harmful than a scandal, which he now sees was a miscalculation. Arden's call to ask him to return.

Next, Jennifer continued, one of the coverts' leaders, preferably Arden, would then speak in support of Kirish. That speaker would highlight the dark forces at work to maintain the status quo, to keep government in the hands of corporate special interests. Possibly they would include a jab at Williams for releasing details on what was supposed to have been a strictly sealed private proceeding intended to protect the privacy of both students. They would close with something moving about people not being defined by their past mistakes but rather by their actions for the greater good.

When Jennifer concluded, everyone around the table turned to look at Arden. She took a long moment imagining herself giving that speech.

"What's Plan B?" she asked and saw Kirish flinch. There was a silence. "Listen, I know that we only want to do this if it's going to be more good than bad. Jennifer's plan is going to alienate some contingent of people—probably mostly women, who have a modern view on consent. I like those voters. I want them on our side. How do we keep them, make them understand? What's the scenario in which we don't support Kirish in the same way? What if I only make the *dark corporate forces* comment, and say that the scandal has been an unfortunate distraction from our work, as its masterminds intended? Challenge voters to make up their mind about 99 for themselves, and not to be manipulated?"

"We did discuss this previously, Arden," Jennifer responded tersely. "We lose the ability to ride the backlash to the same extent if we just encourage voters to keep focused on the policy. Frankly, the policy is too wonky and complicated for most of the general population. You can't expect people to come out on principle for something they don't entirely understand. Anger is going to be what motivates people who wouldn't otherwise vote to go to the polls."

Ophelia cut in, "For the record, I don't necessarily agree that coming out in support of Kirish does that. I mean, you're calibrating to get the support of disenfranchised misogynist dudes? Is that what *riding the backlash* is supposed to be code for?" Her voice had so much contempt in it that people looked shocked.

Although Arden felt the same about the opportunistic strategy, she also feared it was their only way to win. It was strange for her to have someone, Ophelia, be the more idealistic one. She felt the prickly frisson of a compromise: a bit guilty, a bit embarrassed, but it seemed the obvious course. She stalled with a technical question: "What are the demographics again of the voters we think we have, and those we think we can get?"

Based on their informal polling, Jennifer explained that working class, high-school educated white men, representing 30 percent of the state's population, were most likely to vote for 99, but also many were not "likely voters" in that they didn't necessarily make a habit of voting and might not be registered. She was betting that those voters would be galvanized by the blackmail story, and by the Williams story. Of likely voters, Republican college-educated women had been polling in the negative on 99, and Democrat college-educated women (not a large number in the primarily Republican state) had been polling fifty-fifty in favor–against. According to the most recent census, less than 30 percent of the state's population had completed a college bachelor's degree. The state was roughly 40 percent white collar, 60 percent blue collar.

"Arden, we all get it that we risk alienating educated women," Jennifer answered, "but chances are, they're not voting for us anyway."

Arden said, "Are you discounting the impact on the youth vote? Because I think things are changing with younger voters in a way that your old polling models won't capture. For instance, did you poll by calling people's landlines? Because that's going to cut out everyone under thirty."

"Even so," Jennifer allowed, "we think when men, and many women, hear the facts of what happened at Williams, they'll be on Kirish's side. We think people have gotten to the point where they want to understand the facts before rushing to judgment on something like this. We've all seen it used as a political weapon too many times to take anything at face value. And if we aren't there supporting him, standing up against the abuse, it looks like we know something they don't, that he is really to blame. People will suspect they're not getting the whole story."

"And are they getting the whole story?" Jeremy Hatch inserted coolly. "Do we know that Penny Nordin isn't going to pop up with a different version of the story? Do we know there aren't outstanding child-support payments, or an assault charge? Sorry, Kirish, but you haven't been the model of transparency to date."

"You're getting my whole story, which is the only one I know," Kirish responded quietly. "I think I see it clearly, but can anyone ever know that for sure? I suggest that someone call Penny, to see what she will do."

"There are risks associated with calling her, that we might draw her out of the woodwork," Jennifer warned them. "But fine, if people want to do that, we can discuss it. Regardless, I think at this point, with time being short, we should operate as if we have all the facts and make a decision about how to proceed. Arden, will you make the statement? There are a lot of reasons it would be best if it was you. You're the other face of 99. There's the back-story of a possible relationship between you two." Jennifer smirked at their flinches of discomfort. "What? Well, there is. I really don't care if it's true or not. It's been suggested. You two started this thing. If it's not you, Arden, it simply won't be as believable. There will be speculation about why it wasn't you. More noise."

"I'll do it," Arden said, exchanging a meaningful look with Ophelia. "But I'm not promising to read your script. I'll do it in a way that feels right to me. And you have to orchestrate it in a way that I'm not standing beside him. He walks up to the podium, he walks back. Then I walk up." Kirish looked like he'd just been punched. "It's the cheating senator and his dutiful wife—the photo op the media will all be looking for. *I've forgiven him and so should you.* To be avoided," Arden explained, knowing she sounded unforgiving and stone cold.

Arden knew that they had lost crucial time in reaching voters. They had to make a splash with the press confer-ence, and put the whole dirty business behind them. If Arden had to play a role, so be it. She was glad Kirish had come back to try to make things right, but worried that it would be too little, too late.

CHAPTER 23
ELECTION DAY

ELECTION DAY DAWNED COLD AND SHARP. Arden woke early, on just a few hours of sleep, and went to the Church Street headquarters. She sat for five or ten minutes, quietly, thinking of how far they'd come, before the others arrived, first a trickle, then a flood of volunteers. They all knew their job, and got right to work. She didn't have much to say—her voice had gone hoarse from the last week—but shook hand after hand with a quiet and urgent thank you for each of the volunteers. Today was the day.

As planned after Kirish's return the previous week, they had implemented Option A. They were shocked at how many reporters showed up for the press conference they'd announced just the day before, upon Kirish's arrival from DC. Arden remembered them all jammed in the very room where she stood, now filling up with volunteers. It had been horrible to listen to Kirish tell his story, so sordid and stupid, so beneath who she thought he was. His apology diminished him. And her follow-up address was a sham. She shuddered to remember the feeling she had, as she'd fumbled through the address Jennifer had written for her. She'd felt ashamed of herself, not for backing Kirish, but for agreeing to follow the script, especially after declaring she would do it her own way. It had seemed too fraught, too important to leave to chance, and she didn't trust herself not to screw it up. But the words sounded phony, as she recited them, and Arden was certain no one else was convinced either.

Although her words on behalf of the coverts had supported him, she had not joined Kirish at the podium that day. At least that principle she stuck to. It had been a silent reproach that she waited until he stepped away, and waited another beat for the podium to stand empty, before she walked slowly up. She could feel that he hadn't forgiven her for it. But to her mind, he didn't have the right to be angry. She was the one being forced to publicly support him, for show.

The scandal had dominated the media cycle for five days, and then seemed to clear, just two days before Election Day. Coverts still fielded questions about the scandal, on GOTV calls, but it seemed most voters had made up their minds that it was a smear job and decided to believe that Kirish had done nothing wrong. They had never been able to get hold of the girl, Penny Nordin, and she hadn't emerged with recriminations, as they'd feared. Her name had not been released by the media. Although Kirish had been careful to present only the necessary facts, more details had emerged from the school report that had been leaked, and there had been the public back-and-forth of victim blaming and condemnation of Kirish.

The noontime Election Day rally at the capitol building in Pierre was widely televised but less well attended than they had hoped. The small crowd was most enthusiastic when Kirish came to the podium. There were catcalls when he was announced, and deep cries of "We got you, bro!" when he thanked the crowd for the warm welcome, "especially since I've been away."

The enthusiasm waned somewhat when he launched into an explanation of what would happen after 99 was passed. Some in the crowd looked puzzled or worried when he talked about the redistribution process. Arden herself felt worried about what would happen if they won. Worried that they'd come so far only to face defeat in the courts. Worried that, even if 99 survived legal challenge, things would be worse, and they'd been wrong about there being a better way. As she watched the politicos in their business suits hurrying past into the state capitol building, scowling at the coverts, Arden worried that she'd oversimplified things, that she'd romanticized a long-past way of life. Yes, perhaps once there hadn't been the heavy influence of corporations on the American government that there was now. But also, no penicillin. No cars. No internet. She was reminded of something she'd learned in Philosophy 101, something from Hobbes about the reason for government and the social contract: the natural state of human life was solitary, poor, nasty, brutish, and short. Were they taking a step backward? Were they riding a wave of reactionary, misogynist ignorance?

Unfortunately, Arden was up next to speak. Kirish seemed to read her reluctance to come to the elevated stage as continuing unwillingness to stand by his side and gave her a baleful look as he stepped slowly down. She grabbed him as he reached the bottom of the steps, squeezing his wiry bicep, and saying in a low voice, "I'm scared. What if we're wrong?"

He grasped both of her hands with his and leaned down so he was speaking directly into her ear. "This is an experiment. South Dakota is the laboratory. This is how the states are supposed to work. We try things. If it doesn't work, things can be put back the way they were." She nodded. "But this is a good idea," he continued urgently. "This is your vision of a better way." She nodded again and allowed him to gently push her past him and up the stairs.

She stepped behind the podium to modest applause. She cleared her throat to begin, but she was at a loss for what to say. Perhaps it was a testament to her finally getting used to public speaking that she hadn't thought to pre- pare something for this occasion, or perhaps she was just burnt out. In her mind, she ran through her various stories and talking points, well-worn from months on the stump. Nothing seemed fitting. Sweat pricked her armpits. She saw people in the audience checking their phones, looking away.

"What we are proposing, it's . . . something new," she stammered. "And no one knows exactly where it will lead." Her voice sounded as thin and uncertain as she felt, and she shivered in the cold wind. She tried again, more strongly now, stronger than she felt. "But we *do* know where we are now, and many of us feel that it is not doing us justice." Although she didn't even know what she was going to say next, she kept talking. So what if it was off-script, it felt good to simply speak her mind.

"Our efforts should be our own. Our failures are our own. Our disappointments are our own. I want our work to be our own, the fruits of my labor to be my own."

Scattered applause encouraged her. "I want the gov- ernment to do my bidding, not that of corporate interests."

Arden thought about their path to this point, how the coverts had built up so much momentum, only to have it smashed by Kirish and his secrets. Then his return, the reversal of fortunes that had brought. How uneasy she felt about that connection.

"This is our chance to take things back. To take back the land and the profits that should be ours." Arden thought of Emma here and sent out a silent wish that her farm be returned to her, imagining that the gathering energy of the crowd had some force that could be channeled.

"And even if we fail," she continued, her voice building, "either at the ballot or later, our work together on Initiative 99 has been an exercise of our collective power. I urge every one of you"—Arden looked directly into the TV camera in the front row—"for whom this idea touches your imagination, to use that power." She envisioned her words flowing through the camera, into people's living rooms, electrical impulses traveling through time and space, sparking change.

"Perhaps you don't usually bother to vote, because you think it doesn't really make a difference. And you're probably right. Your single vote for any given politician, does it stand up to campaign contributions and lobbyists and influence for sale? No, it doesn't. But that's not how our country is supposed to work." Arden heard a resonance in her voice that felt powerful.

"And you know what? Corporations don't have a vote today." The crowd suddenly went wild. The roar startled Arden, she'd been imagining the faraway abstract audience and had been in a trance forgetting the live crowd. She raised her chin as the energy of the cheers and applause washed over her. She imagined that it lifted her, carrying away her insecurities, her stage fright, her grudges.

"You may have little power in your lives," she said, and like a conductor she could see those words bring down the intensity of the crowd, "but *you* have the power *here*." They surged, lifted up again.

"At the ballot, that is the place where we the people, the real people, have the power. It is your say, yea or nay, that decides our future. If you haven't already, get out and vote. *Yes on 99!*"

As Arden stepped off the stage, she could feel the reverberations of the crowd's cheers in her bones, and imagined it as energy that she had drawn from the crowd. She felt she'd broken through something, and hoped that it would last, that next time she spoke to an audience, she could channel this feeling again. She felt the incredible honor it was to have people's attention, and how lucky she was to have a platform to talk about her ideas.

Later, at covert headquarters, Jeremy sought her out to congratulate her. Even more than the other compliments about the speech, and there were many, Jeremy's meant a lot because she knew he'd tell her if it stunk. But she didn't need the compliments, or even Jeremy's validation. She knew it was great.

"Well, there," Ophelia had hugged her, "you finally figured out how to work an audience, just in time for this thing to be over."

The crowd at headquarters that night was thick and rowdy, which Andrew assured her was a good sign. "Campaign volunteers are like sharks—they can smell blood in the water."

The polls closed at seven o'clock, first in the central time zone areas of the state, with more than 60 percent of the population, covering Pierre, Aberdeen, and Sioux Falls. Then the western third of the state, home to Rapid City, Spearfish, and many of the Native American reservations, closed one hour later, on mountain time. Voting tallies started coming in around nine, with smaller towns reporting first. Although they all knew that the cities would be much closer, it was exhilarating to see the small-town votes rolling in strongly in favor of Initiative 99—67 percent, 56 percent, 71 percent! The results jumped around early on, with a small sample size, but began firming up in the neighborhood of 59 percent. Not enough, they worried, to carry the vote over the expected corporate-friendly and high-population Sioux Falls. The credit card industry, the top employer in Sioux Falls, had come out strongly against 99 in the last two weeks of the campaign with Unibank leading the charge, arguing it would cause massive layoffs and crater property values in the metro area if the banks were forced to pull out. Probably true in the short term, but affordable property values would benefit many, Arden reasoned.

As expected, Sioux Falls voters did not support Initiative 99, although the margins were closer than they'd expected. Local newscasters speculated, based on exit polls, that there had been a stronger turnout of age twenty-five and younger voters, and lower turnout of older voters, since it was a midterm election—no presidential candidates on the ballot to drive turnout. After Sioux Falls and then Pierre, Initiative 99 was no longer carrying the majority of voters needed to pass, hovering at 48 percent. The coverts waited anxiously as the assorted districts ticked in, not moving the needle, waiting on Rapid City and the Native American districts, an hour behind and slow to tally.

Arden could barely breathe as they crowded around the TV, listening to the Sioux Falls newscasters speculating about what looked to be a narrow defeat.

"Listen, there are about thirty thousand Native Americans registered to vote in the state, and we have really strong polling among the tribes," Andrew reminded them as he turned the TV down during a commercial. "Almost two thousand of those were folks we helped to get registered, and we provided assistance with absentee ballots to almost five thousand Native Americans. We're feeling really strong about our support with indigenous voters, and with the new South Dakota Voter Rights Improvement Act for Tribes, many see this as their first chance to affect the outcome on an issue of national interest. The tribes see this as a big *fuck you* to Washington. Many Native Americans are still furious about the Dakota Access Pipeline. Those of you who were with me at the Standing Rock Sioux Tribal Nation meeting in May saw that firsthand. Many tribal leaders see corporations as an extension of government corruption."

Although Arden had missed the Standing Rock meeting, she thought of her visit to the Great Plains Tribal Chairmen's Association, and about her allegory of the parasite. She wondered if that idea had gone out into the world and taken root, like 99 had.

Andrew glanced back at the still muted television and continued, "Moreover, Rapid City is much less beholden to mega-corporations for employment. Its economy is more diversified with tourism, agriculture, and small businesses that would easily transition from corporate-owned to people-owned. Many companies in the western part of the state, except for the oil and gas, and mining operations, are owner operated. It was difficult, but I think we got those folks comfortable that 99 would not take their businesses away. Many are still uneasy, but they also see the upside, not having to compete with the mega-corps."

"How many votes do we need?" someone called out.

Andrew answered with a nod, "Of the 800,000 South Dakota residents, there are almost 530,000 registered to vote. 150,000 Dems, 250,000 Republicans, and 120,000 Independents. If you assume a fifty percent voter turnout, which is common for years without a presidential election, that means there will be about 265,000 people voting. We need fifty-one percent of votes cast, maybe 135,000. Yeah, Sioux Falls is the biggest city, but it's only 153,000 total population to Rapid City's 70,000. And though we didn't carry Sioux Falls," he continued, checking his laptop, "we did get thirty-two percent. That's probably around 25,000 people if we get a fifty-percent voter turnout. And remember, we only need a simple majority of people voting statewide. We're still in the game."

The coverts were cheered by this. After all, Andrew was the pro. Arden and Kirish exchanged encouraged glances from across the crowd, and he smiled at her. This was a relief; things had been awkward between them since his return. Arden had been subdued the last few days, tired, as they all were, but she was also still troubled by the political maneuvering around his return—though by all reports it had been successful. She knew it had been hard on him too. Arden thought of Kirish's kids, if he ever had more, reading the history of 99 and the scandal involving Penny Nordin and their father. Or what some future partner would make of it. If she were that person, that partner, how would she proceed? She entertained the thought for the briefest of moments, while they were still gazing at each other across the room, and then ducked her head and wheeled around, colliding with the person standing behind her.

"Whoa there!" It was Jim Bouchard, grabbing her elbow and steadying her. He grinned at her surprise.

"Jimmy!" she spluttered, "What?! What are you doing here?" She threw her arms around him, and he laughed loudly and squeezed her, lifting her feet almost off the ground. She fought loose, suddenly conscious that they were making a scene, and stepped back, patting his shoulder awkwardly. He looked bemused at her awkwardness.

"I was in the neighborhood and decided to stop by. You gave me the address a couple weeks back, remember?

I walked right in. Security here is shit." He glanced around the crowded room. "You don't mind, do you? Is this a private party?"

"No, of course not! It's great to see you!" Arden meant it. It took her mind off the unbearable suspense, showing him around the office, explaining the voter map and the GOTV process. She was glad for the distraction from staring at the local news and could gather from the cheers and the groans that the results kept rolling in.

"Have you seen Emma?" Arden asked. "I haven't seen her since the foreclosure hearing. She still won't pick up the phone when I call."

"I saw her last week. She's hanging in there. She was not happy about how widely the auction has been advertised, I guess because you kicked up a fuss about AGM at the hearing." He smiled gently down at her. "I tried to explain to her that it's a good thing. Better chance she'll get some money from the sale."

"What did she say to that?" Arden asked.

Jim pitched his voice to a growl and said, "Blood money." He tried to make it funny but she could hear Emma saying it, and it wasn't a joke.

"Well, shit," Arden sighed, "I did the best I could. I think if 99 passes, that should put the sale on hold, since it hasn't happened yet." She put a hand on his arm. "Thanks for checking on her. Sorry I haven't been around. Things have been so crazy."

"I heard," Jim said. "Are you okay?" She knew he was referring to the Kirish scandal.

"I am," Arden answered. "It's been . . . hard. I was really conflicted about how we should respond. How did it seem to you? Did you follow the coverage?"

Jimmy pursed his lips. "Seems like that guy had some bad luck."

"Yeah." Arden thought of Penny Nordin. *She's the one with the bad luck.* She was glad when Ophelia came strolling up.

"Who's this, Arden?" Ophelia drawled, hand extended for shaking to Jimmy, who grabbed it and gave her a grin.

"Uh, Ophelia, this is Jim Bouchard. He's from near Badger, Emma's neighbor," Arden explained.

"Oh-ho, the horse guy!" Ophelia nodded knowingly, which of course Jim thought was hilarious.

"How is Nick?" Arden asked, mostly to get them to stop laughing at her.

"He's fine, thank you," Jim said, fighting back his laughter and rocking back on his heels. "He misses you."

Arden knew she was going to pay for this later when Ophelia got her alone.

A loud cheer erupted from the crowd around the television, and they all rushed over to see. Rapid City results were in, and they'd carried it by 8 percent. The statewide total was now an unbearable 50 percent, with 99 ahead by a mere twenty voters. Most of the cities and towns in the state had reported, with only a handful of towns and tribes remaining, the Standing Rock Sioux among them. An incredulous blond anchorwoman on the local news read from her teleprompter that it was believed that this could be the first ballot initiative in any state that could be decided by the votes of a Native American tribe. The camera cut to a political party leader talking about the difficulty with verifying tribal votes, considering the problems with voter identification, especially with the Standing Rock Sioux, whose reservation straddled the South Dakota border with North Dakota. "Many Standing Rock Sioux claim citizenship in both states," he sniffed. The coverts booed loudly at the television.

"Asshole," Jimmy snorted.

The television then cut to grainy footage from a poorly lit town hall, with the caption "Standing Rock Reservation Polling Place" at the bottom. A Native American man in a blue business suit with a red-and-white feather headdress stepped before the microphone at a low podium, with a serious look on his face. "I'm Daniel Grass, of the Standing Rock Tribal Council. Announcing the election results for the Standing Rock Sioux Tribal residents on *Proposition 99, Voter Initiative To Abolish Corporations*. One thousand and forty-nine votes in favor of the initiative. Zero votes against. This is for you, Energy Transfer Partners." He gave a curt nod and the video feed cut back to the stunned blond anchorwoman.

"I'm being told this puts our tally at 133,569 votes for Initiative Number 99, and 132,317 votes against! That's ninety-six percent of the precincts reporting. My goodness, this is a close one! That was Daniel Grass of the Standing Rock Tribe delivering a message to corporate America, specifically to the Texas-based Energy Transfer Partners, developer of the Dakota Access Pipeline, which the Sioux nation gained national attention protesting in 2016. . . ."

Covert headquarters erupted, with people shrieking and jumping up and down. Arden was caught up in hug after hug, then was propelled toward a camera crew rolling film and pressing a microphone in her face.

"Arden Firth, how are you feeling right now?"

She babbled something predictable about their hard work paying off, thanking the coverts and the Lakota Sioux Tribes, and then grabbed Jennifer and pushed her in front of the camera. Arden fought her way through the crowd to find Kirish and Ophelia, who had tears streaming down her face.

"Holy shit!!!!" Ophelia blubbered, "I can't believe we did it! So amazing that the tribes came in to close the gap!" Andrew and Jeremy joined them with a bottle of champagne and plastic cups, popping the cork and sloshing the frothy warm wine on their hands as they all laughed. Arden saw Jimmy hanging back in the fringe and pulled him into their circle, passing him her cup and filling another.

After the Standing Rock Sioux announcement, victory seemed all but assured, and the celebration went late into the night, with someone bringing in beer and pizza and more cheap champagne.

Arden was ecstatic—she felt that the vote, however uncertain it had seemed or how dirty the media campaign had felt at the end, was a referendum. Yes, it reflected the opinions of so many people, for many different reasons, but those opinions, all together, must represent the right direction. The only off note was Kirish. He was happy, but she could tell he felt isolated. He was downright rude when introduced to Jimmy, and treated him like he was some kind of interloper. The last week had been hard on Kirish. His face was gaunt, and it was clear that the experience had taken a toll on his pride. He performed, as promised, stumping as he had earlier that day at the capitol. But he was otherwise withdrawn, not returning to his former leadership role. Arden knew she could have helped steer him back into the fold, but she had not done so. If it was hard for him, if he'd lost ground or confidence or credibility, it was his own doing.

Arden wasn't so angry anymore about the Williams incident, but she couldn't forgive him for hiding behind it, using it to keep her and everyone away. It was his pride, ultimately, that had caused the real scandal, though she wondered whether the blackmail had actually made him a hero in the eyes of the public. *We got you, bro!*, the crowd this morning had chanted. Perhaps he would have been more humiliated, in the end, if not for the blackmail making him a martyr. But why had he been so closed, so secretive about it—was it guilt or resentment? Why had he been so sure that he'd be misjudged, that Arden couldn't be trusted with the story? The fact that he'd been so keen to draw out and lay bare Arden's secrets at the Legacy Foundation made it all the more unforgivable.

She'd never gone back to him after that night in her apartment when he'd asked for her forgiveness, with Ophelia there chaperoning, and it seemed that part of his isolation was the fact that she had not granted pardon. Should she now release him, now that they'd won? Had he not made amends by coming back to the campaign, helping them win, and doing what she'd asked of him? Part of her wanted to reach out to him, thank him, but she found that she could not. What was her problem? What stopped her? If she were entirely honest with herself, it was the feeling that if he hadn't had his deep, dark secret, and if he hadn't let it scar him so that he was too afraid to engage, something more than a friendship could have grown between them. But instead, he always left her with the feeling that he wasn't interested in her and didn't really like her. Now, when it was too late, it seemed to her that maybe all that hadn't been true. And whatever attraction she'd felt for him had been doused with cold water because she was supposed to feel sorry for him now, because he'd been nursing a trauma of his own making.

Kirish watched her across the room with Jimmy, as if he had a prior claim on her. Was he actually sulking? Arden was exasperated. Seeing that the clock on the wall above the conference room read almost 1:00 a.m., she told Jimmy, "Don't go anywhere," and began the lengthy process of making the rounds to say her goodbyes. She'd already decided she was heading to Badger tomorrow to see Emma and maybe do some horseback riding. Maybe see what else developed.

As she worked her way through the now thinning crowd, she looked over at Jimmy, in an animated conversation with Ophelia, both talking over each other. He caught O's wrist to stabilize her as she lurched, laughing, with his easy way. Arden was glad he was here, that he'd hung around even though she'd been entirely focused on 99 since they'd met. She looked again at the clock, thinking of her texts with Jim when she had been too busy with the campaign, realizing with a smile that this was the date they had promised to have on November 8.

CHAPTER 24   AFTERGLOW

AFTER THE VICTORY PARTY, ARDEN HAD invited Jimmy to sleep on the couch in her apartment. Once she stepped over the threshold, now close to two in the morning, exhaustion overtook her. She found some blankets and a pillow for him, and sat in his lap for a hug on the couch. He stroked back her hair, kissed her forehead and then her mouth, slowly. She felt her intention to go to bed alone waver with that kiss, but then he said, "Congratulations," and stood up, gently displacing her. She was glad to have the spell broken, because she was bone-tired, and wanted their first time together to have her complete attention.

When she woke late the next morning, he'd left her a note that he'd had to leave to get back to his job but hoped he would see her in Badger soon. She wondered if he had picked up on Kirish's strange behavior the night before, but decided it had probably been too subtle to be apparent, amid the chaotic celebration.

Arden packed her things for Badger, and then headed to Church Street, stopping on her way for a quick visit to Ophelia's apartment. Her friend was still in bed, happily nursing a hangover and watching news coverage, both local and national, of the Election Day results. Initiative 99 was mentioned often, with Ophelia carrying on a running commentary of "You got that right," and "You just wait!" Arden hugged her and promised to return after Thanksgiving; she felt a bit guilty for not inviting Ophelia to come with her, but she needed some separation from the coverts. Headquarters was still empty at noon, but Arden felt like the picking up she did, putting plastic cups into a garbage bag, sweeping up confetti and detritus, was a goodbye. After half an hour of straightening up and basking in the glow of victory, she hit the road for Badger, leaving a note of farewell and thanks.

She stayed in Badger for almost three weeks, sleeping late, reading novels, and making pies with Emma. Their sole project was working with the law school clinic lawyers to file a motion to stop the foreclosure auction sale from being held, arguing that 99's passage should halt any corporate bank's rights. For once, talking with the lawyers was a joy.

She loved riding Nick slowly in the snow. She saw Jimmy only three times, and it was markedly low key. She got the sense he was intentionally waiting for some dust to settle in her life. Again, she appreciated his way of giving space and time, of letting things ripen. Maybe that was the farmer in him.

When she did see him, he was warm and immediate, taking her on long drives and holding her hand unself-consciously. He asked her about Kirish, how she felt about the last-minute scandal, and whether there was something between them. Arden tried to be honest, but it ended up sounding dodgy. She could neither confirm nor deny so many things.

The daydream of farming she'd had on their first date morphed into her sharing the Johnson farm with Jim, which he'd be awarded in the distribution of AGM's land. She imagined helping Emma in her orchard, with two horses and a couple of cows in the barn, and chickens in the coop. She found herself returning again and again to the idea, and the dream had such a warmth to it that she had to struggle not to treat it as a vision of the future.

The last evening they got together, they played pool at The Hall. Jimmy was beating her by a lot, when three men walked in. Jimmy knew them and returned their greetings warily. "You guys can have the table after this game, we're all done," he said, though he had already promised Arden a rematch. But then the men had offered to play doubles, and Arden jumped in to accept, enjoying the competition and the clack and rush of the game. After a few minutes of the doubles match, however, Arden realized why Jimmy had been trying to orchestrate an exit.

"Jimmy," one of them said, "you should come up and work in the shale-gas fields with us, you make *bank*, not like wasting your time down here plowing dirt."

"Ya, they're hiring at the pipeline too, I heard," said the other.

Jimmy shrugged and took his shot, hitting the ball too hard. "Nah, I guess I like being a hayseed." Arden had the sense this was not the first time they'd made this suggestion to him.

"Suit yourself," the first one shrugged, dismissively. He turned to Arden, "You're that Proposition 99 chick, aren't you?" one of them asked her, with a friendly smile.

"I sure am," she had smiled back, proudly, not bothering to correct him to "Initiative" or to take offense at "chick." "Did you guys vote for it?"

"I did. Just seemed to me like that guy got screwed. We can't let a guy's life get ruined like that. I felt like I needed to take a stand."

"What about the corporation ban?" she asked hoarsely, afraid of the answer.

The man shrugged and took his shot, banking the ball expertly into a side pocket. Arden stood quietly for a moment, then turned on her heel to stalk out the front door of the bar and stood outside, inhaling the cold air. Jimmy emerged a few minutes later, with her jacket, and they drove home mostly in silence. Although Arden knew that Jimmy had supported 99 for its substance, and had dreamed of what he'd do if it passed, she also remembered him saying something like, "that guy got screwed," just like the jerk playing pool. When he apologized for those guys, calling them meatheads, Arden wasn't proud of her response.

"Why apologize?" she responded acidly. "That's what you all think, isn't it?"

He looked sidelong at her, shaking his head. "You're going to put me in a bucket with those guys to make things easy for you, then? I've been wondering where you're headed, Arden. I would have expected something more honest from you."

Arden struggled to contain her frustration and rage. It was true: it wasn't Jim that she was angry at. She took a deep breath through clenched teeth. "I'm sorry," she managed to choke out. He looked at her, seeing how hard the apology was to pronounce.

"Why does it make you so mad? Everything about Kirish? Did you have a thing for him? Do you still?"

She couldn't answer the last two questions, so she attempted the first.

"The reason I worked so hard for 99 was because I saw it as a way to fight the worst part of what we are as people—the greed, the materialism, the selfishness. But if it passed not because other people felt the same way, but because they wanted to hit back at feminism or sexual-assault allegations, then I can't feel the same way about it. We were fighting the parasite." Arden swallowed, knowing that last bit wouldn't make sense to Jim. "But if we won because people came out for Kirish, *to defend him*, then the whole thing is garbage." The pool hall guys were poison.

"Naw," Jimmy said, "that's not what happened. You can't throw the whole thing away because you don't like some of its elements. You're the leader of this thing. Isn't it for you to say what it's about?"

Arden thought about becoming a leader, all she had learned, over the last year. It was incredible that her ideas had become so large, had really changed things. But she couldn't control the shape her ideas now took, because they were more than just her own. Did she still have the ability or the right to say what 99 meant anymore, now that it had been voted into law by 130,000 people? Did she have that power? Did it mean that she just had to ignore people like the pool hall guys? Or convince them? It shook her confidence in her own vision to have it miss the mark so entirely with people like that. But hadn't they known that not everyone would understand? That people were motivated by so many things. She owed it to herself to make sure that the things that motivated *her* were given a loud enough voice not to be drowned out by everything else.

She realized it was time to be getting back. They had won the first battle with 99's passage, but not the war. There was more work to do, and she had been away too long.

"What do you want out of your life, Arden? What's your next step?" Jimmy asked her. Had he sensed the shift in her?

"I need to see things through with 99. That is clear to me now."

"And what about after that?" Jimmy pressed. "I like you a lot, Arden Firth. More than like. I think we fit together. If you want the kind of life I do, the farming life, I know we could be real happy."

Arden thought about her fantasy of farming with him. She could feel her body warming when she thought of a life with him. They would be happy with each other. But could she be happy in Badger? Would it be enough for her, after 99?

"I like you a lot too. But as far as what kind of life I want . . . I don't know."

He nodded, apparently unsurprised. "When you figure that out, darlin', you know where to find me."

IT WAS TIME TO GO BACK TO VERMILLION. Ophelia called again to ask her to return, to say that they needed her to be there for the legal challenges that had begun almost immediately. There were still strategy calls to make, and hearings and press interviews. Arden's job hadn't ended with the vote. The story had not yet been fully written on 99.

Arden packed up and returned to her apartment, arriving in the evening and parking her car on the street dusted with snow. She heard Kirish in his apartment below, playing music and slamming cabinets.

In the morning, she headed to 99 headquarters, walking slowly in the biting cold. She knew it was time to return, but it wasn't clear to her what she was supposed to do. The coverts were now a skeleton crew, with only

Kirish and Jeremy occupying the large space. Ophelia was rarely there; she was busy cramming for finals trying to make up for long hours spent on the campaign away from her studies. Andrew, Jennifer, and the rest of the Government for the People volunteers had gone back to Massachusetts. Kirish was busy on conference calls with lawyers, reviewing briefs and directing legal research. He was crisp and unemotional in bringing Arden up to speed on recent developments and their strategy for dealing with the legal challenges. She noted a difference in his tone— not rude, but more authoritative. During the campaign, he had deferred to Arden because of her South Dakotan status and connection to the voter base, and because 99 had been her idea. Perhaps also because he had a secret that made him hesitant to be too central to the movement. Then after the scandal, he had been chagrined and doing penance. Now, with the legal phase of the campaign in full swing, Kirish was clearly calling the shots.

When they were alone together, however, Kirish still seemed to be nursing his wounds. He gave her an exaggeratedly wide berth in the kitchen when they were both making tea, being overly formal with "thank you" and "excuse me." As always, he made no offer of small talk or personal details, and neither did Arden. But she kept catching him watching her, with what she read to be reproach in his gaze. To her annoyance, he still seemed to be waiting for forgiveness. Or was he looking for an apology? Why did the two feel like the same thing to her?

Despite all this, Arden was grateful for Kirish; she saw how much they needed his expertise as he managed their response to the numerous legal issues that had arisen. After Election Day, there had been immediate lawsuits filed to prevent Initiative 99 from going into effect, and to keep the lockdown period (preventing corporations from selling their assets before 99 was implemented) from being enforced. There was also a recount action, challenging the tribal votes as invalid. Later in November, the more formal lawsuits were filed, alleging the state and federal unconstitutionality of 99. As expected, the opposition campaign alleged that it violated the interstate commerce rule and due process, was a governmental taking without just compensation, and impeded the political speech of corporations.

Although the coverts had sponsored 99, it was legally considered an action of the state as a voter-initiated law. Once passed by the voters it became a state statute, and therefore it fell to the South Dakota Attorney General to defend 99 in the courts. The attorney general and his political party's elite had hardly been supporters of 99, however, so the coverts sought to intervene to defend 99. They believed that the attorney general would not aggressively or effectively defend the corporation ban and redistribution, but rather would let it succumb to these legal challenges. Kirish and Arden were named as petitioners, together with the ballot committee the coverts had formed to advance 99 through the system.

For the first time, Arden was excited to get in front of the large crowd for the rally at the state capitol. She remembered the rally on Election Day, and the electricity she'd felt flowing from the crowd. This was her chance, she knew, to define what 99 was, what it had been for. She talked about the corporation as a parasite, and about 99 as the exterminator. She talked about white people settling the West, about the Native Americans, the seventh generation. She talked about distributivism, and about giving people three acres and a cow. She talked about self-sufficiency. It didn't matter anymore to stick to the talking points, because she was just describing her own vision.

"I believe that we voted for Initiative 99 because it is a rebuke against our society and our politics. We want to dismantle that which is corrupt, and replace it with something simpler."

The crowd was thoughtful, and paying attention when she spoke. Not going wild as they had when Ophelia had hit the time-tested talking points, but considering what she said. And it was honest. Her vision, and what inspired her.

But there were so many other voices fighting to control the narrative. There was a huge media campaign being pushed by the corporate opposition, now truly awakened after 99 had passed. The Unibank CEO and a state senator coauthored an op-ed piece in the Sioux Falls newspaper—which was picked up statewide, and by the national papers—claiming that South Dakota voters had been duped. The electorate had been tricked by radical out-of-state hucksters, and hadn't understood the ballot question or 99, the op-ed argued. There was renewed talk about the perils of mob rule: uninformed voters made bad, uninformed policy. A legislative committee was formed to look at changing the ballot-initiative process, to make it harder to get an initiative passed. The governing class was in a furor.

Arden was outraged that they were being cast as manipulating voters. She had worked so damn hard to make sure people understood that proposal. What more could she have done?

The anti-99 media blitz continued, with renewed televisions ads splashing bleak warnings of economic collapse and job losses. In seeming support of this predication, the papers reported that Unibank had announced lay-offs impacting South Dakota workers in their credit card operations groups. In light of the new political uncertainty, Unibank was replacing 20 percent of its operations personnel with artificial intelligence processes that could be relocated quickly if needed. Jeremy was livid that his former employer would use 99 to justify the layoffs. He knew, of course, that those plans had been well underway before 99 was conceived.

Kirish asked her to attend the early court hearings so that her face, the face of 99, was present in the courtroom. The legal wrangling drained her. She spent the hours sitting in the courtroom daydreaming of being somewhere else, somewhere outside. She imagined picking apples. She pondered what she would do next with her life. What role did she want to have in the distribution process, if it went forward? She didn't want to be sitting behind a desk, or in a courtroom. She imagined walking the land, dividing it with a survey crew, considering what would be best for a homestead. She imagined meeting with land-use boards, talking with them about property being distributed in the smallest units to the most people, so that they could be self-sufficient and independent. Some people would think she was crazy, and maybe she was, advocating for subsistence farming over buying everything you need (and lots you don't) at your neighborhood Walmart, but that was her vision. That's where she felt like she was heard best, in the small towns, in the Grange halls. Perhaps that was where she'd be the most use, again, out in the rural areas, showing people her ideas, one town hall at a time.

Or maybe it was time for her to live that vision. Maybe she'd had enough of lobbying and persuading others to follow her. Maybe it was time to take a more solitary path. Arden thought of the truly independent homesteading she had read about on the internet, where people lived off the grid. Part of 99 for Arden had been about unplugging from the consumerism and commercialism that dominated

America. And on a personal level, perhaps, it had been about stepping off the hamster wheel of high school, then college, then job, then marriage, then homeownership. And perhaps also it had been about stepping outside of time, the charted course, the well-worn conventional path. Was it inescapable that next she would be an adult? A professional? A wife? A parent? Arden wanted not to be absorbed, worn down by the world. She wanted not to have her priorities twisted and taken away by society, the things that mattered to her fading away. She wanted not to adapt to a deeply flawed world. She remembered Ophelia telling her that it was those people who can compromise that get things done. But how far to go? And if you compromise, a little at a time, over the years, do you find yourself where Jeremy Hatch did, so deep into it that you fear being poisoned by your complicity? Arden tried to imagine a life without complicity.

Late one afternoon, Kirish returned from court looking ashen. Arden had stopped attending every hearing, but she knew that they had been in court that day arguing against the corporate plaintiffs' motion to suspend the implementation of 99 until after the legal challenges were decided.

"This is a heavy loss for us," Kirish explained. "The court has ordered a stay that will effectively counteract the lockdown we had built into 99, during which corporations couldn't move themselves or their assets out of state, or sell off property. So basically, South Dakota corporations will be able to redomesticate, or move to another state, and avoid being dissolved by the law. Also, corporations can sell or move assets to avoid the forfeiture rules."

Arden had known that this was one of the big legal issues they were fighting, but hadn't thought they'd lose.

"Does this mean Emma's foreclosure sale will go through?" Arden asked quietly.

Kirish nodded. Arden couldn't believe it. All they had worked for was crashing down around them, and she thought through the consequences: Corporations like AGM, after it bought the farm, would still have their land distributed, assuming 99 was successful in the courts. However, the cash that the coverts had counted on as a safety net to protect people through the disruption that 99 would bring, the corporate profits, would bleed away as they moved out of state.

"Didn't you say that the courts would consider that our ability to implement 99 would be irreparably harmed if the lockdown didn't hold?" she demanded. "Doesn't this completely undermine our plans to distribute corporate assets?"

He was grim. "We always knew it was a possibility," he said through clenched teeth.

Jeremy looked up from his phone. "The banks are already moving their liquid assets out of the state."

"So that's it? There will be nothing left?" Arden couldn't believe it. Neither man spoke, and she spun on Kirish. "Well?"

He shrugged, looking gray and old in the rumpled blue business suit.

"Why did you tell us this wouldn't happen?" she demanded. All along, he had downplayed the risk of the lockdown period not holding.

"I didn't say that. You heard what you wanted to hear."

Arden narrowed her eyes. She didn't think that was true, but couldn't say for sure.

Had he known all along that the underlying promise of 99, that there would be corporate assets to give to voters, was a falsehood? It slowly dawned on Arden that if it was true, that Kirish had known, then it was also true what the op-ed had claimed, that 99 had passed on false pretenses. Could his betrayal have run that deep?

CHAPTER 25 — REVERSAL

AFTER THE DEVASTATING RULING ON THE lockdown period, the few remaining coverts all went to Sioux Falls to meet with their legal team and evaluate the situation. Arden drove alone, still troubled by whether Kirish had known all along that the lockdown wouldn't hold. It wasn't even so much that she was angry that he might have misled her, although that certainly rankled her. It was that if he knew, and by extension the campaign knew or should have known, it made their work a sham. The promise of corporate assets to sweeten the pot for 99 had been a lie. Even if it wasn't her lie, it turned out not to be true, so in the end what's the difference?

Arden was surprised to hear that Nick Karbal, the well-known appellate lawyer from DC that Kirish had befriended during the campaign, had flown to Sioux Falls to be part of the meeting. He had already arrived at the posh office of a downtown Sioux Falls law firm when Arden arrived. Jeremy and Kirish were there, as were two South Dakota lawyers from the local law firm. As they were all getting settled around the conference table, Arden was shocked to hear the men discuss the likely outcome of the legal challenge as a loss, perhaps not complete, but that it was likely the measure would be found unconstitutional.

"You all are so matter-of-fact about this!" she snapped. "If you were expecting this, why did we just go through all that?" Arden was frustrated and tired. She'd thought things would be moving forward by now, with the redistribution, not endless days in court and law-firm conference rooms.

She turned to Jeremy, who seemed the most certain that 99 would not survive legal challenge. "Why did you put all that money into getting 99 passed if you thought this would be the outcome?"

Jeremy rocked back in his chair. "Even if we'd lost on Election Day, or if we lose later in the courts, we sent a message to those bastards that we're watching and their days are numbered. And if politicians don't hear our message, or continue ignoring us, they won't work for us anymore." He smiled at Arden, but it felt patronizing. "I don't actually think doing away with corporations is a realistic idea, but I love the idea of striking terror into the hearts of those assholes at Unibank. They came to this state because of the favorable banking laws, but who do they think makes those laws? People, that's who, and you can't run a business without people here in South Dakota and expect those laws to still favor you. I did this to stick my finger in their eye. But no corporations at all? We can't turn back time. Guilds and cooperatives?" He chuckled. "I mean, give me a break. The only reason it's possible to even consider abolishing corporations is because it's fucking South Dakota, and because the rest of the states will still be working."

Arden couldn't believe she was hearing this from Jeremy, their main funder. Again, she was dumbstruck that people can be working toward the same thing, but for such different reasons. She looked angrily back and forth between Kirish and Nick Karbal, and stood up quickly, needing to move. They both watched calmly as she paced around the room. "What about you two? Do you feel the same way?"

To her surprise, Nick answered instead of Kirish. She knew that Kirish had been cultivating his relationship with Nick since his first trip to DC, and that he was the constitutional lawyer Kirish admired the most. He'd argued many cases before the US Supreme Court and had been the top Justice Department attorney in an earlier administration. Arden knew they were lucky to have him, and that she shouldn't be stomping around the room like a teenager, acting surprised that they'd gotten sued. She took a deep breath and tried to listen to his response.

"Arden, we've known from the outset that there was a possibility that Initiative 99 would be found to be unconstitutional, either in whole or in part." He paused and looked at her, waiting a beat as if for her to acknowledge this fact. "From my perspective, such a possibility, or even a likelihood, wouldn't stop me from taking a case. For me," pressing his fingers above his heart, "it's not an ideological campaign, as it is for you. For me, it is a question of whether it tests an important area of law, whether the party I represent had an important interest or meaningful goal that I believe should have a strong voice in court. Some of my cases, like fighting for immigrants' rights, are ideological for me in that I strongly believe in my clients' viewpoint. Here, to be completely honest, I probably wouldn't have voted for a corporation ban." He looked apologetic. "Well, I might have voted for one to make a point, as Jeremy said, but not because I would actually ban corporations."

Arden felt like the rug had been pulled out from underneath her.

Karbal held out a palm to her, encouraging her to sit down again, but she didn't budge. He continued, "I do believe that the voters of South Dakota should be able to say they don't want corporations. The exercise of the voter initiative is a hugely important tool in a representative democracy. That's worth fighting for."

He paused, watching Arden as she stood before them, clenching and unclenching her fists.

"The next thing you should know is that the elemental argument that if a state can create something, it should be able to eliminate it, is very compelling. Although this case will hinge on a lot of legal complexities and precedential arguments, it's my experience that cases with compelling elemental arguments tend to be more likely to succeed." Karbal held up his hand, thumb sticking up. "So two points: First, while there is no guarantee that we'll win, please know that it is eminently worth making the argument, and worth having come this far. Second," unfurling his second finger, "you will find supporters who advance your cause on other than ideological grounds. These supporters are crucial and worth having." Nick smiled and invited her again with an open hand to rejoin them at the glossy conference table. The two lawyers from the Sioux Falls firm looked uncomfortable at her outburst, but Nick held her eye until she sat down, took a deep breath, and nodded. Kirish shot her a look, either embarrassed or something else, Arden could not say.

The elder of the Sioux Falls lawyers cleared his throat. "Well, I actually have some bad news. Our contact in the state house tells us that the legislature is calling a special session that may make many of these legal challenges moot." He paused, gauging Arden's composure, but it was Kirish that banged his fist on the table.

"Well," the man continued slowly, "perhaps this isn't a complete surprise to you. It has happened only a few times in our history of voter initiatives that I'm aware of. Usually legislators won't do it because it is pretty much a sure-fire ticket to not getting reelected, but perhaps here enough of them have made a calculation that it's a totally different world after 99 and that nothing will be the same. . . ." He trailed off, and Arden suspected he too had those same concerns.

"What are you talking about?" Arden demanded.

"Well, the laws committee has drawn up a measure undoing 99, to repeal it in its entirety. As I said, it is rare that the legislators would do something so clearly contrary to the will of the voters. But they can do it, without question."

"Wait a minute!" Arden cried. "I don't understand! How can the legislature repeal our voter initiative?"

The lawyer explained, "Initiative 99 was a voter-initiated law, essentially a statute passed by the voters. Any statute, whether it's passed by the legislature or by voter initiative, can be repealed by the legislature. That's what they're going to do."

Arden was flabbergasted. She knew that her grandmother's anti-corporate farming law had been eroded over time when subsequent legislatures had put loopholes in it, but an immediate and complete repeal? No one had ever even told her this was possible.

"How? When?" she sputtered.

"It hasn't been scheduled yet, but we've heard a special session will be set for just before the Christmas break, December 15. We've also been told. . . ." The lawyer paused as if he were truly sorry to be delivering this news. "That the governor is ready to sign it. They have a law professor from USD and another one from Washington DC ready to say that Initiative 99 is fatally unconstitutional and this repeal will save the state hundreds of thousands of dollars in legal fees."

Jeremy snorted. "That's going to be difficult logic to argue with."

Nick Karbal looked disapprovingly at Jeremy. "I hardly think that makes it a principled approach. At any rate, the law's constitutionality won't truly be tested this way. This requires the voters to go back and pass it as a constitutional amendment, which the legislature cannot repeal. That would take another year to get it back on the ballot, but it's simply just a delay tactic by your opposition. They're hoping that you'll lose steam and not be able to collect double the signatures. They'll have more time to mount a well-funded opposition campaign that takes you seriously next time."

"Next time. . . ." Arden echoed, floored. She stared at Kirish, trying to figure out whether he had understood this to be a possibility. "Did you know that this could happen?" She heard the accusation in her voice.

"I knew that it was technically possible, but I never dreamed that they would actually do it." He looked nauseous, and his voice was hollow. "It happened once before in the seventies, but it wasn't immediately after the ballot initiative passed. There, the politicians that repealed the bill campaigned on a repeal platform, and it happened after a subsequent election. Not immediately following."

Arden was furious. "This is a slap in the face to voters. How can these politicians completely disregard the will of the people who elected them?"

There was a morose nodding and commiserating around the table, which further enraged Arden.

"So what are our options?" she demanded. "Can we sue to stop it?"

There was a pause. None of the lawyers at the table seemed to want to deliver the bad news. Nick Karbal looked to the Sioux Falls lawyers, and then gave a disgusted snort. "Well, of course this is a question of *state* law," he sighed, looking annoyed at the others for not responding on their area of expertise.

Arden could see that they were intimidated by Karbal, who continued, "And I haven't looked much into this particular question in this particular state, but as a general rule, the courts cannot intercede to stop the legislature from passing or repealing a law. Challenges can be brought after the fact, but here, as I understand it, it is within the legislature's constitutional purview to do this. We could try to litigate the currently filed challenges against 99, in hopes of getting a final ruling that 99 was constitutional, and therefore, the repeal measure had no rational basis, since it was premised on the idea that 99 was unconstitutional. But the state legislature can easily insulate against that by having as a second reason for the repeal simply that they think 99 is bad policy. Even if they didn't do that, it's most likely that the courts would refuse to reach the question of constitutionality because the point was moot, due to the repeal. The better approach would be to come back next year and pass it as a constitutional amendment. That way it couldn't be repealed. And then the constitutional questions would have to be resolved."

"Uh, actually," the other lawyer spoke up, "I believe you've missed the deadline for filing signatures for a constitutional amendment for next November, so it would need to be the following year."

Arden rested her forehead on the table. Kirish swore under his breath, and other sighs and groans could generally be heard, although Arden couldn't see where they were coming from. After a few minutes, amid muted discussion about the timing of the expected bill, she dragged herself into a standing position and lurched out of the room. Quickly finding the bathroom, fearing that she might vomit, she instead merely used the toilet, splashed water on her face, and stared at herself numbly for a few minutes in the mirror. When she emerged, Nick Karbal was standing with Kirish in the lobby, the two apparently waiting for her. She saw that Kirish had her bag and jacket.

Nick reached out and shook her limp hand. "You both should be proud of what you've accomplished. This kind of voter-initiated policy doesn't happen unless there's a public thirst for change and strong leaders in the movement. As I said before, I don't know if it's the right way to go, as a society, to ban corporations, but if the majority of voters want it, I believe that's how our democracy is supposed to work that we should try it. If you decide to take another run at this, and I hope you will, I would offer to work with you in the planning stages to try to address some of the due process issues. Maybe we can craft an approach that accomplishes your goals but is less likely to be invalidated by the courts. Which you always knew was a possibility. . . ." The DC lawyer trailed off, perhaps not certain Arden always did know that, or perhaps suspecting she'd never really accepted it.

Arden nodded. "Thank you."

Arden and Kirish walked out together, as Nick hung back to say his goodbyes to the other attorneys. She still felt nauseous, buffeted by one piece of terrible news after another. First the lockdown period failed, then she learned Jeremy and possibly others never really believed the corporation ban would work, and now this. Although she'd worried about the corporation ban being undermined with loopholes that lobbyists might insert over the years, she never knew that it could be repealed, in one fell swoop, by the legislature. And again, Kirish had known, and had decided not to tell her.

CHAPTER 26 REDUX

ARDEN AND KIRISH WAITED FOR THE elevator together silently, for what seemed like a long while. They stepped into the glossy mahogany box, with Arden waiting numbly for him to push the button.

Kirish caught her eye. "Can we drive back together? I have to be back here tomorrow anyway—I can catch a ride and collect my car tomorrow. I want to talk to you, and . . . I have this feeling I may not see you for a while." He was looking steadily at her, seeming for the first time since his return unafraid to meet her gaze. When it was time to exit the elevator and she had not moved, he slipped a hand gently around her elbow.

She could see that he was genuinely concerned about her. It made her slightly less put off by him, although there was part of her that wanted to blame him for this unbelievable fatal flaw in their plan. The repeal.

As they paused in the lobby of the law firm building, Arden nodded and rifled through her purse for her keys, shoving them toward him. She wasn't sure she could drive safely. She wondered if this was what high blood pressure felt like—ringing in her ears, a low roar in her head like crowd noise.

They were silent until he pulled onto the narrow north–south highway connecting Sioux Falls and Vermillion. Arden was thinking of the meeting with the Great Plains Tribal Chairmen's Association, the votes cast by the Lakota, and the corporate parasite. She felt Initiative 99 slipping away, and she didn't know if she had the strength to stop it.

She wondered what her mother would have made of the last two years of her life, whether Jill would have been proud of Arden. She thought Emma was proud of her—for working so hard on 99, for being its leader. But she also knew on some level Emma would have preferred her to have stayed in college, to have pursued the safer route. Would Jill have felt the same way? Arden thought not. If Emma had a bit of revolutionary in her, Jill had more than her share. Arden was reminded of a time Jill came home after quitting her waitressing job, walking off the job in the middle of a Friday dinner rush because the boss tried to corner her in the walk-in cooler. She needed that money to pay her rent, but she wasn't going to put up with being groped in order to get it. Although Jill would never have admitted to being a feminist, a dirty word to her, Arden knew that she was one. And when she could focus on being a parent, she drilled into Arden the importance of being independent, not reliant on a man to take care of her. Ultimately, she had been unable to take care of herself and her daughter as she had wanted to. Had she failed because she had been unwilling to compromise? Or was it simply that she didn't have the tools to succeed? She wasn't educated, and she could be crass and impulsive. But also funny and kind.

Arden remembered, as a girl, hearing Jill recount the stories of working customer service at Sears. There had been a family two counties away who'd had a house fire, probably caused by the oven, which had still been under warranty. The woman had been a renter, with no insurance, so all her belongings were lost. Jill had organized a collection for the woman at church, and had driven the pots and pans and towels the two hours to the woman, even though she'd been told not to engage with her any further, by her manager and the company lawyer. She'd almost gotten fired for that, for breaking company policy. Arden thought she would have voted for 99. She had not been afraid of disruption or chaos. She had courted it. She'd had her own demons, at the end, but Arden imagined that if she were still around, she'd be by their side.

"I'm not sure I can do it again," Arden finally spoke. "Two years." On the other hand, she had no idea what she would do otherwise. Staying with Emma back in Badger was great for an escape, but could she really return there for good? Get a job waitressing at The Hall, serving pancakes and beer to the people she went to high school with, to the jerks from the shale fields? No way.

She turned to watch Kirish as he drove. His profile was grave, and his hair was standing up like he'd been raking his hands through it. "Do you think Government for the People will stay involved?" she asked him, really asking if he planned to stay in the fight, but for some reason not wanting to ask him outright.

"I do." He nodded. "Listen, I know it's going to take you some time to get your head around this. I really am sorry that I didn't warn you that this could happen. I guess I was naïve in thinking that politicians wouldn't act against the voters in such an overt way. I feel completely stupid even saying that out loud. But please know that we are all very surprised."

Arden looked out the window. Had he really not told her because he thought it was so remote a chance that it wasn't worth mentioning? Or had he intentionally downplayed the risk of repeal, like he had downplayed the risk of the lockdown period not holding? There were many things he hadn't told her. Whether it was a deception or merely an omission, it showed his lack of faith in her. And if it was a deception, why? Had he wanted Arden and Ophelia to proceed, despite poor chances of success, for his own reasons? She thought of all the networking he'd done in DC under the guise of advocating for 99. Was the point of it all for him self-promotion first, and the success of 99 second?

"I know you'll need time to think about whether you want to sink the next two years of your life into 99, or whatever our next initiative for the constitutional amendment would be," Kirish said. Arden was confused for a moment, and then understood that the next voter initiative, the one to pass the constitutional amendment, would not be number 99. Would it be 100? 105? Arden stared down the road, ruminating on the identity of their cause and its moment in time. Did all the elements come together in a certain way for 99, in a winning way, that couldn't be replicated? The vote had been so close.

Kirish cleared his throat and glanced at her before he continued, "It might actually be three or even four years, with the legal challenges, if we're successful. I know you believe in 99, but I know that for both of us, making it a reality was, well, a lot messier than the ideal."

"I worry that people voted for 99 for the wrong reasons," Arden said, watching him to see how he would react to this reference to the Williams scandal. He nodded, keeping his eyes on the road. Should she tell him about the shale-gas guys? "If that was the case, if enough of those votes really were about something else, would we even win again?" Arden mused.

"Hell, I'm not even sure I was motivated by the right reason," Kirish responded bleakly. "My mother asked me if I wanted to blow things up because of what happened to me at Williams. I don't think so."

Arden found this troubling. His anger, channeled into 99, might have been about his past? Just like hers was, though, she supposed. She felt acid bile rise in her throat, as she thought again of how Kirish had distrusted her, all the while giving her nowhere to hide, pushing her into the Legacy Foundation confession. How after the scandal became public, she'd had to beg him to return, and then he had moped around, watching her reproachfully, like she was somehow to blame.

"Well then, why did you do it? If it wasn't anger about Williams, and it wasn't the right reason, whatever that is, then what was it?" Arden asked in a low voice.

"I think it changed over time. I always thought the idea was fascinating. I thought the whole project was fascinating." He flashed a look at her. "I was stuck here at this fourth-tier law school, without a prayer of getting a law professor job—yes, because of Williams. The University of South Dakota was the only school that didn't ask about the incident. Or maybe they did and they were willing to let me in despite it—I never knew. But I knew that being involved with 99 would establish me in the legal world in a way that a law degree from USD never would."

Just as Arden had begun to suspect. She was surprised that he was admitting it, but when she thought about it, it was obvious. He had been offered an adjunct teaching role at George Washington Law School because of it, hadn't he? He had befriended Nick Karbal, one of the biggest constitutional lawyers in DC. He'd been interviewed by *The New Republic*. Is that what the DC trips had been about, advancing his personal brand? Had 99 served its purpose for him? And in order to accomplish this, had he encouraged her in a losing battle, downplaying the risks and pushing her to drive the campaign forward? If so, then the criticism was true, that they had misled people about 99. She had been misled, and in turn, had unwittingly lied to voters about what 99 could do. She had trusted him above all others, and he had not trusted her.

He continued, unaware of her flare of anger. "But over time, things changed. I began to believe in it, really believe in it. You persuaded me, with your hardheaded certainty that things could be better. Watching you grow into the kind of leader that people would follow was amazing. I feel proud to have been a part of that."

This put Arden off balance, this mix of insults and compliments, of admiration and also his taking credit for her becoming a leader. She did have to admit he had helped her become the leader of 99, both by pushing her and by refusing to step into the void when she would not lead. But his defection and lies by omission had in some ways been her biggest challenge. It had been very lonely, and he hadn't helped her with that.

In the aftermath of the last few weeks, it was hard to feel proud of what she had accomplished with 99. It had all been smashed apart. She thought of what Jeremy had said, that it was worth doing just to send a message to the politicians that they work for the voters, not the corporations. Perhaps it was true, but that's not what she had been working for.

Kirish caught her eye for a moment, and continued, "However I may have started off—in it for myself, I guess—right now I still deeply believe in the work. It matters. And although I'm sick about it, that we have to do it, I'm committed to sign on for round two. And who knows, maybe if we work with Nick Karbal, he can find a way to fix some of the constitutional problems that I'd overlooked."

Arden was surprised he'd made up his mind so quickly to stay in the fight. Would he be able to mobilize the team without her, she wondered? She was struck by his resolve. If she was tired, and felt the campaign had been grueling, how must he feel?

"The other thing I want to say . . ." He looked across the car nervously at her, passing a semi and fumbling the blinker of her car. ". . . is, Arden, I'm so sorry. I haven't been fair to you, or honest with you, or with myself. I've treated you like a child, and I've been punishing on how you present yourself and tell your story. That was work I should have been doing on myself, clearly."

He turned and met her eye before tearing his gaze away and back to the highway. Although he'd just apologized, she said nothing, telling herself that he wasn't done speaking.

After a pause, he continued, "And I manufactured a distance between us because I was afraid to get close to you." He sighed. "I think at this point it's a real distance."

Arden thought of the many times, large and small, that he had pushed her away. The things he had kept from her, about himself and 99. It felt like he was being honest now, but could he be trusted? She closed her eyes.

"You clearly don't like me very much. But obviously you can see now why I kept you away, why I acted like such an asshole." His voice grew bitter, but this time it seemed like that bitterness was directed toward himself.

Arden shook her head. It wasn't that she didn't like

him. He just never acted as a friend. He was the smartest, most effective and strategic ally she'd ever had or could have hoped for with 99, but sadly, never a friend.

"I acted like it was your fault," he said, "or I wasn't interested in you, which couldn't have been further from the truth." Again he looked at her, making her nervous in the traffic as they approached Vermillion, his hand flexing on the steering wheel as if he wanted to reach over and take her hand. Was he saying that he had been interested in her? Or that he was now, still?

"And the really pathetic thing is," Kirish continued, "if I hadn't been such a coward, I think that the two of us working together on 99, building this movement together, would have been incredible. But instead, there was an off-note, a disappointment." His voice grew hoarse as he spoke these last words, and Arden could feel the emotion behind them. She was touched to hear him admit to it—that cowardice that had so angered her. It could have been different.

"Selfishly, there is part of me that relishes the chance to do it again, to do it right. Maybe to correct some of the mistakes we've made. Make our movement stronger. I would be so grateful if you would give me another chance."

Arden watched the snowy countryside fly by out the car window, feeling vertigo, or a sense of the ground shifting. His apology, his honesty, was something new; she was unused to Kirish being this naked. Did she forgive him, or would she? Was it a decision, forgiving someone, or a letting go? She supposed it was the latter. It always came hard to Arden—she knew that. And sometimes, if you couldn't forgive, it just got more painful, like an infected splinter. But she wasn't sure if what she was feeling—the hesitation, the foreboding—was her old stubborn grudge, or something else. Her feelings about Kirish were so tied up in her feelings about 99. The pride, the reliable tension of conflict, the conviction, and now the ambivalence. Once, she would have been thrilled to hear that he had feelings for her, if that's what he was saying. But now, was it too late? She'd been manipulated by him before.

The idea of waging the campaign over again because it had been stolen from her stung. Had Kirish been stolen from her too, or had he been the thief? When she thought back, she realized that the repeal and the Williams assault and the subsequent blackmail all felt like the same wrong turn. Could things be repaired, or was the rot foundational?

She couldn't just walk away from 99, but at the same time, she couldn't find the energy, the zeal, truly, to make it happen again. But what would she feel like if she gave up? Both alternatives felt equally impossible.

Was she required to give Kirish another chance, and if so, what did that mean? If she could not, was she condemning herself as well as him? *Cold, unable to forgive.* She didn't like the feeling of a trap. She had a flash of seeing her mother through a cracked bedroom door, with a black eye, forgiving some nameless boyfriend, abject at her feet.

What was so wrong with wanting a fresh chapter? Arden's thoughts flicked to Jim, lingering on her premonition of a future together. She wanted more of him, with a physical energy. She thought of her warm vision of farming the old Johnson farm, or Emma's, and seeing Jim as part of that future. But that wouldn't be possible without 99 being put into effect. Perhaps if they saved and bought a farm somewhere else. Maybe even in Montana, in the mountains, off-grid. But the idea didn't have the same resonant pull of victory and fate without the success of 99. It did not feel foretold. She would have to choose.

Looking at Kirish in profile as he maneuvered off the highway, she saw that she could forgive him, though not in the way he hoped.

"There are a lot of things you did, and secrets you kept, that were unfair to me. Secrets about yourself, yes, I suppose those were yours to keep, but also information about what could go wrong with 99 that you never told me. I knew that personal stuff was off limits with you, but I trusted you to do the right thing for 99. Now I wonder how much you manipulated me into doing things because they served your own aims."

He nodded as he drove, not meeting her eye.

"I'm not sure what I will do, but whether I come back to do it all over again or not, I can't see that you and I would be together, if that's what you're saying." She watched him for his reaction. He didn't do anything to confirm that his roundabout apology *was* his way of saying that he wanted to be with her, but she thought that was what it meant. Maybe he wanted it to be vague enough that he could pretend it never happened.

"I appreciate your dedication that you can say right now that you'll stay with it. I believe you that 99 matters to you. And I would work with you again, but I don't really trust you anymore. I'm not sure how you rebuild that."

He nodded. "What about between us?"

"We've never been friends, by your choosing. You can make another choice. I'm open to being your friend if you treat me like one."

He had pulled up in front of their apartment building. He cut the engine of her car and turned to face Arden.

"But nothing more than friends?" he asked quietly.

"No," she replied, "I can't see that happening. It's too late."

He nodded and forced a sad smile. "I hope we can be friends. That would mean a lot to me. I hope you can forgive me. And my commitment to seeing 99 through to the end isn't contingent on your being in, or being with me, but I really hope that you will stay in it. The movement needs you to succeed."

Did it? Arden thought of the Lakota, and the message they conveyed with their vote. She thought of their stolen land and broken treaties. The legal treachery, the legislative sleight of hand that Arden had just experienced was a tiny rendition of what the Lakota had seen. She thought of the idea of the rising of the seventh generation. For the Lakota, to honor their support of 99, maybe she had to keep fighting. Claim her role in the rising. Maybe there was a space between forgiving and fighting that she could inhabit, that she could help lead the way through.

ACKNOWLEDGMENTS

WRITING THIS BOOK WAS LIKE HAVING AN affair from my regular life. Thank you first to Mike, for never being jealous, for believing in the book and liking it, and helping me find the time to make it a reality. To Beckett and Paulette, for being proud of me and supporting me in chasing my dream; may you do the same, even if it is hard and takes forever. Even if you forget about it and come back later.

Many thanks to my early readers, who suffered through drafts too rough to impose on people. Beth Hoben, Aimee Houghton, Amanda Mainville, Sarah Gallaher, I know it wasn't always easy going, and I thank you. To Jane Hoben, who wins the prize for reading it the most times, thank you for your endless encouragement and partnership, attention to detail and intellectual curiosity. To my dad, John Hoben, who told me it was the best book ever and read it in one day. Thanks especially to Pat Guiney for your most

thoughtful and insightful reading, editing, and conversation. Magda Berger, thanks for the encouragement when
times grew dark.

Thank you to the many people who helped me along
the way understand the business of publishing books.
First, to Rob McQuilkin and Jade Wong for your kind-
ness and generously sharing the time and insights of your
team to help me find my way. Next time, I'll know better
and will send you a book when it is finished. To Shannon
O'Shaughnessy, Anna Murray, and Sue Hoben, I really
appreciate your readings, shop talk and insight.

Thank you for the creative inspiration, to Frank Waln,
whose powerful music inspired my storyline. Thanks also
to Kishi Bashi, particularly the amazing album 151a, and
my favorite band Vampire Weekend, and to Liz Gilbert's
Big Magic.

To Neal Katyal, thanks for the encouragement when
the seed of the idea was just cracking open.

To Dan Krasner at RepresentUs, who was good
enough to indulge my hundreds of questions about
how ballot initiatives work and to give me the inside
view of South Dakota Initiated Measure 22, where the
South Dakota voters passed an anti-corruption measure
aimed at their legislature, only to have that same legislature repeal it in a midnight session (literally) during
the Trump Inauguration Gala.

To Susan Defreitas, without you I'd never have found
this book in its current form. With your guidance and creative
ideas pulled from the book itself, it became something I am
proud of. Thank you for your encouragement and vision,
and for your superbly constructive suggestions both large
and small. You helped me find meaning and depth in the
story that would have otherwise gone untapped.

To Ruth Hopkins, for your kind words and insight. I was profoundly moved by learning the phrase, *Mitakuye Oyasin*. Thank you for sharing it with me.

In researching the Iroquois Great Law of Peace and its role as a precedent for the US Constitution, I am indebted to Molly Larkin ("The Secret of the U.S. Constitution," https://mollylarkin.com/the-secret-of-the-u-s-constitution/) and to *Forgotten Founders, Benjamin Franklin, the Iroquois and the Rationale for the American Revolution*, Bruce E. Johnson (Gambit, 1982).

Thanks to Katie Kenney for the inspiration on political organizing, the friendship, and horse talk. To Katie Lukas, whose prolific creativity late one night on cover design was a hugely energizing boon—thank you SO MUCH for all your help and support!

Thank you to the team at She Writes Press and the SWP sister authors who helped show the way. Lastly, thank you to Ann-Marie Nieves at Get Red—may our serendipities be good omens.

ABOUT THE AUTHOR

AIMEE HOBEN is a lawyer and writer who lives in Connecticut with her husband, two kids, and their two dogs. She has worked as a land conservation lawyer, a town attorney, and as in-house counsel at the historic fire insurance company (and Fortune 500 corporation) where Wallace Stevens wrote poems as he walked to work. She studied English Literature at the University of Colorado, and law at the University of Connecticut.

Author photo © Michael Ryan

SELECTED TITLES FROM SHE WRITES PRESS

She Writes Press is an independent publishing company founded to serve women writers everywhere. Visit us at www.shewritespress.com.

The Fourteenth of September by Rita Dragonette. $16.95, 978-1-63152-453-0. In 1969, as mounting tensions over the Vietnam War are dividing America, a young woman in college on an Army scholarship risks future and family to go undercover in the anti-war counterculture when she begins to doubt her convictions—and is ultimately forced to make a life-altering choice as fateful as that of any Lottery draftee.

In a Silent Way by Mary Jo Hetzel. $16.95, 978-1-63152-135-5. When Jeanna Kendall—a young white teacher at a progressive urban school—becomes involved with a community activist group, she finds herself grappling with issues of racism, sexism, and oppression of various shades in both her professional and personal life.

The Tolling of Mercedes Bell by Jennifer Dwight. $18.95, 978-1-63152-070-9. When she meets a magnetic lawyer at her work, recently widowed Mercedes Bell unwittingly drinks a noxious cocktail of grief, legal intrigue, desire, and deception—but when she realizes that her life and her daughter's safety hang in the balance, she is jolted into action.

Again and Again by Ellen Bravo. $16.95, 978-1-63152-939-9. When the man who raped her roommate in college becomes a Senate candidate, women's rights leader Deborah Borenstein must make a choice—one that could determine control of the Senate, the course of a friendship, and the fate of a marriage.

Among the Survivors by Ann Z. Leventhal. $16.95, 978-1-63152-236-9. At twenty-one, Karla Most discovers that her recently deceased mother was not the Holocaust survivor she purported herself to be—and she decides to track down the real story.